THE COMPLETE BOOK
OF
BIBLE STORIES

THE COMPLETE BOOK
OF
BIBLE STORIES

A TIMELESS CLASSIC
BY JESSE L. HURLBUT
ILLUSTRATIONS BY JOEL SPECTOR

Zonder**kidz**

To my parents, Isaac and Matilde Spector,
with all my love I dedicate this book.

JOEL SPECTOR

Zonder**kidz**™

The children's group of Zondervan

www.zonderkidz.com

The Complete Book of Bible Stories
Copyright © 1932, 1947, 1952, 1967, 2002 by Zondervan

Illustrations © 2002 by Joel Spector

Requests for information should be addressed to:
Grand Rapids, Michigan 49530

ISBN: 0-310-70207-0

Editor: Gwen Ellis
Art direction: Laura Maitner
Cover design: Lisa Workman
Color illustrations: Joel Spector
Black and white illustrations: Steele Savage
Interior design: Beth Shagene

Printed in the United States of America

02 03 04 05 06 07 /❖DC/ 10 9 8 7 6 5 4 3 2 1

CONTENTS

Old Testament

Jacob

Joseph

Moses

The Tabernacle

Balaam

Joshua

New Testament

The Birth of Jesus

Jesus in Nazareth

John the Baptist

Jesus Calls His Disciples

Jesus Heals

Stories Jesus Told

Miracles of Jesus

Palm Sunday

The Last Supper

Jesus Is Arrested

The Darkest Day of All the World

The Brightest Day of All the World

Stories of the First Christians

Paul's Stories

God's Kingdom

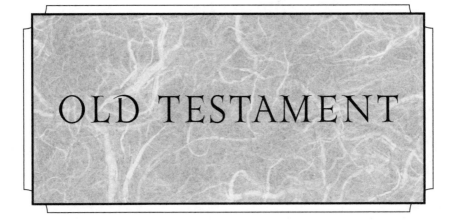

OLD TESTAMENT

Adam and Eve

The Beautiful Garden

n the beginning God created the earth, sun, moon, and stars. But long before anything was created, before there was earth or sun or stars, there was God. God has always been. Then, long, long ago, God spoke, and the earth and heavens came into being. The earth was nothing more than a great, round ball with land and water all mixed into one mass. And it was blacker than midnight, for there was no light anywhere upon the earth. There was no life upon the earth. No man or animal could have lived there.

Then God said, "Let there be light," and the light came. That was the very first day on earth, after a very long night. God separated the light from the dark. God called the light "day." He called the dark "night."

15

At God's command all the dark clouds around the earth began to break up. The sky became visible, and the water that was in the clouds separated from the water that was on the earth. God called the arch of sky over the earth "heaven." The night and the morning made the second day.

"Let the water on the earth come together in one place, and let the dry land rise up," God said. And that's what happened. The water came together in one place, and the dry land rose up from it. God called the great water "sea," and the dry land he named "earth." God saw that the earth and the sea were both good.

Next God said, "Let grass and trees, flowers and fruit trees grow on the earth." At once the earth began to be green and bright with grass, flowers, and fruit-bearing trees. This was the third day on earth.

God said, "Let there be lights in the huge space of the sky." The dark clouds covering the earth rolled back. The sun began to shine by day, and the moon and stars began to shine at night. This happened on the fourth day.

On the fifth day God said, "Let fish swim in the sea and birds fly in the air." So fish began to swim in the sea and birds flew over the land, just as they do today.

Then God said on the sixth day, "Let animals come upon the earth, great ones and small ones, those that walk and those that creep and crawl upon the earth." The woods and fields began to be alive with animals of all kinds. Birds sang in the trees and animals of every kind walked in the forest. The earth was very beautiful with its green fields and bright flowers and trees full of singing birds.

At this time there were no people on earth—no cities or houses and no children playing under the trees. The world was all ready for men and women to enjoy it. God said, "I will make man to be different from all other animals. He shall stand up, have a soul,

and be the master of the earth and all that is in it."
God took some dust from the ground and made a
man and breathed into him the breath of life. The
man came alive and stood up.

But God wasn't through yet. He made a beautiful
garden where four rivers meet. Today we would call
it a park, for it was much larger than any garden you
have ever seen. It went for miles and miles in every
direction. In this park God planted trees and made
the grass grow and the flowers bloom. The park was
called the Garden of Eden, or Paradise.

God gave this garden to the man and told him to
take care of it. He told him to gather fruit from the
trees and plants from the ground for food. Then God
named the first man. He called him Adam. God
brought all the animals to Adam and asked him to
name them.

Adam was all alone in his beautiful garden. Then
God said, "It is not good for man to be alone. I will
make someone to be with Adam to help him." So
when Adam went to sleep, God took a rib from his
side, and from that rib made a woman. He brought
her to Adam and Adam named her Eve. Adam and
Eve loved each other, and they were happy in the
home God had given them.

In six days God had made the heavens, the earth, and all that is in them. On the seventh day God rested.

For a long time Adam and Eve were at peace in their beautiful garden. They did what God asked, they talked with God just as we would talk to a friend, and they did not even know about evil or wickedness. But because it was important for Adam and Eve to understand about obedience, God said to them, "You may eat the fruit of all the trees in the garden except one. Do not even touch the one in the middle of the garden. You must not eat the fruit from that tree. If you do, you will die."

There was a snake living in the garden. One day this snake said to Eve, "Did God really say that you must not eat the fruit of any tree in the garden?"

Eve answered, "We can eat the fruit of all the trees except for the one that stands in the middle of the garden. If we eat the fruit of that tree, God says we must die."

Then the snake said, "No, surely you will not die. God knows that if you eat the fruit of that tree, you will become as wise as he is, for then you will know what is good and what is evil."

Eve listened to the snake, and then she looked at the tree and its fruit. She thought how good the fruit would taste. She wondered if it would really make her wise. She wanted to eat it, even though God had said not to. Then she ate the fruit and gave some to Adam. He ate it, too.

For the first time in their lives Adam and Eve were afraid, because they knew they had done wrong. They tried to hide from God among the trees of the garden. But God called and said, "Adam, where are you?"

Adam said, "Lord, I heard you in the garden, and I was afraid and hid."

God said, "Why were you afraid? Did you eat fruit from the tree that I told you not to touch?"

Adam said, "The woman you put here with me gave me the fruit, and I ate it."

God said to the woman, "What have you done?"

Eve replied, "The snake tricked me. He said it would not harm me. So I ate it."

Then the Lord God said to the snake, "Because you have led Adam and Eve to do wrong, you will not walk as other animals do. You will crawl in the dust and dirt forever. And I will put hatred between you and woman. Your children and her children will be enemies. But one of her children will have the victory over you."

"Adam," God said, "because you listened to your wife when she told you to do wrong, you too must suffer. You must work for everything you get from the ground. There will be thorns, thistles, and weeds growing on the earth. If you want food, you must dig the earth and plant and reap. You must work hard and sweat a lot as long as you live. You came from the dust of the ground, and your body will go back to the dust when you die."

Because Adam and Eve had disobeyed God, they were driven out of their beautiful Garden of Eden home. They were sent out into the world. And just to make sure they could not go back into the garden, God placed angels with swords that flashed like fire at the gate.

So Adam and Eve lost their garden, and no one has ever been able to find it again.

The First Baby in the World

GENESIS 4:1–18

fter Adam and Eve went out into the world to live and work, they were alone for a while. But later God gave them the first baby who ever came into the world. Eve named him Cain. After a time another baby was born. This baby she named Abel. When the boys grew up, they worked with their father, Adam. Cain chose to work in the fields, raising grain and fruit. Abel became a shepherd and had a flock of sheep.

When Adam and Eve lived in the Garden of Eden, they often talked with God and could hear God's voice speaking to them. But now that they had been sent out of the garden, they could no longer talk with God as before. One way they talked with him now was to make a sacrifice. They heaped up a pile of stones for an altar. On the altar they laid their gifts to God and set fire to them. This showed that the offering was no longer theirs. They were giving it to God. Then they would pray and ask God to forgive all that they had done wrong. They would ask God to bless them and do good for them.

Cain and Abel each brought a gift to God. Cain brought the fruit and grain that he had grown. Abel brought a sheep from his flocks. He offered the lamb as a sacrifice. God was pleased with Abel and his offering because Abel had faith, but God was not pleased with Cain's offering. Perhaps Cain had little or no faith in God.

When God showed Cain that he was not pleased with his offering, Cain became very angry with God and with his brother. He did not ask God's forgiveness. One day when Cain and Abel were in the field together, Cain struck Abel. He killed him.

The Lord said to Cain, "Where is your brother Abel?"

Cain answered, "I don't know. Why should I take care of my brother?"

Then the Lord said to Cain, "What have you done? Your brother's blood is crying out to me from the ground. The ground has opened like a mouth to take your brother's blood from your hand. As long as you live, you shall be under God's curse for the murder of your brother. You will wander over the earth and will never find a home, because of the evil you have done."

Cain said, "My punishment is more than I can bear. You have driven me away from the land. I will now be hidden from you. If any man finds me, he will kill me, because I will be alone with no one to be my friend."

God said to Cain, "If anyone harms you, he shall be punished for it." Then the Lord placed a mark on Cain so whoever met him would know him and not harm him.

After that Cain and his wife went away from Adam's home. They lived in a place by themselves and had many children. Later Cain's family built a city and named it after Cain's first child. The name of the child and the city was Enoch.

Noah

The Great Ship That Saved Eight People

Genesis 5:1–9:17

fter Abel died, his brother Cain went to another land. Then God gave Adam and Eve another child. They named him Seth. After that they had many more sons and daughters because they lived a long time. In those early times people lived much longer than they do now. Some people today live to be a little past one hundred years old, but back then some people lived to be eight hundred or nine hundred years old. Even though Adam and Eve lived a long time, they didn't live forever, because they had eaten the fruit that God had forbidden them to eat.

By the time Adam died, there were many people on earth. Adam and Eve's children had many children, and their children had many children. So the earth began to be filled with people. It is sad that as time went on, more and more of these people became wicked. Fewer and fewer of them grew up to become good men and women. As God looked down on the world he had made, he saw how wicked the people had become. He saw that the people thought about evil all the time.

There were a few good people, however. The best of all the men who lived at that time was a man named Enoch. (This was a different man from the one in Cain's story. This one came from the family of Seth, Cain's younger brother.) While others did evil, Enoch did only what was right. He walked and talked with God, and God walked and talked with him. At last, when Enoch was 365 years old, God took him away from earth to heaven. He did not die as all the other people had since Adam disobeyed God. God just came and took Enoch to heaven.

Enoch had a son whose name was Methuselah. We don't know anything about Methuselah except that he lived for 969 years. That is longer than any other person on earth has ever lived. But at last he too died, just like everyone else except his father, Enoch.

By the time Methuselah died, the world was very, very wicked. Then God looked down on the earth

and said, "I will wipe them out. I am very sad that I made man."

But then God saw one good man—Noah. Noah was a man who tried to do right in the sight of God, just as Enoch had done. Noah had three sons: Shem, Ham, and Japheth.

God said to Noah, "I am going to put an end to all people. They have filled the earth with their harmful acts. You and your family will be saved because you have tried to do what is right."

Then God told Noah to build a very large boat. It was very long and very wide and very deep, with a roof over it. It was made like a long, wide house in three stories but built so it would float on the water. It was called an "ark." God told Noah, "I am going to bring a great flood on the earth. It will cover all the land and drown all the wicked people on earth. The animals will be drowned as well as the people, so you must make the ark large enough to hold a pair of each kind of animal and several pairs of some animals that people need, like sheep, goats, and oxen. That way there will be animals as well as people on the earth after the flood. And you must also take into the ark enough food for all the animals and for yourself and your family to last for a year while the floodwaters are on the earth."

Noah did what God told him to do, although it must have seemed strange to all the people around him. Noah was building this great big boat, and there

> *God saw one good man—Noah.*
> *Noah was a man who tried to do right*
> *in the sight of God.*

was no water anyplace on which to float it. It took a long time—120 years—for Noah to build the ark. No doubt, the wicked people all around him wondered and laughed at Noah for building such a great ship.

At last the ark was finished and stood like a great house on the land. There was a door on one side and a window in the roof to let in light. Then God said, "Noah, come into the ark. Bring your wife, your three sons, and their wives, too, for the flood of waters will come very soon. Take with you animals of all kinds and birds and things that creep, seven pairs of those that will be needed by men and one pair of all the rest, so all kinds of animals may be kept alive upon the earth."

So Noah, his wife, and his three sons, Shem, Ham, and Japheth, with their wives, went into the ark. And God brought to the door of the ark all the

animals, birds, and creeping things, and they went
into the ark, too. Noah and his sons put them in their
places and brought in food for all of them. Then the
door of the ark was shut so no more people and no
more animals could come in.

In a few days the rain began to fall. It came down
as never before. It seemed as though the heavens
were split open to pour out great floods upon the
earth. The streams filled, and the rivers rose higher
and higher. The ark began to float on the water.
People who were left behind ran up to the hills, but
soon the hills were covered with water, too. At last
the water was so deep, it covered the whole earth.
The rain fell for forty days.

Then the rain stopped, but because the water was
very deep, it stayed on the earth for more than six
months. The ark and everything in it went on floating on the great sea that covered the land. Then at
last God sent a wind to blow over the waters and dry
them up. The first things to show above the water
were the tops of mountains. The ark finally stopped
floating and came to rest on the top of Mount Ararat.
Noah could not see what had happened on the earth,
because the door of the ark was shut and the window
was on the roof and the water was still deep. So after

a while he opened the window and let loose a bird called a raven. The raven had strong wings. It flew round and round until the waters went down and it could find a place to rest. It did not come back to the ark.

Noah waited awhile for the raven to come back, and then he sent out a dove. The dove came right back because it could not find any place to rest and it does not have strong wings like the raven. After another week went by, Noah sent the dove out again. At evening time the dove came back with a fresh olive leaf in its bill.

Now Noah knew that the water had gone down enough for trees to start growing again. He waited another week and sent the dove out again, but this time the dove did not come back. So Noah knew the earth was drying up. He took off part of the roof and looked out. He saw that there was dry land all around the ark. Noah had been in the ark a little more than a year, and he was glad to see the green land and the trees once more. And God said to Noah, "Come out of the ark with your wife and sons and their wives and all the living things that are with you in the ark."

So Noah opened the door of the ark, and his whole family came out and stood once more on dry ground. All the animals, birds, and creeping things came out as well and began to bring life to the earth.

The first thing Noah did was to give thanks to God for saving all his family. He built an altar and laid upon it an offering to the Lord. He promised that he and his family would do God's will from then on.

God was pleased with Noah's offering and said, "I will never again destroy the earth on account of men, no matter how bad they may be. From this time on, no flood shall ever again cover the earth. There will be seasons of spring, summer, fall, and winter every year. I give you the earth, and you will be the rulers of the ground and of every living thing upon it."

Then God caused a rainbow to appear in the sky. He told Noah and his sons that whenever they or the people after them saw the rainbow, they should remember that God had placed it in the sky as a sign of his promise. He promised that he would never again send a flood to destroy men from the earth.

So whenever we see a beautiful rainbow, we can remember that it is the sign of God's promise to the world.

GOD SAVED NOAH'S FAMILY AND THE ANIMALS ON THE ARK

Noah thanked God for saving him.
He knew the rainbow showed God's promise.

Rebekah Poured Water for Eliezer and His Camels

Eliezer knew God had answered his prayer to help him find a kind and loving wife for Isaac.

Babel

❦

The Tower That Was Never Finished

Genesis 10:1–11:9

fter the great flood Noah's family grew in number. They had children, then grandchildren, then great-grandchildren. The earth began to fill up with people once more. But the people who lived after the flood were different from the people who had lived before it. Before the flood people stayed close together. As far as we know, all the people on earth before the flood lived in one place. They lived in the land where two great rivers, the Tigris River and the Euphrates River, flowed. This part of the world was very full of people. But few or none of the people crossed the mountain on their east or the desert on their west. After the flood families began moving from one place to another. They built new homes in new lands.

The moving was a part of God's plan to have the whole earth used as a home for people. He didn't want them to live in just one small part of it. Families who wished to serve God and do right could move to another land if the people around them became evil. In the new place they could raise their children in the right way.

After the ark came to rest on Mount Ararat, many of Noah's descendants moved south from that mountain to the country between the rivers. They built houses for themselves there. Then they started to build a great city from which to rule all the people around them. They found that the soil in that country was good for making bricks. Those bricks could be used to build strong houses to live in. They could also be used to build a sturdy wall around their city.

The people said to each other, "Let's build a great tower that stands on earth and reaches up to the sky. Then we can stay together and not scatter all over the earth." So they began to build their great tower out of bricks. They piled them up, one story above another. But God did not want all the people on earth to live close together, as they had before the flood. God knew that if they all lived close together, those who were wicked would lead away from him those who were good. All the world would become evil again, as it had been before the flood.

So God caused their speech to change. When they began building this great city and tower from which they intended to rule the world, they were all speaking the same language. But God mixed up their speech into many languages. Then people could not understand each other.

Workers wanted to work with those who spoke the same language they did. They formed groups of those who spoke alike. After a while the groups moved away to other places. The men who were building the great tower could no longer understand each other, so they left the building without finishing it. No one ever came back to finish the tower.

The city was named Babel, a word that means "confusion." Later it was known as Babylon. For a long time it was one of the greatest cities in that part of the world. Some of the people who left Babylon went north and built Nineveh, the most important city of the great land of Assyria. Another group went west and settled by the Nile River. They founded the land of Egypt, with its strange temples and pyramids, its Sphinx and monuments.

Another group wandered northwest until they came to the shore of the great sea we call the Mediterranean Sea. There they founded the cities of Sidon and Tyre. The people became sailors, sailing ships to countries far away. The sailors brought home many things from other lands to sell to the people of Babylon, Assyria, Egypt, and other countries. So after the flood people lived in many lands and spoke many languages.

ABRAM

The Long Journey

Genesis 11:27–13:18

 ot far from Babylon, where the people began to build the Tower of Babel, was another city, called Ur of the Chaldees. Chaldees lived in Chaldea, a country that was right where the Tigris and Euphrates Rivers came together. Living among these people was a man named Abram. He was a good man. He prayed to the Lord God and tried always to do God's will.

But the people who lived in Ur did not pray to God. They prayed to idols—images made of wood and stone. They thought these images were gods who could hear their prayers and help them. And because these people who worshiped the idols did not call on God, they did not know his will. So they did many evil things.

The Lord saw that Abram was good and faithful. God did not want Abram's family to grow up in such an evil place. So the Lord spoke to Abram and said, "Gather together all your family and leave this country and this people. Go to the land I will show you. In that land I will make you into a great nation. I will bless you. I will make your name great. You will be a blessing to others. All the nations on earth will be blessed because of you."

Abram did not know just what this blessing meant. Today we know that Abram's family grew. They became the Israelite people, the family of Jesus, the Savior of the world. Jesus was a descendant of Abram.

Abram did not know just what the blessing God promised to give him would be. He did not know where the land was to which God was sending him.

But he obeyed God's word. He took his father, Terah, who was very old; his wife, whose name was Sarai; his brother Nahor and his wife; and another brother's son, whose name was Lot. Lot's father, Haran, who was Abram's younger brother, had died before this time. Abram took all he had: his tents and his flocks of sheep, his herds of cattle. He went out on the long journey to a land whose name he didn't even know.

He traveled far up the great river Euphrates to a mountain region. He came to a place called Haran in a country named Mesopotamia. The name Mesopotamia means "between the rivers." They all stayed for a time at Haran. Perhaps they stopped there because Terah, Abram's father, was too old to travel farther. They stayed in Haran until Terah died.

Afterward Abram began his journey again. Lot, his brother's son, went with him. Nahor, his brother, stayed in Haran with his family. Nahor's children and grandchildren lived at Haran for many years.

Abram and Lot turned toward the southwest and traveled for a long time. The mountains rose on their right, and the great desert spread out on their left. They crossed over rivers and climbed hills. At last they came into the land of Canaan, which was the land God had told Abram about.

The land was called Canaan because the people who were living in it were the descendants of a man named Canaan who had lived long before. Later this place was called "the land of Israel," and that is what it is called today. Some people today call it "the Holy Land."

When Abram came into the land of Canaan, he found there a few cities and villages. But Abram and his people did not go into the towns to live. They lived instead in tents in the open fields. There they could find grass for their sheep and cattle. Not far from a city called Shechem, Abram set up his tent under an oak tree on the plain. The Lord came to Abram and said, "I will give this land to your children and to their children, and this shall be their land forever."

Abram built an altar and made an offering and worshiped the Lord. Wherever Abram set up his tent, he built an altar and prayed to God. He loved God and served him. He believed all God's promises.

Abram and Lot moved their tents and their flocks to many places where they could find grass for the animals and water to drink. One time they went down to the land of Egypt, where they saw the great river Nile. Perhaps they also saw the Great Pyramids and the Sphinx and the huge temples in that land, for many of them were built before Abram lived.

Abram didn't stay long in Egypt. God didn't want him to live in a land where people worshiped idols.

> *The Lord came to Abram and said,*
> *"I will give this land to your children*
> *and to their children, and*
> *this shall be their land forever."*

God sent Abram back again to the land of Canaan. There he could live apart from cities and bring up his servants and his people to worship the Lord. He came to a place where a city called Bethel would be built in the future. There, as before, he built an altar and prayed to the Lord.

Now Lot, Abram's nephew, had flocks of sheep and herds of cattle and many tents for his people. Abram's shepherds and Lot's shepherds quarreled because there was not enough grass in one place for both of them to feed their flocks. The Canaanites were also in the land, so there was not enough room for them all.

When Abram heard the quarrel between his men and Lot's, he said to Lot, "Let's not argue with each other. The people who take care of your herds and those who take care of mine shouldn't argue with one another. After all, we are part of the same family.

> *God said to Abram, "Lift up*
> *your eyes from this place and look east*
> *and west and north and south.*
> *All the land that you can see, mountains*
> *and valleys and plains, I will give*
> *to you and to your children and*
> *to everyone who comes afterward.*

Let's separate. If you go to the left, I'll go to the right. If you go to the right, I'll go to the left."

This was noble and generous of Abram, for he was the older person and had the right to first choice. Also, God had promised all the land to Abram. He might have said to Lot, "Go away, for this land is all mine." But Abram was kind and good. He gave Lot his choice of the land.

Lot looked over the land from the mountain where they were standing. He saw, down in the valley, the river Jordan flowing between green fields with rich soil. He saw the lively cities of Sodom and

Gomorrah on the plain near the Dead Sea. Lot said, "I will go down there to the plain."

He took his tents, his men, his sheep, his cattle, and everything he had. He left his uncle in the mountains, where the land was not so good. Maybe Lot didn't know that the people in Sodom were the most evil of all the people in the land. But after he went to live near them, he moved his tent closer and closer to Sodom. Soon he was living inside that wicked city.

After Lot left, God said to Abram, "Lift up your eyes from this place and look east and west and north and south. All the land that you can see, mountains and valleys and plains, I will give to you and to your children and to everyone who comes afterward. Your descendants shall have all this land. They shall be as many as the grains of sand on earth. Rise up and walk through the land wherever you please, for it is all yours."

Then Abram moved his tent from Bethel. He went to live near the city of Hebron in the south, setting up his tent under some oak trees. There he built another altar to the Lord.

Lot's Trouble and Abram's Blessing

GENESIS 14:1–15:21

bram lived in his tent on the mountains of Canaan, and Lot moved to Sodom. At that time there were five cities near the Dead Sea. Sodom and Gomorrah were two of the five cities. Each city was ruled by its own king. Over these five kings was another king who lived far away near the land of Chaldea, from which Abram had come. This king ruled all the lands far and near.

After a time these kings in the plain decided not to obey the greater king. So he sent his army to fight them. One battle was fought on the plain not far from Sodom. The kings of Sodom and Gomorrah were beaten in the battle, and all their soldiers were killed. The king who had won the battle came to Sodom and took everything he could find in the city and carried away all the people. He intended to keep them as slaves. That is what used to happen after a battle—people were made slaves and everything they owned was taken.

So Lot and everything he owned was carried away by the enemy. The army with their slaves did not stop to rest until they came to the headwaters of the river Jordan, at a place that was later called Dan. Lot had been very selfish when he chose to live on the plain in the city of Sodom and made his uncle, Abram, live in the mountains. But he lost everything he gained by his selfish choice, and he became a prisoner as well.

Someone escaped and ran away from the battle. He went straight to Abram, who sat in his tent under the oak tree near Hebron. As soon as Abram heard what had happened, he called together all his men, his servants, his shepherds, and his friends. He led

them out to pursue the enemy who had taken Lot. Abram went as fast as possible and caught up with the enemy, who still had all the prisoners and goods they had taken away with them.

Abram rushed up to the enemy at night while they were sleeping. He fought them and drove them away. As they fled, they left everything behind. They ran to hide in the mountains. In their camp Abram found his nephew, Lot. He and his wife and daughters were safe. Lot got back all his goods. There too were all the other people from Sodom with their goods.

The king of Sodom came to meet Abram at a place near the city of Salem, which is now called

> *The Lord spoke to Abram and said,*
> *"I am like a shield to you.*
> *I will give you a very great reward*
> *for serving me."*

Jerusalem. With him came the King of Jerusalem, Melchizedek. Melchizedek, unlike most other kings in the land at that time, was a worshiper of the Lord God. King Melchizedek blessed Abram and said, "May the Lord God Most High bless Abram. May the Creator of heaven and earth bless him. Give praise to God Most High. He gave your enemies into your hand."

Then Abram gave King Melchizedek a present because he worshiped the Lord. Abram gave back to the king of Sodom all the people and goods that had been taken away, and he would not take any reward for bringing them back.

You would think that after all this, Lot would have seen that it was wrong for him to live in Sodom. But he went right back there. Even though his heart was sad because of the wickedness that he saw all around him, he made his home in Sodom once again.

One day after Abram had gone back to his tent under the oak trees at Hebron, the Lord spoke to him and said, "I am like a shield to you. I will give you a very great reward for serving me."

Abram said, "O Lord God, what can you give me? I have no child to whom I can give it. After I die, my servant, not my son, will own everything that I have." Abram had a large family of people around him and many servants, but he had no son. Now he was an old man and his wife, Sarai, was also old.

God said, "The one who will receive what you own will not be a stranger but will be your own son."

That night God brought Abram out of his tent under the stars and said to him, "Look up at the sky and count the stars, if you can. The people who are

> *Abram looked and saw smoke and fire that looked like a flaming torch passing between the pieces of the offering.*

going to be your descendants in the years to come will be more than all the stars that you can see."

Abram did not see how God could keep his promise, but he believed God's word. He did not doubt it. God loved Abram because he believed the promise. He had faith even when he could not understand how God's promise could be kept. Today we know that God did keep his promise. All the Jewish people in the world have come from Abram.

One day, just as the sun was going down, God came to Abram again. God told him about many things that would happen in the future. God said, "After your life is ended, your descendants will go into a strange land. The people of that land will make slaves of them and will be cruel to them. They will stay in that strange land four hundred years.

Afterward they will come out of the land, not as slaves but as very rich people. They will come back to this land, and it will be their home. All this is going to happen after your life, for you will die in peace and be buried when you are old. All this land where you are living will belong to your people."

God wanted Abram to remember this promise. God told him to make an offering of a lamb, a goat, and a pair of pigeons. That night Abram looked and saw smoke and fire that looked like a flaming torch passing between the pieces of the offering.

That was the way the promise between God and Abram was made. God promised to give Abram a son and to give the people a land. Abram promised to serve God faithfully.

Such a promise as this is called a "covenant." This was God's covenant with Abram.

Hagar

The Angel by the Well

Genesis 16:1–17:27

bram's wife, Sarai, had a maid—a servant who waited on her. The servant's name was Hagar. She had come from the land of Egypt, where there were pyramids and temples. Sarai and her maid, Hagar, had some trouble. They could not agree, and Sarai was so sharp and severe with Hagar that she ran away from Sarai's tent.

Hagar went out into the desert and took the road that led toward Egypt, her own country. On the way she stopped beside a spring of water. An angel from the Lord met her there and said, "Hagar, what are you doing here? Where are you going?"

Hagar answered, "I am going away from my mistress, Sarai, because I do not wish to stay with her and serve her any longer."

Then the angel told her, "Go back to your mistress and submit to her. It is better for you to go back than to leave. God knows all your troubles. He sees and hears you, and he will help you. You shall have a son, and you shall call him Ishmael, because God has heard you."

The name Ishmael means "God hears." So whenever Hagar would speak her son's name, she would think, *God has heard me.* Then the angel told Hagar that her son Ishmael would be strong and fierce and that no one would be able to overcome him or any of his descendants.

So Hagar was comforted and returned to serve Sarai. The well where she saw the angel was called by a name that means "the well of the Living One who sees me."

In time Hagar had a son, just as the angel told her. She called him Ishmael.

After this happened, Abram was living near Hebron. The Lord came to him again and spoke to him. Abram bowed his face to the ground, and God said, "I am the Almighty God. Walk before me and be perfect, and I will make you a father of many nations. And your name will be changed. You will no more be called Abram but Abraham, a word that means 'father of a multitude,' because you will be the father of many nations of people. Your wife's name

> *The name Ishmael means "God hears." So whenever Hagar would speak her son's name, she would think, God has heard me.*

will be changed also. She will no longer be called Sarai but Sarah, and that means 'princess.' You and Sarah will have a son, and you shall name him Isaac. He will have many sons when he becomes a man, and his descendants, those who come from him, will be very many people."

So Abram's and Sarai's names were changed.

LOT

Sodom and Gomorrah and the Rain of Fire

ne day Abraham was sitting in the door of his tent when he saw three men coming toward him. Although he did not know it at the time, they were angels. One of them seems to have been the Lord himself in the form of a man.

When Abraham saw these men coming, he went out to meet them and bowed to them. He said to the one who was the leader, "My Lord, do not pass by. Come and rest a little under the tree. Let me send for water to wash your feet. Let me get you some food. Stay with us a little while."

So this person, who seemed to have been God in the form of a man, sat with his two followers in Abraham's tent under the oak trees at Hebron. They ate some food which Sarah, Abraham's wife, had prepared for them. Then the Lord talked with Abraham. He told Abraham again that in a short time God would send him and Sarah a little boy whose name should be Isaac. In Abraham's language Isaac means "laughing." God chose it because Abraham and Sarah laughed when they heard the news. They were so happy, they could hardly believe it.

Then the three persons got up to leave Abraham's tent. Two of them went on the road that led toward Sodom. The one that Abraham called "my Lord" stopped after the others had gone. He said, "Shall I hide from Abraham what I am going to do? Abraham is to be the father of a great people. The entire world will be blessed through him. I know that Abraham will teach his children and all those who live with him to obey the will of the Lord and to do right. I will tell Abraham what I am going to do. I am going down to the city of Sodom and the other cities that are near it. I am going to see if the city is as bad as it seems to be. The wickedness of that city is like a cry coming up before the Lord."

Abraham knew that Sodom was very evil. He feared that God was about to destroy it. He said, "Will you destroy the righteous with the wicked? Will the good die with the bad in Sodom? Perhaps

there may be fifty good people in the city. Will you spare the city for the sake of fifty good men who may be in it? Will the Judge and Ruler of all the earth do what is right?"

The Lord answered, "If I find fifty good people in Sodom, I will not destroy the city. I will spare it for their sake."

Then Abraham said, "Perhaps I ought not to ask anything more. I am only a common man talking with the Lord God. But suppose you find forty-five good people in Sodom. Will you destroy the city because it lacks only five good men to make up the fifty?"

The Lord said, "I will not destroy it if there are forty-five good men in it."

Abraham said, "Suppose there are forty good people there. What then?"

> *Then Abraham said, "Oh, don't be angry with me. I'm only going to ask once more. Maybe there are ten good men found in the city."*

The Lord answered, "I will spare the city if I find forty good men in it."

Abraham said, "O Lord, do not be angry. If there are thirty good men in the city, it may be spared?"

The Lord answered, "I will not harm the city if I find thirty good men there."

Abraham said, "Let me venture to ask that you spare it if twenty good men are there."

The Lord agreed. "I will not destroy it for the sake of twenty good men if they are there."

Then Abraham said, "Oh, don't be angry with me. I'm only going to ask once more. Maybe there are ten good men found in the city."

The Lord said, "If I find ten good men in Sodom, I will spare the city."

Abraham had no more to say. The Lord in the form of a man went on his way toward Sodom. Abraham turned back and went to his tent.

Lot, Abraham's nephew, had chosen to live in Sodom even though the people were very wicked. Once Lot had been carried away as a prisoner when Sodom was taken by its enemies. Abraham rescued him. But after all that happened, Lot went right back to live in Sodom again. He was there when the angels came to Abraham's tent.

Two of the angels who had visited Abraham went down to Sodom and walked through the city, trying to find some good men. If they could find ten good men, the city would be saved. But the only good man they found was Lot. He took the angels, who looked like men, into his house. He treated them kindly and made supper for them.

The men of Sodom came to Lot's house and tried to take the two men out. They wanted to harm them. The men of Sodom were very wicked and cruel. But they couldn't do anything evil against the angels. When they tried to break open Lot's door, the two angels struck all those wicked men blind. They felt around in the dark for the door.

Then one of the angels said to Lot, "Are there any others besides you in the city—any sons or sons-in-law or daughters? If you have any, get them out of this city quickly. We are here to destroy this place because it is so evil."

Lot went quickly to the houses where the young men who had been engaged to his daughters lived and said to them, "Hurry, get out of the city, for the Lord is going to destroy it." But the young men would not believe his words. They only laughed at him. What a mistake it was for Lot to choose to live in a wicked city where his daughters became engaged to men living there.

When morning was coming, the two angels tried to get poor Lot to hurry away. They said, "Get up quickly. Take your wife and your two daughters and leave. If you do not hurry, you will be destroyed along with the city. "

But Lot was slow to leave his house and all that he had. The angels dragged them out of the city. God was good to Lot. He took him out of the city before he destroyed it.

When the angels had brought Lot, his wife, and his daughters out of the city, one of the angels said to him, "Run for your lives and escape! Do not look behind you. Do not stop anywhere in the plain. Climb up the mountain, or you may be destroyed!"

Lot begged the angels not to send him so far away. He said, "O my Lord, I cannot climb the mountain. Have mercy on me. Let me go to that little city that lies yonder. It is only a little city. You can spare it. Please let me be safe there."

The angel told him, "We will spare that city for your sake. We will wait until you are safe before we destroy these other cities."

So Lot ran to the little city called Zoar, and there he found safety. In the language of that time the word *zoar* means "little." Lot came to Zoar at sunrise.

As soon as Lot and his family were safely out of Sodom, the Lord caused a rain of fire to fall upon Sodom and the other cities on the plain. With the fire came great clouds of sulfur smoke covering all the plain. So the cities were destroyed and all the people in them. Not one man, woman, or child was left.

While Lot's family was fleeing from Sodom, his wife stopped and looked back. The Bible says she became a "pillar of salt" standing there on the plain. Lot and his daughters escaped, but now they were afraid to stay in the little city of Zoar. They climbed up the mountain, away from the plain, and found a cave. They lived there. Lot lost his wife and all that he had, because he had made his home among the wicked people of Sodom.

Abraham, standing in his tent door on the mountain, looked down toward the plain. He saw the smoke rising from it like the smoke of a great furnace.

That was the end of the cities of the plain. Sodom and Gomorrah and all the other cities were destroyed. Only Zoar was saved, because Lot, a good man, asked for it.

ISHMAEL

The Boy Who Became an Archer

GENESIS 21:1–21

fter Sodom and Gomorrah were destroyed, Abraham moved his tent and camp far away from that part of the land. He went southwest to live near a place called Gerar, not far from the Mediterranean Sea. And there at last the child God had promised was born. Abraham was one hundred years old.

Sarah and Abraham named their son Isaac, just as the angel told them to do. They were so happy to have a little boy that they invited all the people to a great feast in honor of little Isaac.

Hagar the Egyptian, Sarah's maid, had run away from her mistress and had seen an angel by the well. The angel sent her back to her mistress. After that happened, Hagar had a child and named him Ishmael. So now there were two boys in Abraham's tent—Ishmael, the son of Hagar, and Isaac, the son of Sarah.

Ishmael was a rough, wild boy. He did not like Isaac, who was quiet and gentle. He was not kind to him. This made Sarah very angry. She said to Abraham, "I don't want this boy Ishmael growing up with my son, Isaac. Send Hagar and her boy away, for they trouble me."

Abraham felt very sorry to have trouble between Sarah and Hagar and between Isaac and Ishmael. Abraham was a good, kind man. But the Lord said to Abraham, "Don't be troubled about Ishmael and his mother. Do as Sarah asked you to do. Send Hagar and Ishmael away. It is best that Isaac be alone in your tent, for he is to receive everything that is yours. I, the Lord, will take care of Ishmael and will make a great people of his descendants."

So Hagar, leading her little boy, left Abraham's tent. Somehow she lost the road and wandered into the desert. She did not know where she was. Soon Hagar and Ishmael used up all the water in her bottle. Her poor boy was thirsty in the hot sun and the burning sand. She had nothing to give him to drink. She thought Ishmael was going to die of thirst. She laid him down in the shade of a little bush, and then

she went off a little way by herself. "I can't bear to look at my poor boy suffering and dying of thirst," she said.

At just the moment when Hagar was crying and her boy was moaning with thirst, she heard a voice. It said to her, "Hagar, what's wrong? Don't be afraid. God has heard your cry and the cry of your child. God will take care of both of you and will make your boy into a great nation of people."

It was the voice of an angel from heaven. Just then Hagar looked, and right there close by was a spring of water. Hagar was so glad. She filled the bottle with water and took it to her suffering boy under the bush.

Hagar did not go to Egypt. Instead she found a place near this spring. She lived there and brought up her son far from other people. God was with

Ishmael and cared for him. As Ishmael grew up, he learned to shoot with a bow and arrow. He became a wild man, and his children after him were wild, too. They became the Arabians of the desert. They did not want to live in cities or to be ruled by other people. They wandered through the desert and lived as they pleased.

So Ishmael became the father of many people, and his descendants are living in that land today. Isaac also became a great nation. His descendants are living all over the world.

ISAAC

How an Angel's Voice
Saved a Boy's Life

GENESIS 22:1–23:20

n Abraham's time men worshiped God by building an altar of earth or stone and then placing an offering on it as a gift to God. The offering was usually an animal such as a sheep, a goat, or a young ox. Such an offering was called a "sacrifice." This was pleasing to God.

On the other hand, the people who worshiped idols often did terrible things that God hated. They thought it would please their gods if they offered as a sacrifice the most precious living thing they owned. They would sometimes take their own little children and kill them upon their altars as offerings. They gave up their little ones to the gods of wood and stone that were not really gods at all but only images.

God wanted to show Abraham and all his descendants that he was not pleased with the offerings of living people. God found a way to teach Abraham that he would always provide a sacrifice for man's sins. In this story it was a ram caught by his horns in the bushes, but later on it was his Son who was provided to cover man's sins. He also tested Abraham to see if he would faithful and obedient no matter what God asked him to do.

God gave a command that would test Abraham. He said, "Take your son, Isaac, whom you love so much, and go to the land of Moriah. There, on a mountain that I will point out to you, sacrifice him as a burnt offering to me." This command filled Abraham's heart with pain. But he was not as surprised to receive such a command as a father might be in our day because of what the people who lived around him did. Abraham never for one moment doubted or disobeyed God's word. He knew that Isaac was the child God had promised to him. He remembered that God had promised that Isaac would have children and have many descendants. He did not see how God could keep his promise about Isaac if Isaac died as an offering. Perhaps God would raise him from the dead afterward.

Abraham obeyed God's command right away. He took Isaac, two young men, and a donkey loaded with firewood. They went toward the mountain in the north. Isaac walked by his father's side. For two days they walked, sleeping under trees at night in the open country. On the third day Abraham saw the mountain far away. As they came near it, Abraham said to the young men, "Stay here with the donkey while I go up the mountain with Isaac to worship. When we have worshiped, we will come back to you."

Abraham believed with all his heart that God would bring Isaac back to life. He took the wood from the donkey and put it on Isaac's back. The two went up the mountain together. As they were walking, Isaac said, "Father, here is the wood, but where is the lamb for the offering?" And Abraham said, "My son, God will provide the lamb."

Finally they came to the place on the top of the mountain. Abraham built an altar of stones and earth. On it he placed the wood. Then he tied the hands and feet of Isaac and laid him on the wood on the altar. Abraham picked up a knife and lifted his hand to kill Isaac. But just at that moment the angel of the Lord called out of heaven, "Abraham! Abraham!"

Abraham answered, "Here I am, Lord."

Then the angel of the Lord said, "Do not lay a hand on your son. Don't harm him. I know now that you love God more than you love your only son. I know you are obedient to God. You are ready to give up your son, your only son, to God."

What relief and joy these words from heaven brought to Abraham's heart. How glad he was to know it was not God's will for him to sacrifice his son! Then Abraham looked around, and there in the bushes was a ram caught by his horns. Abraham took the ram and offered it as a sacrifice in place of his son. So Abraham's words came true when he said that God would provide a lamb. Abraham gave the place a name—Jehova-jireh. In the language that Abraham spoke that means "the Lord will provide."

This offering, which seemed so strange, did much good. It showed Abraham and Isaac that Isaac belonged to God, for he had been offered to God. It

showed them that all those who would later come from Isaac, his descendants, had been given to God. It showed Abraham and all the people after him that God did not wish people to be killed as offerings for worship, even though all the people living around them made such sacrifices. And this offering looked forward to the time when God would give his Son, Jesus Christ, to die for the sins of the world. All this was taught in Abraham's act of obedience and worship on the top of Mount Moriah.

Some people think that at the very place where Abraham made his offering, another altar later stood when God's people built a temple to worship him. If that is true, the rock is still there, and over it is a building called the Dome of the Rock. Many people now visit this rock under the dome and think about what happened there so long ago.

After Abraham made his sacrifice, he went home to Beersheba, a place south of the land of Canaan. This is where he lived during his later years. After a time Sarah died. She was 120 years old. Abraham bought a cave and called it the cave of Machpelah. He buried his wife, Sarah, there.

Isaac and Rebekah

GENESIS 24:1–25:18

fter Sarah died, her son, Isaac, was lonely. He was old enough to marry, so his father, Abraham, started looking for a wife for him. Long ago in the country where Abraham lived, parents chose wives for their sons and husbands for their daughters. The children did not choose for themselves.

Abraham did not want Isaac to marry a woman from the land where they were living. All the people of that land worshiped idols. He knew that a wife from that land would never teach her children the ways of the Lord.

When Abraham had come to the land of Canaan, on the way he stayed for a while at Haran in Mesopotamia. When Abraham left Haran to go to Canaan, his brother Nahor and his family stayed in Haran. They worshiped the Lord, just as Abraham and his family did. Abraham thought that perhaps he could find a wife for Isaac among his brother's family.

Abraham could not go to Haran to find a wife for his son. So he called his chief servant, Eliezer. This was the man he most trusted. Eliezer cared for all

Abraham's flocks and cattle. It was his job to rule over all the other servants. So Abraham sent Eliezer to Haran to find a wife for Isaac.

The servant took ten camels and many presents and went toward Haran. It was a long journey, but at last one day he came near the city. In the evening he stopped at the well just outside the city. Eliezer made his camels kneel down. Then he prayed to the Lord to send just the right young woman to be a wife for Isaac.

Just as the servant was praying, a beautiful young woman came to the well with a water jar on her shoulder. As she drew water and filled her jar, Eliezer

came to her. He bowed and said, "Will you kindly give me a drink of water from your jar?"

She answered, "Drink, my lord." She held her jar for him to drink. Then she said, "I will draw some water for your camels also to drink." She emptied her jar into the trough by the well and drew more water until she had given all the camels a drink.

Eliezer looked at her and wondered if she might be the right woman for Isaac to marry. He said to her, "Will you tell me your name, young lady? Whose daughter are you? And do you suppose that I could find a place to stay at your father's house?" Then he gave her a gold ring and golden bracelets for her wrists.

The beautiful young woman said, "My name is Rebekah, and my father is Bethuel, who is the son of Nahor. You can come to our house. We have room for you, and a place and food for your camels."

Eliezer bowed his head and thanked God, for he saw that the Lord had answered his prayer. This kind and lovely young woman was a cousin to Isaac. He told Rebekah that he was the servant of Abraham— a near relative of her own family.

Rebekah ran home and told her parents about the stranger. She showed them the presents he had given her. Then her brother Laban went out to the well to find the man and bring him home. He also found a place for his camels. They washed Eliezer's feet. In that land where sandals were worn instead of shoes, people always welcomed guests by washing the dust of the road off their feet. Then Laban asked Eliezer to join them for supper. But Eliezer said, "I will not eat until I have told you why I've come."

So Eliezer told them all about Abraham and his riches and how Abraham had sent him to Haran to find a wife for Isaac. Then he told how he had met Rebekah at the well. He felt sure that Rebekah was the one the Lord had chosen to become Isaac's wife. He asked that they let Rebekah go with him to Abraham's home so she could be married to Isaac.

As soon as he had told them his errand, Rebekah's brother Laban and her father, Bethuel, said, "This comes from the Lord. It is his will. You may take Rebekah to be the wife of your master's son. The Lord has shown that it is his will." Then Abraham's servant gave rich presents to Rebekah and to her mother and to her brother Laban. That night they had a joyful feast.

In the morning Eliezer said, "Now I must go home to my master."

But they said, "Oh, not so soon! Let Rebekah stay with us for a few more days—ten days at least before she leaves her home."

But Eliezer said to them, "Don't stop me, since God has answered my prayer. Now I must go back to my master."

They called Rebekah and asked her, "Will you go with this man?"

And she said, "I will go."

So Eliezer went home and took Rebekah with him, with good wishes, blessings, and prayers from all in her father's house. After a long journey they came to the place where Abraham and Isaac were living. When Isaac saw Rebekah, he loved her. She became his wife, and they were faithful to each other as long as they both lived.

Later Abraham died. He was almost 180 years old. Isaac and Ishmael buried Abraham in the cave at Hebron where Sarah, Abraham's wife, was buried. Isaac became the owner of all the riches of his father. He inherited his father's tents, his flocks of sheep, his herds of cattle and camels, and all his servants. Isaac was a peaceful, quiet man. He did not move his tents often, as his father had done, but stayed in one place nearly all of his life.

JACOB

How Jacob Stole His Brother's Blessing

GENESIS 25:27–27:40

fter Abraham died, his son Isaac lived in Canaan. Like his father, Isaac lived in a tent, and around him were the tents of all his people. There were many sheep and herds of cattle feeding wherever they could find grass to eat and water to drink.

Isaac and his wife, Rebekah, had two sons. The older was named Esau, and the younger was named Jacob. Esau was a man of the woods who loved to hunt. He was rough and covered with hair. Jacob was quiet and thoughtful. He liked to stay home and care for his father's flocks. Isaac loved Esau more than Jacob, because Esau always brought his father the game he killed when hunting. But Rebekah liked Jacob because she saw that he was wise and careful in his work.

In those days when a man died, his oldest son received twice as much as the younger sons. This was his right as the firstborn son. This was called his "birthright." Esau was the older son and so had a birthright to more of his father's wealth. Besides the wealth, Esau had the promise of God that his family should receive great blessings.

When Esau grew up, he didn't care at all about his birthright or the blessing God had promised. But Jacob, who was a wise man, wanted Esau's birthright. One day when Esau came home hungry and tired from hunting in the fields, he saw that Jacob had a bowl of food cooked for dinner. Esau said, "Give me some of that red stuff in the dish, won't you? I am really hungry."

Jacob answered, "I will give it to you if you will first sell me your birthright."

Esau said, "What good is a birthright if I starve to death from hunger? You can have my birthright if you will give me something to eat."

Esau then promised Jacob that he would give Jacob his birthright for a bowl of food. It was not right for Jacob to deal so selfishly with his brother. But it was very wrong for Esau to care so little for his birthright and God's special blessing.

Sometime later, when Esau was forty years old, he married two wives. Although it would be a wicked thing to do in our time, it was a common practice among many people in Bible times. Many good men had more than one wife. But Esau's two wives were women from the people of Canaan. They worshiped idols, and they did not worship the true God. These wives taught their children to pray to idols. After a while Esau's descendants lost all knowledge of God and became very wicked.

Isaac and Rebekah were very sorry to have their son Esau marry women who prayed to idols and not to God. But still Isaac loved Esau more than Jacob.

In those days when a man died,
his oldest son received twice
as much as the younger sons.
This was his right as the firstborn son.
This was called his "birthright."

At last Isaac became very old and feeble and so blind that he could scarcely see anything. One day he said to Esau, "My son, I am very old, and soon I must die. But before I die, I wish to give you, my older son,

God's blessing upon you and your children and your descendants. Go out into the fields and with your bow and arrows shoot some animal that is good for food. Make me a dish of cooked meat—the kind you know I love. After I have eaten, I will give you the blessing."

Right then Esau ought to have told his father that the blessing did not belong to him. He should have said that he had sold it to Jacob. But instead he went hunting to find the kind of meat his father liked most.

Rebekah was listening and heard all that Isaac said to Esau. She knew that it would be better for Jacob to have the blessing than for Esau to have it. She loved Jacob more than Esau. So she called Jacob and told him what Isaac had said to Esau.

"Now, my son, do what I tell you," she said. "You will get the blessing instead of your brother. Go to the flocks and bring me two young goats from the goat herd. I will cook them just like the meat Esau cooks for your father. You will take it in to your father, and he will think that you are Esau. He will give you the blessing that really belongs to you."

But Jacob said, "You know that Esau and I are not alike. His neck and arms are covered with hair. Mine are smooth. My father will feel my arms and neck and will know that I am not Esau. I am afraid he will curse me."

But Rebekah said, "Never mind. You do as I have told you, and I will take care of you. If any harm comes, it will come to me, so do not be afraid. Just go and bring me the meat."

So Jacob went and brought a pair of young goats from the flock. His mother made a dish of food just the way Isaac liked it. Then Rebekah found some of Esau's clothes and dressed Jacob in them. She placed on his neck and hands some of the skins from the goats so his neck and hands would feel rough and hairy to the touch.

Jacob went into his father's tent carrying the dinner and speaking as much like Esau as he could. "Here I am, my father."

Isaac said, "Who are you, my son?"

Jacob answered, "I am Esau, your older son. I have done as you bade me. Now sit up and eat the dinner I have made. Then give me your blessing as you promised."

Isaac said, "How is it that you have found it so quickly?"

Jacob answered, "Because the Lord your God showed me where to go and gave me good success."

Isaac still wasn't sure that it was Esau who was speaking. He said, "Come nearer and let me feel you so I may know that you are really my son Esau."

Jacob went close to Isaac's bed. Isaac reached out and touched him and said, "The voice sounds like Jacob, but the hands are the hands of Esau. Are you really my son Esau?"

Jacob again told his father a lie and said, "I am."

Then the old man ate the food that Jacob had brought him. He kissed Jacob because he believed he was Esau, and he gave Jacob the blessing. Isaac said to him, "May God give you the dew of heaven and the richness of the earth and plenty of grain and wine. May nations bow down to you and become your servants. May you be the master over your brother. May your family and descendants rule over his family and his descendants. Blessed be those who bless you. Cursed be those who curse you."

As soon as Jacob had received the blessing, he rose and hurried away. He had scarcely gone out when Esau came in from hunting. He had a dish of food that he had cooked. He said, "Father, sit up and eat the food that I have brought. And give me the blessing."

Isaac said, "Why? Who are you?"

Esau answered, "I am your older son, Esau."

Then Isaac trembled and said, "Who then came in and brought me food? I have eaten his food and blessed him. Yes, and he shall be blessed."

When Esau heard this, he knew he had been cheated. He cried aloud with a bitter cry and said, "O my father, my brother has taken away my blessing and my birthright! Can't you give me a blessing, too? Have you given everything to my brother?"

Then Isaac told him all that he had said to Jacob. "I have told Jacob that he shall be the ruler. I have put all his brothers and their children under him. I have promised him the richest ground for his crops, and rains from heaven to make them grow. All these things have been spoken and they must come to pass. What is left for me to promise you, my son?"

But Esau begged for another blessing, and Isaac said, "My son, your dwelling shall be of the riches of the earth and the dew of heaven. You will live by your sword, and your descendants shall serve his descendants. But in time to come they shall break loose and shake off your brother's rule. They shall be free."

Hundreds of years later it all came true just as Isaac had said it would. The blessing of God's covenant or promise came to the people of Israel, Jacob's descendants, instead of the people from Esau, the Edomites. It was best that the blessing came to Jacob and his descendants, for they worshiped God. Esau's people worshiped idols. But it was very wrong for Jacob to get the blessing in the way that he did.

Jacob's Wonderful Dream

GENESIS 27:41–28:22

hen he realized he had lost his birthright and his blessing, Esau was very angry with Jacob, his brother. He said, "My father, Isaac, is very old and will not live long. As soon as he is dead, I will kill Jacob for robbing me."

When Rebekah, their mother, heard this, she said to Jacob, "Before it is too late, go away from home. Get out of Esau's sight. Perhaps when he can no longer see you, he will forget his anger and then you can come home again. Go visit my brother Laban, your uncle in Haran, and stay with him for a while."

It was a long distance to Haran, where Rebekah's brother lived. One evening Jacob went out of Beersheba, on the border of the desert, and walked alone toward a land far to the northeast. He carried his staff in his hand. One evening, just about sunset, he came to a place among the mountains more than sixty miles from his home. As he had no bed to lie upon, he took a stone and rested his head on it as you would a pillow. He lay down to sleep. We would think that was a very hard pillow, but Jacob was very tired and soon fell asleep.

In the night he had a wonderful dream. In his dream he saw stairs leading from earth up to heaven. Angels were coming down and going up the stairs. Above the stairs he saw the Lord God standing.

God said to Jacob, "I am the Lord, the God of Abraham and the God of Isaac, your father. I will be your God, too. The land where you are lying all alone will belong to you and your children after you. Your children will spread abroad over the lands east and west, north and south. They will be like the dust of the earth, and through your family all the world

will be blessed. I am going with you on your journey, and I will watch over you everywhere you go. I will

> *God said to Jacob, "I will bring you back to this land. I will never leave you, and I will surely keep my promise to you."*

bring you back to this land. I will never leave you, and I will surely keep my promise to you."

In the morning Jacob woke up and said, "Surely the Lord is in this place, and I didn't even know it! I thought I was alone, but God has been with me. This place is the house of God. It is the gate of heaven!" Then Jacob took the stone he had used for a pillow and set it up as a pillar. He poured oil on it as an offering to God. Jacob named the place Bethel, which in his language means "the house of God."

Jacob made a promise to God at that time. He said, "If God really will go with me and will watch over me on my journey and give me bread to eat and will bring me to my father's house in peace, then the Lord shall be my God. This stone shall be the house of God. And I will give back to God as an offering one-tenth of all he gives me."

Jacob Meets Rachel

GENESIS 29:1–30:24

acob continued his long journey. He waded across the river Jordan at a shallow place, feeling his way with his staff. He climbed mountains and journeyed beside the great desert on the east. At last he came to the city of Haran. There beside the city was the well where Abraham's servant had first met Jacob's mother, Rebekah. After a while a young woman with a band of sheep came to the well. It was Rachel.

Jacob took off the flat stone that covered the well. He drew water out of the well and gave it to all of Rachel's sheep. Then he learned that this young woman was his own cousin, Rachel, the daughter of Laban. He was so glad to meet her that he wept for joy. Right then he began to love Rachel and longed to have her for his wife.

Rachel's father, Laban, who was also Jacob's uncle, welcomed Jacob and took him into the house. Jacob asked Laban if he could marry Rachel. He said, "If you will give me Rachel, I will work for you seven years."

Laban said, "It is better that you should have her than that a stranger marry her."

So Jacob lived for seven years in Laban's house, caring for his sheep, oxen, and camels. He loved Rachel so much that the seven years seemed like only a few days.

At last the day came for the wedding. They brought in the bride, and she was covered from head to toe with a thick veil, so her face could not be seen. She and Jacob were married. But when Jacob lifted

> *He was so glad to meet her that he wept for joy. Right then he began to love Rachel and longed to have her for his wife.*

her veil to look at his beautiful Rachel, under the veil was Rachel's older sister, Leah, who was not beautiful. Jacob did not love Leah. He had not asked to marry her. Jacob was very angry. He had been tricked. He did not remember that he himself had tricked his father and cheated his brother Esau.

Laban explained, "In our land we never allow the younger daughter to be married before the older daughter. Keep Leah for your wife and work for me seven years longer, and you shall have Rachel also."

Even though God did not approve of it, people in those times did not think it was wrong to have more than one wife. No one thought it was wrong to have more than one wife, as we do today. So Jacob stayed seven years more before Rachel became his wife.

While Jacob was living at Haran, eleven sons were born to him. Only one of these was the child of his beloved Rachel. This son, Joseph, was dearer to Jacob than any of his other children because he was the youngest and because he was Rachel's child.

A Midnight Wrestling Match

GENESIS 30:25–33:20

 acob lived in the land of Haran for a long time. He was there much longer than he had expected to stay. He became very rich. Laban paid Jacob's wages by giving him a share of his sheep and oxen and camels. Jacob was very wise and careful in his work, so his share grew larger until he owned a great flock and many cattle. At last, after twenty years, Jacob decided to go back to the land of Canaan. He missed his father, Isaac, who was still living though now very old and feeble.

Jacob did not tell his uncle Laban that he was leaving. While Laban was away from home, Jacob quietly gathered his wives and children and all his sheep, cattle, and camels and left Haran. When Laban learned that Jacob had left him, he was not pleased. He wanted Jacob to continue taking care of everything for him. Jacob was a better manager than Laban. God blessed everything Jacob did. Laban also did not want Jacob to take his daughters so far away.

So Laban and his men followed Jacob. But that night God spoke to Laban in a dream and said,

"Don't harm Jacob when you meet him." So when Laban came to Jacob's camp on Mount Gilead, on the east side of the river Jordan, Laban spoke kindly to Jacob. The two men made a covenant—a promise—to each other. They piled up a heap of stones. On top of the stones they set a large rock like a pillar. Then Jacob and Laban sat down and ate a meal together. Jacob said to Laban, "I promise not to go past this heap of stones and this pillar to do you any harm. May the God of your grandfather, Nahor, and the God of my grandfather, Abraham, be the judge between us."

Laban made the same promise to Jacob. Then he kissed his daughters and all his grandchildren goodbye. Laban went back to Haran, and Jacob went on to Canaan.

Jacob gave two names to the heap of stones where they had made the covenant. One name was Galeed, a word that means "the heap of witness." The other was Mizpeh, which means "watchtower." Jacob said, "The Lord watch between you and me when we are absent from each other."

Shortly after this, while Jacob was still on his way to Canaan, he heard news that filled him with fear. He heard that Esau, his brother, was coming to meet him, leading an army of four hundred men. He knew how angry Esau had been long before and how he had threatened to kill him. Jacob feared that Esau would now come and kill him and his wives and children.

If Jacob had acted in a right way toward his brother, he would not have been afraid of Esau's coming. But Jacob knew he had wronged Esau. He was terribly afraid to meet him.

That night Jacob divided all that were with him into two parts. If one part were captured, the other might escape. Then he sent a great many oxen, cows, sheep, goats, camels, and donkeys to his brother as a present. He hoped that the present would make his brother be kind to him. He then sent all his family across the brook called Jabbok. He stayed behind to pray.

While Jacob was praying alone, a man grabbed him and fought with him. Jacob wrestled with this

strange man all night. The man was an angel from God. They wrestled so hard that Jacob's hip was strained in the struggle. The angel said, "Let me go, for it is daybreak."

Jacob answered, "I will not let you go until you bless me."

Then the angel said, "What is your name?"

He answered, "My name is Jacob."

Then the angel said, "Your name will no longer be Jacob but Israel, which means 'he who wrestles with God.' For you have wrestled with God and have won the victory."

Then the angel blessed him. As the sun rose, the angel left. Jacob named the place Peniel, a word that means "the face of God." He said, "I have met God face to face." After this Jacob (Israel) walked with a limp because of the strain.

Early the next morning as Jacob crossed the brook, he looked up, and there was Esau coming right toward him. Jacob bowed seven times before Esau with his face to the ground. It was the custom in that land that when meeting someone of higher rank, you bowed. Esau ran to meet Jacob. He put his arms around Jacob and kissed him. The two brothers wept. Esau forgave Jacob for all the wrong that he had done. At first Esau would not receive Jacob's presents. He said, "I have enough, my brother." But Jacob urged him until at last he took the gifts. That ended the quarrel between the two brothers. They were at peace.

Soon afterward Jacob came to Shechem, a place in the middle of Canaan. There he set up his tents at the foot of a mountain. Although there were streams of water all around, he dug his own well, great and deep. This is the well where many hundreds of years later Jesus sat down and talked with a woman. The well may still be seen today.

Sometimes Jacob was called Jacob and sometimes he was called Israel. But all who came from him—all his descendants—were called Israelites.

Not long after Jacob returned, Isaac died and was buried by his sons Jacob and Esau. They placed him in the cave at Hebron where Abraham and Sarah were buried. Then Esau took his family and cattle and went away to a land on the southeast of Canaan, which was called Edom. Jacob, or Israel, and his family lived in the land of Canaan. They lived in tents and moved from place to place to find the best pasture for their flocks.

JOSEPH

The Dreamer

GENESIS 35–37

fter Jacob came back to the land of Canaan with his eleven sons and two wives, another son was born to him and Rachel. Jacob had worked long and hard for Laban, Rachel's father, so she could become his wife. Jacob loved her very much. But now a great sorrow came to him. Soon after the baby was born, Rachel died. Jacob was filled with sadness. Jacob named the baby Benjamin. Now Jacob had twelve sons. By the time Benjamin was born, most of Jacob's sons were grown men. But the two sons his wife Rachel had, Joseph and Benjamin, were still young boys.

Of all his children, Jacob loved Joseph the best. Joseph was Rachel's child, and he was born when Jacob was old. Jacob made a beautiful robe of many colors of cloth and gave it to Joseph. It was a long coat with wide sleeves. This special gift was a sign of Jacob's love for Joseph, and it made the older brothers very jealous.

The brothers didn't like Joseph because he obeyed their father, while they often did not follow their father's instructions. They did whatever they felt like doing. Sometimes Joseph told on them, and that made the brothers very angry with him. But they hated him most because of two strange dreams he told them about. He said, "I dreamed that we were out in the field binding sheaves when suddenly my sheaf stood up and all your sheaves came around mine and bowed down to it."

The brothers sneered, saying, "Do you think the dream means you will rule over us in the future? Do you think we will bow down to you?"

Then Joseph had another dream, and he told them about this one, too. "This time I saw in my dream the sun, the moon, and eleven stars all come and bow down to me."

His father said, "What is this dream you had? Will your mother and I and your brothers come and bow down before you as if you were a king?"

> *The brothers saw him coming in his bright coat, and they started plotting. "Look, the dreamer is coming! Let's kill him and throw his body into a pit. Then we can tell Father that some wild animal ate him. We will see if his great dreams come true."*

So his brothers hated Joseph and would not speak a kind word to him, but his father thought about what Joseph had dreamed. He kept it in mind.

One day Joseph's older brothers were taking care of their father's flocks near a town called Shechem.

JOSEPH'S FATHER GAVE HIM A COLORFUL COAT

Joseph's older brothers were angry because their father
didn't give them a beautiful coat.

JOSEPH FORGAVE HIS BROTHERS

The whole family came to live with Joseph.
They were happy together in Egypt.

Jacob sent Joseph to see how the brothers were doing and to bring back a report. It was fifty miles away—quite a long trip for a boy to take all alone. Joseph walked all the way there but could not find his brothers! Finally he met a man who told him they had gone on to Dothan, a city that was fifteen miles farther. Joseph must have been tired, but he kept walking until he found them.

The brothers saw him coming in his bright coat, and they started plotting. "Look, the dreamer is coming! Let's kill him and throw his body into a pit. Then we can tell Father that some wild animal ate him. We will see if his great dreams come true."

One of his brothers, whose name was Reuben, felt more kindly toward Joseph than the others did. He hoped to rescue Joseph after the others had gone away, so he said, "We don't have to kill him ourselves. All we have to do is throw him into this empty well and leave him here in the wilderness to die." Reuben wanted to secretly come back later and take Joseph home to their father.

Since the other brothers didn't know Reuben's plan, they went along with it. First they tore off Joseph's colorful coat, and then they threw him into the empty pit, even though he cried and begged them not to do it. Then they calmly sat down to eat their dinner on the grass nearby.

After dinner Reuben had to go to another part of the field, so he was away when a group of men passed by with camels loaded with bundles. They were merchants going to Egypt to sell spices, lotions, and myrrh. Judah, another of Joseph's older brothers, had a new idea. "Instead of letting Joseph die and go to waste, why don't we sell him to these traders and make ourselves some money? That way we won't have to cover up what we've done, because he will be gone. And after all, he is our brother!"

The others agreed and made a deal with the merchants. Joseph's own brothers sold him as a slave for eight ounces of silver. When Reuben came back and found out what they had done, he was very upset, but he finally agreed with the others to tell their father a lie.

The brothers killed one of the goats from their father's flock. Then they dipped Joseph's beautiful colored coat in the goat's blood. They took the coat back to Jacob and said, "We found this coat out in the wilderness. Look at it and see if you think it was your son's."

The minute Jacob saw it, his heart broke because he knew it was the special coat he had made for

Joseph. "It is my son's robe!" he cried. "Some wild animal has eaten him. It must have torn him to pieces." He wept for many days, thinking of how he

> *The minute Jacob saw it, his heart broke because he knew it was the special coat he had made for Joseph. "It is my son's robe!" he cried. "Some wild animal has eaten him."*

had sent young Joseph alone on the journey through the wilderness. Everyone tried to comfort him, but he would not be comforted. "I will go down to my grave mourning for my poor lost son," he said, sobbing.

So the old man lived in sadness, missing his son, because of the lie those wicked brothers told. They knew that Joseph was not dead, but to keep themselves from getting into trouble, they would not confess to their father the dreadful deed they had done. But trouble came to them just the same.

In the meantime Joseph found himself living in a very different place. Instead of sleeping in tents and herding goats, he lived and worked in an Egyptian palace! The traders had sold him to the captain of the guard of the king of Egypt.

Prison to Palace

GENESIS 40:1–41:44

oseph's brothers sold him as a slave to some men from Midian who were on their way to Egypt. Joseph saw many sights as they traveled that must have seemed strange to him. He had always lived in tents with his family, but in Egypt the people made large buildings to live in. They also made huge pyramids and temples full of statues and color. There were crowds of people everywhere.

The Midianites sold Joseph to a man named Potiphar, an officer in the Egyptian army. He was the captain of the palace guard for Egypt's ruler, the pharaoh. Potiphar was pleased with Joseph because he was cheerful and hardworking. God blessed all that Joseph did. Before long Potiphar put Joseph in charge of his house and everything in it. Although Joseph had been bought as a slave, Potiphar treated him as the ruler of all the other servants in his house.

At first Potiphar's wife was friendly to Joseph. But she became his enemy because Joseph would not obey her when she asked him to do things that were wrong. She lied to her husband about Joseph to get him into trouble. Potiphar believed his wife when she said Joseph had done wrong. He was angry because he had trusted Joseph with everything and it looked as if Joseph had tricked him. Poor Joseph was thrown in prison even though he had done nothing wrong.

Joseph had faith in God. He believed that everything would work out all right for him in the end. He believed that God knew he was innocent. That was the most important thing for Joseph. He stayed cheerful and helpful. Soon the keeper of the prison put him in charge of all the other prisoners. Joseph took care of them just as he had taken care of everything in Potiphar's house. Joseph was faithful and wise, and God blessed everything he did.

The pharaoh sent two new men to the prison because they had angered him. One was the royal butler, who served the king's wine. The other was the royal baker, who made the king's bread. Joseph took care of both men and waited on them because they had been in royal offices.

One morning Joseph saw that the butler and baker looked sad. He asked them what was wrong. One of them told him, "Each of us dreamed a very strange dream last night. There is no one here who can tell us what our dreams mean."

In those times most people believed that dreams were sent as messages from God. They didn't have Bibles to read to find out what God wanted them to do with their lives. They were worried that God would send them a dream and they wouldn't understand what he wanted them to do. They went to wise men who could sometimes tell them what the dreams meant.

Joseph knew about dreams and their meaning. His brothers had called him "the dreamer" because he believed that God spoke to him in dreams. So he said to the men, "Tell me your dreams. Maybe my God will help me understand them."

The royal butler told his dream first. "In my dream," he said, "I saw a grapevine with three branches. As I looked, the branches shot out buds. The buds opened into flowers. The flowers turned into clusters of ripe grapes. I picked the grapes and squeezed their juice into Pharaoh's cup. The juice turned into wine. I gave it to the king to drink, just as I used to do when I served his table in the palace."

Then Joseph said, "Here is what your dream means: The three branches stand for three days. In three days the king will call you out of prison. He will give your old job back. You will serve his table and give him his wine as you used to do. When you get out of prison, please remember me. Try to find some way to help me get out of prison, too. Please speak to the king for me."

Of course the royal butler felt very happy to hear that the first man's dream had such a good meaning. So the royal baker told his dream. He hoped for a good meaning as well. "In my dream," he said, "I carried three baskets of breads on my head, piled one on top of the other. The basket on top held all kinds of

baked goods for Pharaoh. But birds came and ate the food out of the baskets."

Joseph said to the baker, "Here is the meaning of your dream: I am sorry to tell you that Pharaoh will sentence you to death. The three baskets on your head mean that in three days the king will have your head cut off. The birds eating the bread mean you will be eaten by birds after you are dead."

In three days both things happened just as Joseph had told the men. It was Pharaoh's birthday, and he held a party for all his officials. He called the royal butler and the royal baker out of prison. In front of everyone he gave the royal butler his job back. Then he sentenced the royal baker to have his head cut off.

The royal butler was so glad to be back at his job. He came and stood by the king every day, serving his table. But he forgot all about Joseph and his promise to help get him out of prison. Two more years passed, and Joseph turned thirty years old in the prison.

Then one night Pharaoh himself dreamed two dreams. In the morning he sent for all the wise men of Egypt and told them his dreams. No one could explain the meaning of the dreams. The king was upset. He felt his dreams had some important meaning.

Suddenly the chief butler remembered the young man who had explained his dream's meaning. He said, "I remember something I'd forgotten until

> *Pharaoh told Joseph, "I have dreamed dreams, and there is no one who can tell me what they mean. I was told you have the power to understand dreams and explain their meaning."*

today. Two years ago Pharaoh was angry with his servants. He sent me and the chief baker to prison. When we were there, we each dreamed a dream. The next day a young Hebrew man told us what our dreams meant. In three days they came true, just as the man had said. I think that if the king sends for this man who is in prison, he could explain the meaning of the king's dreams."

The butler and other Egyptians called Joseph and his people "Hebrew." The people of Israel were called Hebrew as well as Israelite. The word *Hebrew* means "one who crosses over." It was given to the Israelites because Abraham, their ancestor, had come from a land on the other side of the Euphrates River.

He and his family had crossed over on their way to
Canaan.

Pharaoh quickly sent for Joseph. The guards took
him out of prison and gave him new clothes to wear.

> *Pharaoh said to Joseph, "There is
> no other man as wise as you. God has
> shown you all this. I will put you in
> charge of the crops and land in Egypt.
> All the people will obey you. I will be the
> only one higher than you in all of Egypt,
> because I sit on the throne."*

Then they brought him to the king at his palace.
Pharaoh told Joseph, "I have dreamed dreams, and
there is no one who can tell me what they mean. I
was told you have the power to understand dreams
and explain their meaning."

Joseph answered, "The power is not in me, but
God will give Pharaoh a good answer. What are the
dreams?"

"In my first dream," said Pharaoh, "I stood by the
river. I saw seven fat and handsome cows come up
from the river to feed on grass. While they were eat-

ing, seven thin and bony cows followed them up from the river. I have never seen such ugly cows in all the land of Egypt. These seven thin cows ate the seven fat cows. But after they had eaten the fat cows, the thin cows still looked just as bony and ugly as before. Then I woke up."

Then Pharaoh told his second dream. "I went back to sleep and dreamed again. I saw seven large, strong heads of grain growing on one stalk. Then seven thin, weak heads grew up after them. The seven thin heads of grain swallowed the seven large heads. But afterward they were just as thin as before."

Pharaoh said to Joseph, "I told these two dreams to all the wise men. There was no one who could explain their meaning. Can you tell me what these dreams mean?"

Joseph said to the king, "Pharaoh's two dreams mean the same thing. God has been showing the king what he will do in this land. The seven fat cows and the seven large heads of grain stand for seven years when there will be plenty of food. There are seven years coming when Egypt will have more crops from their fields than they have ever seen. The seven thin cows and the seven thin heads of grain stand for seven poor years. After the seven good years there will be seven bad years. In the bad years the fields will hardly grow any crops for people to eat. Things will be so bad that the people will forget all about the seven good years.

"God gave Pharaoh two dreams about these years because they are coming soon. Let the king find some wise man to be in charge of the land. During the first seven years, when there is plenty of food, he can store away part of the crops. Then the people can use the stored crops for food during the seven bad years. Egypt will have plenty of food in all the years so the people will not starve."

Then Pharaoh said to Joseph, "There is no other man as wise as you. God has shown you all this. I will put you in charge of the crops and land in Egypt. All the people will obey you. I will be the only one higher than you in all of Egypt, because I sit on the throne."

Pharaoh took off his signet ring and gave it to Joseph so he could give orders from the king to everyone in Egypt. The pharaoh dressed Joseph in royal robes and put a gold chain around his neck. He had Joseph ride in a chariot next to his own royal chariot. All the Egyptians cried out, "Make way!" when they saw the man who had once been a slave boy. God had not forgotten Joseph after all.

Joseph's Dreams Come True

GENESIS 41:46–42:38

hen Joseph was made ruler over the land of Egypt, he did as he had always done. It was not Joseph's way to sit down and rest and enjoy himself. He did not make others wait on him. He began to do his work faithfully. He went all over the land of Egypt and saw how rich the grain fields were. The people had much more grain than they needed. He told them not to waste it. He told them to save it for the time of need that was coming.

Joseph asked the people to give him one bushel of grain out of every five they harvested. This would be stored in the king's storehouses. So the people kept as much grain as they needed to eat, and they brought their extra grain to Joseph to store. Every city had a storehouse.

The king of Egypt gave Joseph a wife from the noble young women of his kingdom. Her name was Asenath. God blessed her and Joseph with two sons. He named the older son Manasseh, a word that means "making to forget." Joseph said, "God has made me forget all my troubles and my life as a slave." He named the second son Ephraim, a word that means "fruitful." Joseph said, "God has not only made the land fruitful, but he has made me fruitful in the land of my troubles."

The seven years of plenty soon passed. The years when there was little food came right after the good years. In all the lands around Egypt people were hungry. There was no food for them to eat. But in the land of Egypt everyone had enough food. When their fields ran out of grain, they went to Joseph. He opened the storehouses and sold grain to them. People came from the other countries to buy from him as well.

The land of Canaan, where Jacob lived, also needed food. Jacob had many animals and lots of money, but his fields would not grow much grain. His family and people would starve if they did not find a place to buy some.

Jacob told his sons, "I have been told there is grain in Egypt. Go down to that land and take money to buy grain. Then we will be able to make bread and live."

So the ten older brothers of Joseph went down to the land of Egypt. They rode all the way on donkeys, and they brought money with them. Jacob would not let Benjamin, Joseph's younger brother, go with them. He was very special to his father now that Joseph was gone. Jacob feared that harm might come to Benjamin.

The ten brothers went right to Joseph to buy food. They did not know him now that he was a grown man. He dressed like a prince, and he sat on a throne. Joseph was almost forty years old. It had been almost twenty-three years since they had sold him as a slave. Joseph knew his brothers as soon as he saw them. He decided to be sharp and stern with them. He wanted to see what they were like now. He wondered if they were as selfish and mean as they had been when he was with them.

The brothers came before Joseph and bowed with their faces on the ground. Joseph remembered the dream he had about his brothers' bundles of grain bowing down to his. He spoke to them as if he were a stranger. He even pretended not to understand their language. A servant told him what their language meant in Egyptian words.

"Who are you? Where do you come from?" Joseph asked them in Egyptian. He tried to sound angry.

They answered him very meekly, "We have come from the land of Canaan to buy food."

"I don't believe you," Joseph replied. "You must be spies. You came to see how helpless our land is so you can make war on us."

"No, no," said Joseph's ten brothers. "We are not spies. We are all sons of one man who lives in Canaan. We have come to buy food because we have none at home."

"You say you are the sons of one man. Who is your father? Is he living? Do you have any more brothers? Tell me about yourselves."

So they said, "Our father is an old man. We did have a younger brother, but he was lost. We have one brother left, who is the youngest of all. Our father could not spare him to come with us."

Joseph pretended he did not believe his brothers. He put them in prison for three days. Then he sent for them again. They did not know he could understand their language. They talked together about what to say to him. Joseph listened but pretended he did not understand. They said, "This bad thing has happened because of what we did to our brother Joseph. We heard him cry for help when we threw him into the pit. We did not have mercy on him, and God is punishing us."

Reuben, who had tried to save Joseph, said, "Didn't I tell you not to harm the boy? You would not listen. God is bringing this on us all now."

When Joseph heard this, his heart was touched. He saw that his brothers were really sorry for what they had done to him. He turned away from them so they could not see his face, and he cried. Then he turned back to them and said angrily, "I serve God, so I will let you all go home except for one man. I will keep him here in prison. The rest may go home and take food for your people. You must come back and bring your youngest brother with you. Then I will know you have told me the truth about yourselves."

Joseph ordered his servants to tie up one of the brothers, named Simeon, and take him off to the prison. Then he told them to fill up his brothers' sacks with the grain they had bought. But before they tied the sacks shut, Joseph had his servants secretly put each brother's money back in the top of his sack. The brothers loaded their bundles on their donkeys and left for home without their brother Simeon.

On the way home the brothers stopped to eat. One of them opened his grain sack. When he saw his money lying on top of the grain, he showed the others. They were all afraid that the stern Egyptian ruler would be angry with them if they tried to explain that a mistake had been made. He had already accused them of being spies. Would he think they were also thieves if he found out about the money?

When they got home, they told Jacob about the problem. They told him about the stern Egyptian who was keeping Simeon prisoner until they came back and showed him Benjamin. Jacob was very upset. He did not want them to take Benjamin to Egypt. He was afraid he would never see his youngest son again. For a time he would not let the brothers go back. But soon they had used up all the food and needed to get more.

A Lost Brother Found

GENESIS 43:1–45:28

oon Joseph's brothers and their families had eaten almost all of the food they had bought in Egypt. Jacob told them, "Go down to Egypt again and buy some more food for us." The brothers knew that the stern Egyptian ruler (who was really their lost brother Joseph) would never sell them more food unless Benjamin came with them as he had asked. So the brothers talked Jacob into letting Benjamin go with them. Jacob sent presents he hoped would make the Egyptian ruler happy instead of angry. The brothers even took twice as much money so they could pay back the money Joseph had hidden in their grain sacks last time.

They came to Joseph's office where he sold grain to all the people. They bowed to their brother, and he saw that they had brought Benjamin with them. He told his servant to take the brothers to his house and make a big dinner for them. The brothers tried to give the extra money to the servant, but he would not take it. The servant told them, "Don't be afraid. Your God must have sent you this as a gift. I got the money for the grain you bought last time."

The servant took care of the brothers until Joseph got home. They bowed to him again and gave him the gifts their father had sent. Joseph asked them if they were well. He asked about their father. They said, "Our father is living and well." Joseph looked at his younger brother, Benjamin. He was the child of his own mother, Rachel. Joseph said, "Is this your youngest brother you told me about? God bless you, my son." Then Joseph's heart was so full of love, he could not stop his tears. He ran to another room and cried. Then he washed his face and returned to have dinner. He had his servants give Benjamin five times as much food as the other brothers. Maybe he wanted to see if the brothers were as jealous of Benjamin as they had been of him.

After dinner Joseph told his servant, "Fill the men's sacks with as much grain as they can carry. Put each man's money back in his sack again. And put my own silver cup in the youngest brother's sack with his money."

After the brothers left for home, Joseph told his servant to follow them. He had the servant stop the brothers and tell them he knew they had stolen his master's silver cup. The brothers didn't know the cup was in Benjamin's sack. They told the servant to search all their sacks. They said he could put to death anyone whose sack had the cup hidden inside. When the servant opened Benjamin's sack and pulled out the silver cup, the brothers were sad and afraid. They all went back to Joseph's house thinking they would be put to death or made into his slaves.

Joseph pretended to be angry and said, "What evil thing is this that you have done? Didn't you know I would find out about it?"

Then Judah said, "O my lord, what can we say? God has punished us for our sins. We must all be your slaves."

But Joseph replied, "No, only one of you is guilty. I will keep the one who took my cup as my slave. The rest of you can go back to your father." He wanted

> *Joseph said, "I am Joseph your brother, whom you sold into Egypt. But don't feel afraid. God sent me before you to save your lives."*

to see if his brothers were still selfish enough to let Benjamin suffer while they escaped. Then Judah fell at Joseph's feet and begged him to let Benjamin go. Judah was the brother who had told the others to sell Joseph as a slave when he was a boy. Now he offered to take Benjamin's place. Joseph had found out what he wanted to know. His brothers were no longer mean and selfish. One of them was willing to suffer so Benjamin could go free. Joseph was so happy that he couldn't keep his secret any longer.

He sent all his Egyptian servants out of the room. When he was alone with his brothers, he said to them in their own language, "Come here to me. I am your brother Joseph. Is my father really alive?"

The brothers were even more afraid then. They thought Joseph would be very angry. But he forgave them instead. He said, "I am Joseph your brother, whom you sold into Egypt. But don't feel afraid. God sent me before you to save your lives. For two years food has been hard to find. It will be five more years before the fields grow grain. You were not the ones who sent me to Egypt. God has made me like a father to Pharaoh. I am ruler over all the land of Egypt. Now go home and bring my father and all his family to Egypt. That is the only way to save their lives."

Joseph and his brothers hugged and kissed and cried together. The brothers went home with good news, rich gifts, and lots of food. Joseph sent wagons with them to use to bring his father and all his family to Egypt. Jacob was full of joy to learn that his son Joseph was still alive. He and his family rode to Egypt on royal wagons to live with him. They were all happy together for many years.

MOSES

⁂

The Beautiful Baby Found in a River

EXODUS 1–2

he children of Israel stayed in the land of Egypt much longer than they had expected to stay. They were in that land about four hundred years. Going down to Egypt was a great blessing to them. It saved their lives during the years of famine and need. The soil in the land of Goshen, that part of Egypt where they were living, was very rich. They could gather three or four crops every year.

The other thing they liked about living in Goshen was that they lived apart from the other people of Egypt. Their children didn't learn about the idols the other nations worshiped. They learned to worship only the Lord God. They were happy and healthy and grew from just seventy people to such a great number that they filled the land.

As long as Joseph was alive, the Egyptians treated his family kindly. They loved him because he had saved Egypt from starving during the famine. But after Joseph died, a new king became ruler. He didn't remember all that Joseph had done to help the pharaoh in the past. He became afraid of the Israelites because there were so many of them. He wanted to make them weaker so they would not be able to take over his land. He made them become slaves and work for cruel slave drivers. These men made Israel's children work very hard with little food.

But that didn't stop their numbers from growing. So the pharaoh ordered that all boy babies born to Israelite families had to be thrown into the Nile River, and only girl babies would be allowed to live.

One mother hid her boy baby for three months after he was born. He was such a lovely child that she could not bear to follow Pharaoh's cruel order. When she could no longer hide him, she thought of a plan to save his life.

The mother believed that God would help her save her beautiful little boy. So she got a little basket made from some long, sturdy grass. She covered it with tar that would keep out the cold river water. Then she put her baby in the basket. It was like a little boat. She slipped the little boat bed in among the tall reeds that grew along the banks of the Nile. She sent her little girl named Miriam to hide and see what would happen to her brother.

As Miriam watched, Pharaoh's daughter came to the river with her maids to take a bath. They saw the basket floating on the water among the reeds, and the princess sent one of her maids to bring it to her so she might see what was in the mysterious basket. When she opened it, she saw a beautiful baby. He looked up at her and began to cry.

The princess loved him at once. She said, "This is one of the Hebrews' children." But even though she knew about Pharaoh's order, she felt sorry for the tiny baby all alone on the river. At that moment Miriam came out of her hiding place and offered to help.

"Shall I go find a Hebrew woman to be a nurse to the child for you?" she asked.

"Yes," said the princess. "Go and find a nurse for me."

So the girl ran as quickly as she could and brought her own mother to the princess. Miriam showed that she was a wise and brave girl by speaking up and helping her brother. The princess commanded the baby's real mother, "Take this child and nurse him for me, and I will pay you wages for it."

How glad the mother was to take her own child home! No one could harm him now, for the princess of Egypt protected him.

When he was grown enough to leave his mother, Pharaoh's daughter took him into her own home in the palace. She named him Moses, a word that means

"drawn out." She said, "I pulled him out of the water."

So Moses the Hebrew boy lived in the palace among the nobles of the land. He became the son of the princess. He learned from wise royal teachers all the knowledge of the Egyptians. He grew up free in the court of the cruel king who had made slaves of his people.

When he became a grown man, Moses felt a call from God to help set the Israelites free. Because of this the Pharaoh became his enemy, and Moses had to leave the riches of the Egyptian palace. He had to hide from the angry king, so he went to live with kind shepherds in the land of Midian. That was where he met his wife. He stayed there until God brought him back to Egypt to do the work he had planned for Moses from the beginning.

The Voice from the Burning Bush

Exodus 3:1–4:31

oses lived in a palace as a prince of Egypt for forty years. But later the Egyptians became his enemies. So he left the palace and became a shepherd in the land of Midian. For forty more years Moses wandered with his flock of sheep. He lived alone and often slept on the ground instead of in a palace. He lived in wild country surrounded by mountains instead of in cities full of people surrounded by pyramids and big buildings. He wore a rough leather robe and carried a shepherd's staff that looked like a walking stick. He wore sandals on his feet, but he took them off when he stood by an altar to worship God. That was the way his people showed respect for God. It was like the way men today may take off their hats to show respect.

Moses was a wise man. He was one of the greatest men who ever lived. But he did not think of himself as great or wise. He was content with the work he was doing. He sought no higher place. God, however, had other work for Moses to do. During all those years in the wilderness God was getting Moses ready for God's special work.

While Moses was wandering with his flock of sheep in Midian, the people of Israel were bearing heavy burdens as slaves in Egypt. They made bricks and built cities for Pharaoh.

One day Moses was feeding his flock on Mount Horeb. This mountain was also called Mount Sinai in the Bible. Moses saw a bush that seemed to be on fire. He watched to see it burn up to ashes. But the bush just kept burning and did not disappear. Moses said to himself, "I will go closer and look at this strange thing. Why doesn't the bush burn up?"

As Moses went to the bush, he heard a voice coming out of the bush. It called him by name. "Moses, Moses!"

He answered, "Here I am."

The voice said, "Moses, do not come near. Take off your shoes first. You are standing on holy ground."

So Moses took off his shoes. He stood near the burning bush. The voice from the bush said, "I am the God of your father Abraham. I am the God of Isaac and of Jacob. I have seen my people suffering in Egypt. I have heard their cries for help. I am coming to set them free from the Egyptians. I will bring them up to their own land. It is the land of Canaan,

> *The voice said, "Moses, do not come near. Take off your shoes first. You are standing on holy ground."*

a good, large land. Come now, and I will send you to Pharaoh. You will lead my people out of Egypt."

Moses knew what a great work this would be. He said, "O Lord, who am I to do such a great thing? I'm just a shepherd here in the wilderness."

Then God said to Moses, "I will be with you. I will help you do this great work. I will give you a sign that I have been with you. After you have led my people out of Egypt, you will bring them to this mountain, and they will worship me. Then you will know that I have been with you."

Moses said to God, "When I go to the children of Israel, I will tell them that the God of their fathers has sent me. They will ask me, 'Who is this God? What is his name?'"

God told Moses, "My name is I AM, the One who is always living. Tell your people, 'I AM has sent me.' Then they will believe you. Gather the elders of

Israel and go to Pharaoh. Say to him, 'Let my people go, that they may worship God in the wilderness.' At first Pharaoh will not let you go. But afterward I will show my power in Egypt. Then he will let you go out of the land."

But Moses wanted God to give him a sign that he could show his people and the Egyptians. He wanted to make sure they would believe that God had sent him.

God asked Moses, "What are you holding in your hand?"

Moses answered, "A stick made of wood. It is my shepherd's staff. I use it to lead the sheep."

Then God told him to throw it on the ground. When he threw it, the stick turned into a snake. Moses was afraid to go near it. He ran away from it.

But God said, "Don't be afraid. Take hold of it by the tail." Moses did, and the snake turned back into a stick of wood in his hand.

God told Moses to put his hand inside his robe and then take it out. When Moses did that, his hand turned white and became covered with scales. It looked as if his hand suddenly had a skin disease called leprosy. Moses was afraid. Everyone was afraid of getting sick from leprosy in those days. God told

The Princess of Egypt
Found Baby Moses

She lifted him out of the little basket-boat where his mother
had hidden him. She decided to raise Moses as her own son.

MOSES OBEYED GOD AND
THE RED SEA PARTED

Moses helped God bring his people into a new land
by a path through the sea.

him to put his hand back inside his robe and take it out again. When Moses obeyed, his hand looked normal once more.

Then God told Moses, "When you go to speak my words, show them the first sign. Make your staff

> *God told Moses, "I am the Lord who made man's mouth. Go, and I will help your lips talk. I will help you know what to say."*

become a snake. If they do not believe you, show them the second sign. If they still do not believe, take some water from the river. Pour it on the ground. It will turn into blood. Don't be afraid. Go and speak my words to your own people and the Egyptians."

Moses still did not want to go. He did not feel he was a great enough man to do such a great work. He said, "Lord, you know I am not a good speaker. My speech is slow. I can't talk in front of people."

God told Moses, "I am the Lord who made man's mouth. Go, and I will help your lips talk. I will help you know what to say."

Moses still did not want to speak for God. He said, "Lord, choose some other man for this great work. I can't do it."

And God answered, "You have a brother named Aaron. He can speak well. He is coming to see you right now. Let him help. He can do the talking. You can show the signs I gave you."

At last Moses agreed to obey God and go do the work God had asked him to do. He left Mount Sinai with his sheep and took them to his father-in-law, Jethro. Then he started walking to Egypt. On his way Moses saw his brother, Aaron, coming to see him. He and Aaron went to the leaders of their people in Egypt. They told them what God had said and showed them the signs he had given them. The people believed and were glad. They said, "God has seen all our troubles! At last he is going to set us free!"

Moses and Signs from God

EXODUS 6–10

oses and Aaron gave the people of Israel the message from God. Then they went to meet Pharaoh. Pharaoh was angry that God wanted him to let the Hebrews go free. He needed many slaves to make the bricks he used to build his cities. He punished the Hebrews when he heard Moses' and Aaron's words. He made them work harder to make more bricks for his cities.

This made the slaves angry with Moses and Aaron. "You promised to set us free," they complained. "Instead you have made our lives harder than ever." So Moses prayed to God for help. God told him, "Take Aaron and go to Pharaoh again. Show him the signs I gave you."

So the two men went back to see the king of Egypt. They told him God wanted him to let their people go. But Pharaoh asked, "Who is the Lord? Why should I obey his commands? What sign can you show that God has sent you?"

Then Aaron threw down his rod, and it turned into a snake. But the magicians in Pharaoh's palace knew a trick to make it look as if they could turn their sticks into snakes, too. They may have had tame snakes hidden in their long robes or some other trick. But God gave Aaron a new sign. His snake caught the magicians' snakes and swallowed them all. Then the snake became a stick again when Aaron picked it up. Still Pharaoh refused to obey God's command.

Moses told Aaron, "Take your rod and wave it over the waters of Egypt, over the Nile River and the lakes and streams." When Aaron obeyed, all the water turned to blood for seven days. The fish that lived in the river died. It smelled so bad that the Egyptians couldn't drink the water. Then Pharaoh's magicians used a trick to make some water look like blood. When they did, the king hardened his heart. He would not let God's people go.

So God sent Moses to see Pharaoh with another message. Moses warned the king that God would

send another plague if he didn't let his people go. Pharaoh would not obey. So Aaron held out his rod again, and suddenly the land was covered with frogs. They hopped all over the fields like troops in an army. They came into the houses and got on the Egyptians' beds. They fell into the Egyptians' food, and the frogs even got baked into their bread.

Then Pharaoh asked Moses, "Pray to your God for me. Ask him to take the frogs away. Then I will let your people go."

When Moses prayed, the frogs died. But Pharaoh did not keep his promise. He would not let the Hebrews go.

So God told Moses to have Aaron strike the dust on the ground with his rod. When he did, gnats crawled out of the dust and landed everywhere. For the next plague God sent swarms of flies that buzzed everywhere in the land. Pharaoh's magicians couldn't make gnats or flies appear. They told Pharaoh that Moses' God was more powerful than they were. But Pharaoh still wouldn't let the people go.

Then God sent another plague. Thousands of the Egyptians' horses, camels, sheep, and oxen died in one day. None of the Hebrews' animals died. But the king was stubborn. He would not change his mind and let the people go.

Things just got worse when a plague of boils came to all the people. It was so bad that the king's magicians could even stand before him. But Pharaoh's heart was stubborn and he wouldn't listen to Moses.

Then Moses pointed his rod toward the sky. At once black storm clouds came. Thunder rumbled and lightning struck. In that desert land where it rains very little, heavy rain and hail fell. It destroyed crops growing in the fields and fruit growing on the trees. Pharaoh was frightened and promised to let the children of Israel go. But when God stopped the storm, the king broke his promise and did not let them leave.

Next God sent swarms of locusts. Those bugs ate up every green thing that had not been killed by the hailstorm. After the locusts he sent a plague of darkness. For three days no one in Egypt could see the sun shining. They could not even see the moon or stars in the sky. But still Pharaoh would not let the people go. He told Moses, "Get out of my sight! Never come to see me again. If you do, you will be killed!"

Moses answered, "It will be as you say. I will never see your face again."

Then God told Moses, "There will be one more plague. When it happens, Pharaoh will be glad to let the people go. He will drive them out of the land. Get your people ready to go. Their time here will soon be over."

The Last Sign

EXODUS 11–13

hile all the plagues were happening to the Egyptians, God kept the children of Israel safe in the part of Egypt called Goshen. The water there did not turn into blood. Frogs, flies, and locusts did not bother the people there. When darkness covered Egypt, the sun still shone in the land of Goshen. Many of the Egyptians saw this and thought God might protect them too if they gave their Hebrew neighbors gifts like gold and silver and jewels. So the children of Israel suddenly went from being very poor to being very rich. When they were getting ready to leave, they asked the Egyptians if they could have clothes and other things of value. The Egyptians were glad to give them whatever they wanted so they would leave and take away the plagues with them.

Moses told the Hebrews that God was about to send one more plague. It would be worse than the others. They would have to obey God's orders if they wanted to be saved from it. He said each family had to kill a lamb and sprinkle some of its blood on the doorway of their house. At midnight an angel was going to go through the land and stop at every house that did not have lamb's blood on its doorway. Wherever the angel stopped, the oldest child in the house would die.

He also told the Hebrews to make a special supper out of the lamb they had killed. They were to eat it standing up, to show they were ready to leave Egypt as soon as Moses told them to go. This meal was called "the Passover supper" because when God's angel saw the lamb's blood, he passed over those houses and the oldest child did not die.

The people of Israel were told to eat this meal every year from that time on to remember what God had done for them. It became a great feast day in Israel, called "the Passover." Many years later the

Passover supper was the last meal Jesus ate with his disciples before he was crucified. Christ has been offered up for us. He is our Passover lamb.

That night in Egypt a loud cry came from every Egyptian house. Every house lost its oldest child. Even Pharaoh's oldest child died. The king sent a message to Moses and Aaron. "Hurry and get out of the land," he said. "Take everything you have. Don't leave anything. Pray to your God to have mercy on us and not to harm us anymore."

So after four hundred years in Egypt the children of Israel went out of the land. They went in order

> *The king sent a message to Moses and Aaron. "Hurry and get out of the land," he said. "Take everything you have. Don't leave anything. Pray to your God to have mercy on us and not to harm us anymore."*

like a great army. They lined up family by family. They left so quickly that they baked their bread without waiting for it to raise and get fluffy. The bread they made that way turned out flat, like a cracker.

They took it with them to eat on their trip and called it "unleavened bread." Unleavened bread has been made every year since then for the Passover, to remember how the Hebrews had to hurry out of Egypt.

God went before the people as they marched out of Egypt. In the daytime he led them by a great cloud that looked like a tall church pillar. At night the pillar turned into fire so everyone could see it and follow. Whenever the pillar stopped, the people knew it was time to rest. They set up their tents and waited until the pillar started to move again. This great cloud or fire probably scared away anyone who thought of doing harm to the Hebrews. It was like a guide and a guard for them.

The Path Through the Sea

hen the children of Israel marched out of Egypt, they started toward the land of Canaan, where their people lived four hundred years before. The shortest road to follow would have taken them through the land of the Philistines. They did not want to go that way, because the Philistines were very strong and always tried to make war with others. They were glad to see the pillar of cloud and fire leading them another way. God took his people through the land of Midian instead. Moses knew his way to Midian because it was where he had lived as a shepherd for forty years. The people who lived there had been friendly to him, and he had married a woman from their land.

The Hebrew people were surprised to see the pillar turn right toward the Red Sea instead of going around it. When it stopped for them to rest, there was a sea full of water in front of them, mountains on each side of them, and soon they heard the sound of horses and chariots behind them.

After the children of Israel left, Pharaoh changed his mind again. He decided to march out after the Hebrew people with his army. He wanted to bring them back to go on working as his slaves. The trapped people cried out to Moses, "Why did you bring us out to this terrible place to die? It would have been better to stay in Egypt as slaves!"

"Don't be afraid," Moses answered. "Stand still and see how God will save you. You will never see those Egyptians again. The Lord will fight for you."

That night the pillar of fire moved behind the people of Israel instead of in front of them. It stood

> *"Don't be afraid," Moses answered. "Stand still and see how God will save you. The Lord will fight for you."*

between them and the army of Egypt. To the Hebrews the pillar was bright with God's glory. To the Egyptians it was dark and terrible. They didn't dare go near it.

Then God told Moses to hold out his wooden rod over the Red Sea. When Moses obeyed, God sent a strong east wind, and the water split apart to leave a path of dry sand through the middle of the sea. The

people of Israel went through the sea on dry ground, with a wall of water on both sides of their path.

When the Egyptians saw the path, they decided to keep chasing the Hebrews and went right onto the sea path. But the sand was no longer hard. It had become soft. Their chariot wheels sank into it and broke off. Their horses got stuck in the deep sand and fell down. The army was frightened of the walls of water and cried out, "The Lord is fighting for them! Let's run away!"

By this time the Hebrews had reached the other side of the sea. They stood on a hill watching the enemy army struggle through the sand. Then Moses lifted up his hand, and the water walls closed

> *The army was frightened of the walls of water and cried out, "The Lord is fighting for them! Let's run away!"*

together over the path through the sea. Water covered the Egyptian army and its chariots and horses. Not one of them was left to chase after the children of Israel.

Moses and his people knew God had saved them. They sang a song of victory:

I will sing to the Lord.
    He has triumphed gloriously.
The horse and his rider
    he has thrown into the sea.
The Lord is my strength and song,
    and he has become my salvation.

The Sky Rains Bread

After the people of Israel crossed the Red Sea, they began to walk through valleys between great mountains and through the desert. There were many of them: men, women, children, and all their flocks. They all needed food and water, but this land was not as rich as the land of Goshen, where they had lived in Egypt. When they could not find fresh water or much food, some of the people began to complain. They wondered if they were going to starve or die of thirst in this land that seemed so harsh compared with Egypt. Some felt so hungry and tired that they even wondered if they should go back to Egypt and be slaves again.

Moses called out to God for help. The Lord said, "I will rain bread from heaven for you."

The next morning the people looked out of their tents and saw a wonderful sight. On the sand all around the camp they saw little white flakes, like snow or frost. They had never seen anything like it before, so they said, "What is it?" And that word in the Hebrew language was what they called the bread from heaven—manna.

Moses told them, "This is the bread the Lord has given you to eat. Go out and gather as much as you need. But take only as much as you will use in one day. You cannot save it for tomorrow."

So the people gathered the manna. They cooked it in different ways. They baked it and boiled it. It tasted like wafers flavored with honey. They lived in the wilderness for forty years and ate the fresh manna that God gave each day. As Moses had said, they could not save it for the next day or it would become rotten and smell bad. The one exception was the Sabbath. This was God's way of teaching them that they needed to trust him for daily bread.

The Ten Commandments

Exodus 17:1–31:18

hile the Israelites were traveling in the desert, they had trouble finding enough water for all the people and animals. Leaders came to Moses and cried, "Give us some water, or we will die! Did you bring us out of Egypt to kill us here in the desert?"

Moses called out to God, "Lord, what should I do? These people are angry and almost ready to kill me. How can I give them water?"

Then the Lord told Moses what to do. He told him to bring everyone together near a large rock. Moses struck the rock with his wooden rod. Enough water poured out of it for all the people and animals to drink.

While they were camped near this rock, some wild people who lived in the desert attacked them. They were called the Amalekites. Moses made a young man named Joshua the captain of all the men who were fit to be in an army. They fought a great battle against the Amalekites. Moses stood on the rock where everyone could see him. He held his hands high in the air. When his arms got tired and dropped at his sides, the enemy army would start to win. So Aaron and Hur stood beside Moses and held up his hands until the Israelites won the battle.

Three months after they left Egypt, the Israelites came to the great mountain called Mount Sinai. It was the place where long before then Moses had first heard God's voice from the burning bush. The Hebrew people now camped in front of the mountain. They were there for many days.

Moses went up to God, and the Lord called to him. God told Moses, "Don't let the people go up on the mountain. Don't even let them touch it. This is a holy place." God told Moses that the people of Israel were his special treasure and would be his priests. He told them to wait to hear his words and see his glory on the mountain. A few days after this the people saw clouds and smoke covering the mountain. Lightning flashed and thunder rolled and crashed. The mountain shook.

The people stood far off, shivering with fear. They heard God speak to them, saying, "I am the Lord, who brought you out of the land of Egypt."

Then God told the people the words of the Ten Commandments. They were the ten most important laws for his special people to obey:

"Do not put any other gods in place of me.

"Do not make statues of gods that look like anything in the sky or on the earth or in the waters. Do not bow down to worship them.

"Do not misuse the name of the Lord God.

"Remember to keep the Sabbath day holy. Do your work on the other days.

"Honor your father and mother. Then you will live a long time in the land.

"Do not commit murder.

"Do not commit adultery.

"Do not steal.

"Do not give false witness against your neighbor.

"Do not long to have anything that belongs to your neighbor."

All the people heard these words spoken by the Lord God. They saw the mountain full of smoke and lightning and heard the thunder. They were afraid. So they told Moses, "Let God speak to you, Moses. Then you can tell us God's words. But don't let God speak to us anymore, or we may die."

Moses said, "Don't be afraid. God has come to you to speak to you because he wants you to have respect for him. Make sure you obey his words."

THE TABERNACLE

God's Tent

t seems strange that the Israelites could forget all that God had done for them. God had led them out of Egypt and had done many miracles for them. He had made a dry path through the Red Sea for them to walk on. But after all the miracles, they wanted to worship idols instead of God. In those times the people of all the lands around them worshiped idols. Those people carried into battle statues of gods made of gold or wood. They would hold them up like flags to frighten their enemies. They believed that putting statues in their homes and fields would keep them healthy and make their crops grow.

The Hebrews had seen their rich and powerful masters in Egypt bow down to idols. They may have thought the idols made the Egyptian people strong. They may have felt that it was too difficult to understand an invisible God and his truth without something they could see with their eyes and touch with their hands. So God gave Moses a plan for something that would teach his people about him. It was something they could see, but it was not an idol.

God's plan was this: In the middle of the camp of Israel there would be a place called "the house of God." People could come there to worship. They could see it and say, "That is the house where God lives among his people." They would know that God was there, even though no statue of him would be put there.

All the Hebrews lived in tents so they could move from place to place and get food for their cattle. So their house of worship would also be like a large tent, but it would be made of boards covered with gold. It could be taken down and moved as often as their camp moved. This kind of tent was called a "tabernacle." God would live among his people in the tabernacle, and there they could meet God.

We know God is a spirit and he is everywhere. He didn't have to stay inside a tabernacle. But God chose to show his presence among his people in a special way. People put beautiful curtains and golden decorations in the tabernacle and all around it. The tabernacle was the size of a big house with two rooms. There was a large open yard all around the tabernacle. The yard was fenced all around with white cloth hanging from metal posts. The yard was big enough so many people could come inside. It was called the "court." The court had a great altar made of wood and brass that could be carried on poles when the people moved. It did not have a top or bottom so it would not be too heavy to move. There priests offered animals as sacrifices to God for the sins of all the people.

The two rooms inside the tabernacle were called the Holy Place and the Holy of Holies. Only the priests could go into the Holy Place to serve God. The priests lit the seven golden oil lamps and burned

incense and prayed to God for all the people. Also in that room was a table with twelve loaves of bread on it to represent an offering of food to the Lord from each of the twelve tribes, that is, the descendants of the twelve sons of Israel. The only other furniture in the room was a small golden altar called the altar of incense, where sweet-smelling incense was burned. Everything in the Holy Place was made of gold or covered with gold.

The inner room of the tabernacle was the Holy of Holies. Only the high priest was allowed to go into the Holy of Holies, and that was only once a year. In that room was one thing—the ark of the covenant. The ark was a beautiful gold box with carved angels on top, and it held the stone tablets of the Ten Commandments that God gave Moses. In this room God lived and showed his glory.

Whenever the camp of Israel moved, the priests and their helpers from the tribe of Levi first covered all the furniture of the temple with cloths. Then they took down the tabernacle and carried all the pieces of it. They moved it with care and respect. The twelve tribes marched behind the priests and Levites carrying the tabernacle and the ark of the covenant. The people could not see the ark of the covenant because of its cloth wrappings. God did not want them to be tempted to worship any golden thing. But the people knew that God's special presence was with them, because they could see the pillar of cloud from God that floated in front them as they marched.

When the Hebrews got to their new camping place, the first thing they set up was the tabernacle, the court around it, and the altar. They traveled and moved the tabernacle for forty years.

BALAAM

The Donkey That Talked

NUMBERS 22:1–35

he Israelites marched through the desert for many years. They had a rugged life. It was like living in a training camp for soldiers. They learned how to be an army for God. After being slaves in Egypt for four hundred years, they had forgotten how to think for themselves. After many years in the desert and many battles, they became strong and started to win battles they fought with their enemies. They took back the land that their ancestors Joseph and his brothers had left when they came to Egypt. They remembered how God had promised their grandfathers this land if the people would follow him. They even fought giants to take back their land. Finally the children of Israel recaptured all the land on the east side of the Jordan River and north of the Arnon Brook.

The people who lived south of the Arnon Brook were called Moabites. They were afraid when they heard that the Israelites were coming to fight and take over their land. Their king was named Balak. Balak sent for a man who was a prophet to come and help him. The prophet's name was Balaam. Balaam only spoke what God told him to, so whenever he gave a message to people, it came true. King Balak hoped to give Balaam money to say something bad against the Israelites so he could beat them in battles.

When Balak's men arrived, they promised Balaam money if he would go with them to the king. Balaam told them, "Stay here tonight. I will ask the Lord what to do."

That night God came to Balaam and said, "You must not go with these men. You shall not curse these people. They are to be blessed."

So the next morning Balaam told the men, "Go back to your land. The Lord will not let me go with you."

The Moabite men went back and told their king what Balaam had said. But the king thought that Balaam might come anyway if he offered more money. So he sent his own princes as messengers with larger gifts. They told Balaam the king would give him anything he asked to come and curse the Israelites.

Balaam said, "Even if Balak gives me his house full of silver and gold, I can only speak what God gives me to speak. Stay here tonight. I will ask my God what I may say to you."

Now Balaam knew very well what God wished him to say. But he wanted to be rich even though he was a prophet of God. He wanted to go with the men and get Balak's money. But he didn't dare go against God's command.

That night God told him, "If these men ask you to go with them, you may go. But when you get to

Balak's country, you must only speak the words I give you to speak."

Balaam was glad to hear that he could go with the princes of Moab. But God was not pleased. He knew that Balaam hoped to get the king's money even though he could not do what the king asked.

God sent his angel to meet Balaam on the road and teach him a lesson. The angel showed himself first to the donkey Balaam was riding. The poor donkey saw a bright angel with a sword of fire standing in the road. The donkey wanted to go around the angel. Balaam could not see the angel, so he beat his donkey to make it go back on the road.

The angel appeared again in another place, where the road was narrow. There was a stone wall on each side. The donkey turned to one side and crushed Balaam's foot against one of the walls. Balaam was angry and beat the poor donkey again.

The angel of the Lord appeared to the donkey again in a place where it could not turn to the right or left. This time the donkey was so frightened, he fell down on the ground. Balaam beat him again and again, but the donkey would not get up. That was when the Lord allowed the donkey to speak aloud. The beast said to Balaam, "What have I done wrong that you have beat me three times?"

Balaam was so angry that he never thought how strange it was for his animal to talk. He said, "I beat you because you would not go where you should. If I had a sword instead of a stick, I'd kill you!"

Then the donkey spoke again. "Aren't I your donkey, the one that has always carried you where you wanted to go? Did I ever disobey you before? Why do you treat me so cruelly?"

At that moment God opened Balaam's eyes to let him see the angel holding a fiery sword and standing in front of him. Then Balaam leaped off the donkey and fell on his face on the ground in front of the angel. The angel said, "Balaam, you know you are going the wrong way. If your donkey had not stopped, I would have killed you. The road that you are taking will lead you to death."

Balaam said, "I have sinned against God. Please forgive me. I will go back home instead."

But the angel knew that Balaam really wanted to go on to meet King Balak. The angel said to Balaam, "You may go with these men to Moab, but be sure to say only the words God gives you to say."

The Prophet Speaks

Numbers 22:36–25:18; 31:1–9

hen Balaam went on to the land of Moab, King Balak said to him, "So you have come at last! Why did you wait until I sent the second group of messengers? Didn't you know I'd pay you the amount you want?"

Balaam answered, "I have come as you asked, but I have no power to speak anything except the words God gives me."

King Balak thought that Balaam was just saying this to get more money. He did not understand that a true prophet of God would only speak the words God wanted. Balak took Balaam up to the top of a mountain so they could look down on the camp of the Israelites. Their tents were spread out all over the plain, and the white cloud of God's special presence was over the tabernacle in the center.

Balaam said, "Build seven altars for me. Then bring me seven young oxen and seven rams for offerings."

They did as he asked. Then God gave a message to Balaam, and Balaam spoke God's words:

"The king of Moab has brought me from the east, saying, 'Come and curse Jacob for me. Come and speak against Israel.' How can I curse those God has

> *Balaam said, "How beautiful are your tents, O Israel! God brought him out of Egypt, and God will give him the land he promised."*

not cursed? How can I speak against God's own people? From the mountaintops I see this people living alone, different from other nations. Who can count the men of Israel? There are so many, like the dust of the earth. Let me live my last days and die like these godly people."

Well! The king of Moab was very surprised by Balaam's words. "What have you done?" he cried. "I brought you to curse my enemies, and you have blessed them instead!"

Balaam answered, "I told you beforehand that I could speak only the words God puts in my mouth."

But the king thought he would try again to get Balaam to curse Israel. He brought him to another place where they could look down on the camp. Again God gave Balaam a message to say:

GOD TOLD GIDEON TO USE
A LIGHT AS A WEAPON

God wanted Gideon to depend on him.
He would help Gideon win the battle.

GOD MADE SAMSON AS STRONG AS A LION

Samson saved Israel by the super strength that God gave him.

"Get up, King Balak, and hear. God is not a man, that he should lie or change his mind. God will do what he has said. He has commanded me to bless these people and they will be blessed. The Lord God is their king. He will lead them in victory."

Then King Balak said to Balaam, "If you can't curse these people, let them alone. Don't bless them!"

And Balaam answered, "Didn't I tell you that what God gives me to say, I must say?"

But King Balak wanted to try again. He brought Balaam to another place to see if God would let him curse Israel there. Balaam looked down on the camp again and said:

"How beautiful are your tents, O Israel! God brought him out of Egypt, and God will give him the land he promised. God will destroy Israel's enemies like a lion. Everyone who blesses him will be blessed. Everyone who curses him will be cursed."

Of course, King Balak was angry with Balaam. "I called you to curse my enemies, and you have blessed them," Balak said. "Go back to your own home. I was going to give you great riches, but your God has kept you from your reward."

And Balaam answered, "I told your messengers, 'Even if Balak gives me his house full of silver and gold, I can speak only what God gives me to speak.' What God speaks, I must speak. Now let me tell you what these people will do to your people in the years to come. A star will come out of the people of Jacob. A king will rise up out of Israel. He will rule over Moab. All these lands will be under the rule of Israel."

And all Balaam said happened many years later. King David of Israel ruled over all those countries.

But Balaam's heart was still greedy for money, and he sadly went back to his home. Even though God had used Balaam's lips to speak for him, Balaam was not a true servant of God in his heart.

JOSHUA

The Walls of Jericho

After Moses died, the Israelites were still camped on the east side of the Jordan River. God told Joshua, "Now that my servant Moses is dead, you must rule the people. Do not wait any longer to lead them across the Jordan River and conquer the land I promised them."

God told Joshua that he would give the Israelites a large area of land to live in if they would follow his commands. Their land would reach from the Euphrates River in the north down to the border of Egypt in the south. It would go from the desert on the east to the Great Sea on the west. Then God told Joshua, "Be strong and full of courage. I will be with you as I was with Moses. Obey what is written in the Book of the Law Moses gave you. Then you will have success."

So Joshua told his officers to go through the camp and tell the people to get ready to take a journey. "In three days we will cross the Jordan River and go into the land the Lord promised to us."

God had said to be full of courage. They were going to need to be brave. The Jordan River was much larger at that time of year because of the spring rain. Water overflowed all its banks, and the currents were deep and powerful. Even a very strong man could have trouble swimming all the way across. And the Israelites didn't have boats that could cross it.

They could see the high walls of the city of Jericho standing near the foot of the mountains on the other side. Before the rest of the land could be won, they would have to take over Jericho, because it guarded the road leading up the mountains.

Joshua sent two strong men as spies to swim across the river and find out all they could about the city. The king of Jericho found out about the spies and tried to capture them. The spies hid from the king and his men in a house that was built into the wall of the city. It was the home of a woman named Rahab. She believed that the God of the Israelites was the true God, because she had heard the stories of the Israelites' journey. She knew how God dried up the Red Sea so they could get away from Pharaoh and how he led them through the desert with a pillar of cloud and fire. She was sure God was going to give them her city as well. She told the spies that all the people inside the city were afraid of the Israelites because of the stories. She agreed to hide them from the king if they would do something for her.

"Promise me," said Rahab, "in the name of the Lord, that you will save my life and the lives of my father and mother and my brothers and sisters when you take over this city."

So the spies agreed, and Rahab hid them under piles of flax stalks, which look like long grasses. After

the king's men had gone away, she let the spies climb down the outside of the wall on a red rope that she hung from her window. The men told her to put the rope outside her window again when the army of Israel came to take over the city. They promised to tell their army not to kill the people inside the house with a red rope hanging from the window.

The spies swam back across the river and reported to Joshua. They said, "God has given us all the land. The people there are afraid and don't want to fight us."

Unlike the people who lived across the Jordan River, God made the twelve tribes of Israel united and strong. The people of Canaan had many small nations, and each little tribe or city had its own king. This kept them from being one people.

God's Rocks

o Joshua told the Israelites it was time to march. They took down their tents, and the priests took the tabernacle tent apart. The priests led the people to the Jordan River, carrying the ark of the covenant high on their shoulders on its carrying poles. As soon as their feet touched the water at the edge of the rolling river, a wonderful thing happened. The water up the river stopped flowing downstream.

The water just piled up in a great heap and left the riverbed a giant, dry path.

The priests stood in the middle of the dry river, holding the ark as all the people walked across to the other side. Joshua told one man from each of the twelve tribes to bring one large stone from the place in the riverbed near where the priests were standing. Joshua told the men to pile up the twelve large stones on the bank of the river. Joshua said, "Let this heap of stones stand here to remind us of what God has done for us today. When our children ask what the stones are for, we will tell them, 'They are here because the Lord God made the river dry up before the ark of the covenant so the people could cross over into the Promised Land."

God's Trumpets

he children of Israel set up their new camp in the land God had promised to their ancestors five hundred years before. The camp was on the plain of Jordan called Gilgal. They found grain and barley growing in the fields. It was ready to harvest, so they gathered it and made bread. On that harvest day God stopped giving them the manna from heaven with which he had fed them for forty years.

Joshua went out to look at the high walls around the city of Jericho. He saw a man dressed in battle armor coming toward him. "Are you on our side, or are you one of the enemies?" Joshua asked the man.

The man answered, "I come as captain of the Lord's host."

Then Joshua knew it was the angel of the Lord. He bowed and asked, "What word has my Lord for his servant?"

The angel told Joshua a special battle plan from the Lord. Joshua followed the directions the angel gave him, even though he may have thought it sounded like a strange way to win a battle.

First he brought out his army as if they were going to fight against Jericho. Behind them came priests blowing as loud as they could on trumpets made from rams' horns. Then came priests carrying the ark of the covenant, holding it high on their shoulders by its carrying poles. Last came all the families of Israel, marching in order.

Everyone was quiet except for the priests blowing on the rams' horns. They marched all the way around the walls of Jericho, and then they went back to their camp. They did this same thing every day for six days. On the seventh day they did not stop after they had gone all the way around the city once. They

kept on marching round and round until they had gone around the city seven times. Then they all stood still. The priests stopped blowing on their trumpets.

After a moment Joshua called out, "Shout, for the Lord has given you the city!"

Then a loud shout rang out from the army and all the people. The walls of Jericho began to shake and crumble and fall. They fell down flat at every place except one. In that place a bright red rope was hanging from a window in a house that was built on the wall. Joshua told his two spies to go there to Rahab's house and bring her and everyone in her family out to a safe place. They took care of Rahab's family and welcomed them into the camp of Israel.

The army of Israel took over the city. No one tried to defend it—they were all afraid of the army of the Lord. Joshua and the people offered all the treasures of the city to God. Rahab and her family became part of the people of Israel, as if they had been born among them. She married one of the nobles of the tribe of Judah, named Salmon. One of their grandchildren grew up to be King David, who was also an ancestor of Jesus.

The Story of a Wedge of Gold

JOSHUA 7–8

he Israelites were to destroy the city of Jericho, as God commanded them. A man named Achan of the tribe of Judah was a soldier in the Israelite army. When he was in a house in Jericho, he saw a wedge-shaped piece of gold, some silver, and a beautiful garment that had come from Babylon. He looked at them and wanted to have them for his own. So he took them secretly to his tent and hid them. He thought no one saw him do it. But God saw it all. Because Achan stole from God, to whom everything in Jericho belonged, great trouble came on Israel.

From Jericho there was a road up the ravines and valleys leading to the mountain country. On one of the hills above the plain stood a little city called Ai. Joshua did not think it was necessary for all the army to go fight the battle of Ai. It was just a little place. So he sent a small army of three thousand men. But the men of Ai came out and killed a number of them and drove the rest away. Joshua's men failed to take the city.

When the rest of the people heard about this defeat, they were afraid. Joshua was alarmed, not because he was afraid of the Canaanites but because he knew God was not pleased with the Israelites. Joshua fell on his face before the Lord. He said, "O Lord, why have you led us across the Jordan only to let us fall before our enemies? What shall I say now that the men of Israel have been beaten in battle?"

God said to Joshua, "Israel has sinned. They have disobeyed my words and have broken their promise. They have taken treasure that belongs to me, and they have lied. That is why they cannot stand against their enemies. I will not be with you anymore unless you bring back what is stolen and punish the thief."

God said to Joshua, "Israel has sinned. They have disobeyed my words and have broken their promise. They have taken treasure that belongs to me, and they have lied. That is why they cannot stand against their enemies. I will not be with you anymore unless you bring back what is stolen and punish the thief."

The next morning Joshua called all the tribes of Israel to come before him. When the tribe of Judah came, God showed Joshua that this was the guilty tribe. Then as the divisions of Judah came by, God pointed out one division, and in that division, one family, and in that family, one man. Achan!

Joshua said to Achan, "Confess your sin to God. Tell me what you have done. Do not hide it from me."

Then Achan told Joshua what he had done. Joshua sent messengers to Achan's tent. They found the hidden things and brought them before all the people.

Achan's crime had harmed all the people. His family had helped him hide the crime. The people of Israel sentenced Achan and his family to death. Then they burned everything that belonged to that family. They piled stones over the top of the ashes so anyone who saw the pile of stones would remember what happened to Achan for his sin.

God showed his people how careful they must be to keep his commands. After this Joshua sent a larger army to Ai, and it was totally destroyed. Then God allowed the people to take for themselves anything they wanted from the city of Ai.

Now when they marched over the mountains to the city of Shechem, in the middle of the land of

Canaan, the people of the land were so filled with fear that none of them resisted the Israelites.

Near Shechem are two mountains, named Ebal and Gerizim. In between is a deep valley. There Joshua gathered all the people of Israel. They had left their tabernacle and their altar behind when they went into battle. So they built another altar of stones. They used the new altar to offer sacrifices and offerings to the Lord. Joshua read the Law of Moses to

the people. All the people, even the little children, listened to the reading. Then half the tribes stood on the slope of Mount Ebal on the north, and half stood on the slope of Mount Gerizim on the south. As Joshua read God's words of warning about what would happen if they sinned, the people on Mount Ebal answered all together, "Amen." When he read about the blessing of God to those who obey God's law, the people on Mount Gerizim answered all together, "Amen."

In doing this, they gave the land to the Lord. They promised to serve God. They marched down the mountains, past the smoldering ruins of Ai. They marched past the heap of stones that covered Achan. They marched past the broken walls of Jericho and back to the camp at Gilgal beside the river Jordan.

DEBORAH

A Mighty Woman of God

ifteen different judges led the people of Israel during the time when they had no king. One of them was a wise woman named Deborah. Deborah was the only judge who was a woman. She was so good and so wise that all the people came to see her when they needed advice or help in settling a problem. She sat under a palm tree north of Jerusalem and ruled over the land. She did not need an army or a throne to make her a ruler. All the people saw that God's Spirit was upon her. They wanted to obey her wise words.

Deborah heard how cruelly the Canaanites were treating the Israelite tribes in the north. She sent a message to a brave man named Barak who lived in the land of Naphtali. It read, "Barak, call out the tribes of Israel who live near you. Raise an army and lead the men to Mount Tabor. The Lord has told me that he will give you victory over the armies of Canaan and their leader Sisera."

But Barak felt afraid to raise an army to go into battle. He was afraid to be their leader. He sent Deborah an answer: "If you will go with me, I will go. But if you will not go with me, I will not go."

Deborah agreed to go with Barak, but she told him, "Because you did not trust God and go when he called you, the honor of this war will not be yours. The Lord will hand over Sisera to a woman!"

Then Deborah got up from her seat under the palm tree and went to Kedesh, where Barak lived.

Together Deborah and Barak sent out a call for the men of the north. Ten thousand men met together and brought all the weapons they could find or make. This was a small army compared with the huge army of the Canaanites. They followed Deborah as their general and made camp on the top of Mount Tabor, where they could look down on the great chariots and horses and men in General Sisera's army. Deborah was not afraid. She told Barak, "Go! This is the day the Lord has given Sisera and his army into your hands. The Lord has gone ahead of you. He will give you the victory."

Then Barak blew a trumpet and called out his men. They ran down the side of Mount Tabor and rushed upon their enemies. The Canaanites were so surprised that they didn't have time to get to their warhorses or to get into their mighty chariots. They were afraid and ran away so fast, they stepped on top of each other and knocked each other down.

The Israelites knew that the Lord helped them, because there had been a heavy rain and the brook Kishon was full of rushing water. Many Canaanites who tried to swim across it to get away were drowned, and the Israelites were able to beat those who stayed to fight in battle.

Deborah's prophecy about Sisera came true. He saw that his army was losing, and he tried to hide in the tent of a woman named Jael. She pretended she wanted to help him. She gave him a bottle of milk and hid him under some rugs. Sisera was very tired and fell asleep there. When he did, Jael killed the wicked general. Barak and all the people found out what she had done and honored her as a hero.

GIDEON

Gideon and His Brave Three Hundred

JUDGES 6:11–8:23

ne day a man named Gideon was threshing his wheat when suddenly he saw an angel sitting under an oak tree. The angel said to him, "Mighty warrior, the Lord is with you.... Go and save Israel."

Gideon answered, "How can I possibly save Israel? My family group is the weakest in the tribe of Manasseh. And I'm the least important member of my family."

The angel answered, "I will be with you. So you will strike down the men of Midian all at one time." The Midianites were Israel's enemy.

Gideon felt that the one talking with him was the Lord in the form of an angel. Gideon brought an offering and laid it on a rock. The angel touched the offering with his staff, and at once a fire leaped up and burned it. Then the angel vanished. Gideon was frightened, but the Lord said, "Do not be afraid. You are not going to die."

Then the angel told Gideon that the first thing he needed to do was to help his people get over worshiping idols. He was to destroy their altars to other gods and to build a new altar to the Lord. Gideon was to make an offering on the new altar. So Gideon did all that the Lord told him to do. He broke up the idols and used the wood for a fire to burn up the offering.

When the people got up in the morning and went to worship, their idols were gone. The people said, "Who did this? Someone told them, "Gideon, the son of Joash, did it."

The men of the town wanted to kill Gideon and went to his father. "Bring your son out here. He must die," they said.

But Gideon's father was wise and answered, "Is your idol really a god? If he is, he can stand up for himself when someone tears down his altar." So Gideon went on living.

After a while the Spirit of the Lord came on Gideon, and he gathered together all the men of his

own tribe and other tribes in that area to fight with
the Midianites. The people of Israel didn't have any
swords or other weapons. They were usually a peace-
loving people and didn't need weapons.

Gideon said to God, "You promised you would
use me to save Israel. Please do something for me.
I'll put a piece of wool on the threshing floor.
Suppose dew is only on the wool tomorrow morning. And suppose the ground all around it is dry.

> *After a while the Spirit of the Lord*
> *came on Gideon, and he gathered*
> *together all the men of his own tribe*
> *and other tribes in that area to fight*
> *with the Midianites.*

Then I will know that you will use me to save Israel.
I'll know that your promise will come true."

And that is exactly what the Lord did for Gideon.
In the morning Gideon squeezed water out of the
wool, but the ground was dry.

Then Gideon said to God, "Don't be angry with
me. Let me use the wool for one more test. This time
make the wool dry. And cover the ground with dew."

So once more God did what Gideon asked. The wool was dry, and the ground was wet. Now Gideon knew that God was going to be with him and would give him the victory over his enemies.

Then the Lord told Gideon his army was too large. God said, "You have too many men. I do not

> *When Gideon did what the Lord said, there were only three hundred men left. These were the men who had not laid down their swords and shields to drink water. These were the men who stood watchful for any enemy who might appear while they were getting a drink.*

want Israel to brag that their own strength has saved them. So here is what I want you to announce to your men. Tell them, 'Those who tremble with fear can turn back.' Let them leave."

So Gideon did what the Lord asked, and 22,000 men went home. There were only 10,000 left.

Then the Lord spoke to Gideon again and said, "There are still too many men. So take them down to the water. I will sort them out for you there."

So once again Gideon did what the Lord asked and took his men to the water. There the Lord spoke again and said, "Some men will drink the way dogs do. They will lap up the water with their tongues. Separate them from those who get down on their knees to drink." Gideon watched and sure enough, some men got down on their knees to drink and some cupped water in their hands and lapped it like a dog.

The Lord then told Gideon to keep those who lapped the water in their hands and to send the rest home. When Gideon did what the Lord said, there were only three hundred men left. These were the men who had not laid down their swords and shields to drink water. These were the men who stood watchful for any enemy who might appear while they were getting a drink.

Then God did one more thing to encourage Gideon's heart. One night the Lord said to him. "Get up. . . . Go down to the camp with your servant. Listen to what they are saying. After that, you will not be afraid to attack the camp."

So Gideon and his servant went down to the edge of the camp. The Midianites had been joined by the Amalakites and all of the other tribes from the east.

There were so many of them that they looked like huge numbers of locusts. They looked like grains of sand on the seashore. They had so many camels you couldn't even count them.

When Gideon got to the edge of the camp, he heard one man telling another about a dream he had. "A round loaf of barley bread came rolling into our camp. It hit a tent with great force. The tent turned over and fell down flat."

His friend replied, "That can only be the sword of Gideon from Israel. God has handed us over to him. He has given him the whole camp."

Well, when Gideon heard that, he worshipped God. He went back to his camp and said, "Get up! The Lord has handed the Midianites over to you."

Gideon divided the three hundred men into three groups. He gave each man a trumpet and a jar with a torch in it. "Watch me," he told them. Do what I do. I'll go to the edge of the Midianite camp. I and everyone who is with me will blow our trumpets. Blow your trumpets from your positions all around the camp. And shout the battle cry, 'For the Lord and for Gideon!'"

It was about ten o'clock at night when they arrived at the Midianite camp. The guard had just been changed. Gideon and his men got into position all around the camp. Then they broke their jars, blew their trumpets, and shouted the battle cry, "A sword for the Lord and for Gideon."

When the Midianites heard the commotion and saw the lights all around them, they started fighting each other with swords. They were filled with terror and thought only of escape, not of fighting. But wherever they turned, their enemies seemed to be standing with swords drawn. They trampled each other to death trying to get away. The army ran away toward their own land east of the Jordan River. They were crying out in fear as they went. Then Gideon called the rest of the troops, and they chased the Midianites. The armies of Israel took control of all the lands of the Midianites.

Gideon lived a long time after this battle, and he judged the people. They wanted to make him king, but he said to them, "I will not rule over you. My son won't rule over you either. The Lord will rule over you."

SAMSON

A Mighty Man of God

JUDGES 13–16

here were times when the people of Israel began to worship idols instead of the true God. When they did that, God did not protect them. Enemy armies were able to defeat them and take over their land. God allowed this to happen so his children would see that they needed his help and turn back to him.

After the thirteenth judge to lead Israel died, the people turned back to worshiping idols, and the Philistine army defeated them. The Philistines lived on the west side of Israel by the Great Sea. They were strong and always ready to go to war. They worshiped an idol called Dagon who had a body like a man's with a head like a fish.

When the Philistine army took over Israel, they took away all the Israelites' swords and spears so they could not fight. Then they took all the crops and food for themselves. The children of Israel were very hungry, and they cried out to the true God for help. God heard them and sent help.

A child named Samson was born. God sent an angel to tell Samson's parents that their boy would grow up to save Israel. But the angel warned them that Samson must never have his hair cut or drink any wine or strong drink as long as he lived. When someone was dedicated to the Lord in this way, he was known as a "Nazarite." Samson grew stronger and stronger. He became known as the strongest man in the Bible. Instead of leading an army, Samson saved Israel by the super strength God gave him.

When Samson was a young man, he fell in love with a Philistine woman. Of course, his parents were unhappy about this because of the angel's message. How could Samson save Israel from the Philistines if he married one of their women? It seemed as if he wanted to make friends with Israel's enemies instead of saving his people from them. But God used Samson's marriage to help Israel get free from the Philistines in a way no one could have imagined.

One day Samson was going down to the town of Timnath to see the Philistine woman. Suddenly a hungry lion came down from the mountain, growling and roaring. The Spirit of the Lord came upon Samson, and he grabbed the lion and tore it to pieces as if it were made of paper. Then he went on his way to Timnath and back home again. He hadn't been frightened of the lion one bit. He didn't tell anyone what had happened.

Sometime later when Samson went back to Timnath to marry the Philistine woman, he remembered killing the lion. He stopped to look at the lion's body. He saw that all the lion's flesh had been eaten by a swarm of bees that had made a nest in its bones. There was honey in the nest. He scooped out some of the honey and ate it as he walked. He still didn't tell anyone about what had happened.

The wedding feast for Samson and his bride lasted a whole week. The young Philistine men who came liked to play guessing games using riddles and questions. Samson thought of a riddle he could tell them.

"I will give you a riddle," said Samson. "If you answer it before the feast is over, I will give you thirty sets of clothes. If you can't answer it, then you must give me thirty sets of clothes."

"Let us hear your riddle," they said.

Samson replied,

"Out of the eater, something to eat;
    out of the strong, something sweet."

The Philistine men couldn't think of the answer. They tried to find out all day and kept trying for two more days. At last they went to Samson's new wife and said, "Get your husband to tell you the answer. If you don't, we will set your house on fire and burn everyone up!"

So Samson's wife begged him to tell her the answer. She cried, "If you really love me, you wouldn't keep a secret from me."

At last Samson gave in. He told his wife how he had killed the lion and then found the honey in its

> *The Spirit of the Lord*
> *came upon Samson, and he grabbed*
> *the lion and tore it to pieces*
> *as if it were made of paper.*

bones. She went and told the young men what he had said. Just before the feast was ending, the young men came to Samson and said they knew the answer to his riddle. "What could be sweeter than honey? And what could be stronger than a lion?" But Samson knew they had cheated and told them so. He angrily went out and killed the first thirty Philistine men he found. Then he took their clothes and gave them to the young men at his wedding. He was angry with his new wife for telling his secret. He left her there and went home to his father's house. His Philistine wife's parents thought Samson had gone for good, so they gave their daughter to another man as his wife.

After a time Samson's anger cooled off. He decided to go back to Timnath to see his wife. But when he got there, her father told him they had already given her to someone else.

Samson was very angry. He wanted to do something to hurt all the Philistines because of what had happened. He caught all the wild foxes he could find until he had three hundred of them. Then he tied pairs of them together by their tails. Next he tied a piece of dry wood to their tails and set it on fire. He turned the foxes loose in the Philistine grain fields. The foxes ran wildly over the fields and set all the grain on fire. The fire spread to the Philistine olive groves and burned them down, too.

DAVID SHOT A STONE AT GOLIATH WITH HIS SHEPHERD'S SLING

His aim was good.
The giant fell down to the ground like a tall tree.

KING DAVID TAUGHT HIS SON,
SOLOMON, TO LOVE GOD

Solomon grew up to build a beautiful temple for the Lord.

When the Philistines found out why Samson had done this, they killed both the woman Samson had married and her father. This didn't make Samson happy. He came back and killed a company of Philistine soldiers by himself. The Philistine army chased him into the land of the tribe of Judah, but they could not capture him or keep him locked up. He broke free of every rope and broke down walls and gates when they tried to imprison him.

Samson met another Philistine woman and fell in love with her. Her name was Delilah. The Philistine rulers came secretly to her and said, "If you find out what makes Samson so strong, we will give you money."

Delilah agreed. She begged and cried to get Samson to tell her the secret of his strength. At first Samson did not tell her the truth. He said that if she tied him up with seven green twigs from a willow, he would lose his strength. Delilah tested this story by tying Samson up with willow twigs while he was sleeping. Then she called out, "The Philistines are coming!" and Samson woke up. He easily broke the twigs and was free.

Delilah pretended to have hurt feelings. She said, "You are making fun of me. Tell me the truth about how you can be bound."

But Samson told her another lie. He said, "If they tie me with new ropes that have never been used before, I will not be able to get away."

So when Samson fell asleep again, Delilah tied him up with new ropes. Then she called out again, "Samson, the Philistines are coming!" Samson jumped up, and the ropes broke as if they were made of thread.

Delilah begged him again to tell her the secret of his strength. This time Samson told her something close to the truth. He said, "See how my hair is braided into seven locks? If you weave it together like a piece of cloth, I will lose my strength."

While he was asleep, Delilah wove his hair into her weaving loom and pinned it with a large pin to the loom's frame. But when Samson woke up, he carried away the pin and the loom's frame. He was just as strong as before.

Delilah cried and said, "How can you tell me that you love me, when you trick me and hide your secret from me?"

She begged him day after day until he at last gave in to her and told her the real secret of his strength. He said, "I am a Nazarite. I am under a vow to God not to drink wine or allow my hair to be cut. If I let my hair be cut short, then God's strength would leave me and I would be as weak as any other man."

Delilah knew he had finally told her the truth. She sent a message to the Philistine rulers, saying, "Come up here at once. I am sure Samson has told me all that is in his heart."

The Philistines hid and watched outside her house. When Samson fell asleep, Delilah called a man with a razor to come and shave off Samson's seven locks of hair. When he was finished, Delilah called out, "Samson, the Philistines are coming!" Samson woke up. At first he did not know that his long hair had been cut off. He thought he could get away as easily as before. But the Philistines easily made him their prisoner. They were so cruel, they hurt Samson's eyes so that he was blind. They chained him with heavy chains and put him in prison in a place called Gaza. While he was in prison, they made him push a heavy millstone and grind grain like an ox.

But while Samson was suffering in prison, his hair was growing back. He made a promise to give himself back to God. When his hair became long again, Samson's super strength came back.

One day the Philistines held a great feast in the temple of their fish god, Dagon. They said, "We thank Dagon because he has given us power over our enemy." Then they had Samson brought out for the three thousand Philistines to laugh at him. Samson told a boy who was leading him to put his hands on the main pillars of the temple. He said he just wanted something strong to lean on, but Samson had a plan. He prayed, "O Lord God, remember me just one last time and give me strength." He put one arm around one pillar and the other arm around the other pillar. Then he said, "Let me die with the Philistines."

Samson bowed forward with all his might. He pushed the pillars right over. The heavy roof fell down on all the Philistines and killed them along with Samson. In his death Samson killed more Philistines than he had during his life. His whole family came to Gaza and took his body home to bury. Samson's deeds of courage and strength kept the Philistines from getting control over the lands of Judah and Benjamin. He helped save Israel from its enemies.

RUTH

Ruth Meets Boaz

 woman named Ruth was born and lived in the land of Moab. When she grew up, she married a Hebrew man who also lived in Moab, with his brother and his mother, Naomi. His brother married another Moabite woman named Orpah. Naomi's husband had died. She was a widow. Everyone in the family had to work hard to grow even a little food to eat. After a time Ruth's husband and his brother died. Now Naomi, Ruth, and Orpah were all widows, and they were very sad.

Naomi decided to go back to Israel, where she had other relatives living. She had heard that God had blessed the land of Judah with plenty of good food. Naomi told Ruth and Orpah, "My daughters, you may go back to your mothers' homes. You have been kind to my sons and to me. May the Lord bless

each of you with a new husband and a happy home."

Naomi kissed her daughters-in-law good-bye, and they all cried together. Orpah left and went back to her parents' home. But Ruth wanted to stay with Naomi and take care of her. She said, "Do not ask me to leave you, for I never will. Where you go, I will go. Where you live, I will live. Your people will be my people. Your God will be my God. Where you die, I will die and be buried. Nothing but death itself will part you and me."

Naomi could see that Ruth meant what she said, so she allowed her to travel back to Judah with her. They had to walk around the Dead Sea, and they had to cross the Jordan River. They climbed the mountains of Judah and came to the town of Bethlehem. All of Naomi's friends and relatives were glad to see her again.

One of Naomi's relatives was a very rich man named Boaz. He owned large fields and grew a lot of grain. When farmers in Israel picked their crops, they always left some of the food in the field unharvested. God had commanded the farmers to allow poor people to go through the field behind the workers and gather what was left over. This was called "gleaning." Ruth was young and strong, so she went out into the fields that belonged to Boaz and gleaned grain to get food for herself and Naomi. One day Boaz saw her there and asked one of his workers who she was. The man answered, "It is the young woman from Moab who came home with Naomi."

Boaz went to Ruth and said, "Listen to me. Stay here with my servant girls and don't go to any other field to glean. No one will harm you here. When you are thirsty, go and get a drink from our water containers."

Ruth bowed to Boaz and thanked him for his kindness. She knew that not everyone was kind to outsiders. Boaz said, "I have heard how kind you have been to Naomi. You left your own land and came with her to a new country. You have come under God's protection like a chick under a mother bird's wings. May he give you a reward!"

At mealtime Boaz gave Ruth some of his own food. She ate all she wanted and had some left over. Later he told his workers, "Leave some extra grain for her. As you gather, drop bunches of it where she will find it."

That evening Ruth showed Naomi how much grain she had gleaned and told her the story of how

> *Boaz said, "I have heard how*
> *kind you have been to Naomi.*
> *You left your own land and came*
> *with her to a new country.*
> *You have come under God's protection*
> *like a chick under a mother bird's wings.*
> *May he give you a reward!"*

Boaz had been so kind and friendly. Naomi said, "This man is a relative of ours. Stay in his fields as long as the harvest lasts." So Ruth gleaned in his fields until the harvest had all been gathered.

At the end of harvest, Boaz held a feast at the threshing floor to celebrate. The threshing floor was the place where they separated the grain from the straw. That night Ruth went to Boaz and said something Naomi had told her to say: "You are a near relative of my husband and his father. Will you do good to us for his sake?" Those words meant that Ruth was willing to marry Boaz. Boaz looked at Ruth and realized what a kind woman she was. Ruth could have stayed in her own country. She could have looked for a younger or richer man to marry. But instead she took a long, dangerous trip to help Naomi, and then she was willing to marry a man who would welcome Naomi as well as herself into his home.

Ruth chose Boaz because he was kind, and Boaz loved Ruth because she was kind! They both knew what was important to God. After they were married, Naomi came to live in their house with them. Soon they had a son they named Obed. When he grew up, Obed became the father of Jesse. And Jesse was the father of David, the shepherd boy who became king of all Israel. Naomi became a happy grandmother, and Ruth became the mother of kings.

SAMUEL

Samuel Hears God's Voice

1 SAMUEL 1–7

A woman named Hannah went to worship at the house of the Lord in a city called Shiloh. She needed God's help, so she prayed a special prayer: "O Lord, if you will hear me and give me a son, I will give him back to you to serve you as long as he lives."

The Lord heard Hannah's prayer and gave her a little boy. She named him Samuel because that name means "asked of God." Hannah knew God had answered her prayer and given her the baby.

At that time a man named Eli was a high priest at Shiloh and a judge in Israel. Hannah kept her promise to God, and when Samuel was still very young, she brought him to Eli. She said, "My lord, I stood here praying and asked God for this child. I promised that he would belong to the Lord as long as he lives. Let him stay here with you and grow up in God's house."

So Samuel stayed with Eli and lived in one of the tents beside the tabernacle of the Lord. Every year his mother made him a little linen coat, just like the ones worn by the priests. He worked in the tabernacle along with the men who were priests. He lit lamps and opened doors. He helped Eli, whose old eyes were becoming blind. It was a blessing for Eli to have Samuel to help him, because his own sons were not kind to him and did not obey God's laws. They made Eli very sad.

One night when Samuel was still a little boy, he heard a voice calling him in the night. He thought the voice was Eli's, so he got up from his bed and ran to him. He asked Eli, "What do you want me to do?"

"My child," answered Eli, "I did not call you. Go back to bed."

Samuel lay down, but he soon heard the voice calling again, "Samuel! Samuel!"

So Samuel got up and went back to Eli. "Here I am," he said. "This time I'm sure I heard you call me."

"No," said Eli, "I did not call you. Go back to bed."

The third time the voice called, Samuel got up and went to Eli. The little boy was very sure Eli had called him. Eli knew that it must have been God calling Samuel, so he told Samuel, "Go lie down once more. If the voice speaks to you again, say, 'Speak, Lord, for your servant is listening.'"

Samuel obeyed Eli. He waited in his bed, listening for the voice. The voice spoke as if someone he could not see were standing by his bed. "Samuel! Samuel!"

Then Samuel answered, "Speak, Lord, for your servant is listening."

The Lord said, "Listen to what I say. I have seen Eli's wicked sons. I have seen that their father did not punish them when they were doing evil. I am going to punish them myself, and the story of what I have done will make everyone's ears tingle when they hear it!"

Samuel lay in his bed until morning. He got up and did his usual work. He said nothing of God's message until Eli asked him. "Samuel, my son," Eli said, "tell me what the Lord said to you last night. Don't hide anything from me."

So Samuel told Eli everything that God had said. It was a sad message for Eli, but he understood it. He told Samuel, "It is from the Lord. Let him do what seems good to him."

The good news was that God had spoken to his people. Hannah, the lonely mother in the mountains of Ephraim, heard that her son was the prophet God had chosen to be his messenger to all Israel. From that time on, God spoke to Samuel, and Samuel told God's word to the twelve tribes of Israel.

When he was a grown man, Samuel went to the people in all the tribes of Israel to tell them God's word. Their country had lost battles and had been taken over by the Philistine nation. Samuel knew this happened because the people worshiped idols instead of the true God. He said, "If you will truly come back to the Lord God with all your heart, he will set you free from the Philistines. Quit worshiping false gods and statues."

When they heard Samuel's words, the people of Israel broke the statues of false gods and began to pray to the true God. They confessed that they had

> *God spoke to Samuel, and Samuel told God's word to the twelve tribes of Israel.*

sinned, and Samuel asked God to forgive them. God did forgive his people. He helped them win one of their battles against the Philistines, by sending a powerful storm. Samuel set up a great stone on the battlefield so they would always remember how God had set them free. He wrote the word *Ebenezer* on the stone because that name means "the stone of help."

The people of Israel had peace during the time they followed Samuel. He taught them to obey and love God. He was the last of the great judges who ruled the land.

The First King of Israel

1 SAMUEL 8–15

amuel lived to be an old man and a wise judge for all the people of Israel. He wanted his sons to become judges and take care of the people, too. But Samuel's sons did not follow God's laws. They were not wise and honest. They did not always give judgments according to what was right. Sometimes when they judged a case, they would decide in favor of the person who would give them bribe money.

The elders of all the tribes of Israel were unhappy with Samuel's sons as judges. They came to Samuel and said, "You are growing old, and your sons do not rule as well as you have ruled. All the lands around us have kings. Choose a king for us as well."

Samuel was not happy, because he thought the people should look to God as their king. He prayed about their request, and God gave him an answer for the elders. God said, "If you choose a man to be king as the other nations do, he will take some of your sons away from you and make them his soldiers. He will take your other sons and make them wait upon him, work his fields, and make his chariots and weapons of war. A king will take the best fields and farms from you and give them to his friends. He will take your daughters to cook for him and to be servants in his palace. You will cry out to the Lord because of the king you have chosen, but the Lord will not help you."

But the people would not listen to Samuel's warning. They really wanted to have a royal king, as the other nations had. They wanted a strong man who would lead them to win in battle. They dreamed of becoming a rich and powerful nation. So the Lord said to Samuel, "Do as the people ask. Choose a king for them."

Samuel sent the people home and promised he would find a king for them. He chose a man named

Saul to be the first king of Israel. Saul was a big, handsome man from the tribe of Benjamin. Although he grew up as a humble farmer's son, Saul became a mighty king who led the people to victory in battle. The nation of Israel became strong and rich. The people were pleased with King Saul. They sang songs about him and shouted, "Long live the king!" whenever they saw him coming.

Saul loved to hear their praise, and he listened carefully to what the people wanted him to do. He hoped they would always like him and sing more songs about the battles he had won. Saul began to care more about what the people thought of him than about what God thought. One day Samuel told Saul that God was going to choose a new king who would obey his laws instead of doing things to please the crowds. Saul tried to get Samuel to change his mind, but it was too late.

DAVID

A Shepherd Boy Is Chosen King

1 SAMUEL 16:1–13

fter a while, God sent Samuel to choose a new king. He traveled to Bethlehem and visited the home of a man named Jesse, because God had told him that one of Jesse's sons should take Saul's place as king. Samuel told Jesse that God wanted to choose one of the boys to serve him in a special way. Jesse brought seven strong, handsome sons to stand before Samuel. They all looked as if they would make great kings. But God spoke to Samuel as Jesse's sons stood before him. God told him, "Do not look at his face or the height of his body. Man judges by the outward looks, but God looks at the heart."

After Samuel had seen all these young men, he told Jesse, "None of these is the man God wants me to meet. Are these all the children you have?"

Then Jesse told Samuel about his youngest son. "I have one more son, but he is just a boy. He is out in the field caring for our sheep."

Samuel had them call the boy to the house. His name was David, a word that meant "darling," and he was a handsome boy. He may have been about fifteen years old. As soon as Samuel saw David, God told him that this boy was the one to be king. Samuel gave David a blessing and poured olive oil on his head, but he didn't tell anyone that God had chosen David to be the new king. From that day on, God's Spirit was strong in David's life. God gave him

courage and wisdom. He grew so strong that he killed wild bears and lions that tried to harm his sheep. He played a harp and made up beautiful songs about the goodness of God. One of the songs of David is called the Shepherd Psalm.

Psalm 23

The LORD is my shepherd. He gives me
    everything I need.
  He lets me lie down in fields of green grass.
He leads me beside quiet waters.
  He gives me new strength.
He guides me in the right paths
  for the honor of his name.
Even though I walk
  through the darkest valley,
I will not be afraid.
  You are with me.
Your shepherd's rod and staff
  comfort me.

You prepare a feast for me
  right in front of my enemies.

You pour oil on my head.
   My cup runs over.
I am sure that your goodness and love will follow me
   all the days of my life.
And I will live in the house of the LORD
   forever.

David and Goliath

1 SAMUEL 16:14–17:54

hile David was singing songs to God in the fields, King Saul was having more and more trouble. God's Spirit had left him because he no longer obeyed God's words. He was so unhappy that he seemed to have no peace. People were saying he had lost his mind, because he acted so strangely. Saul told his servants to find someone to play the harp and sing to him. Listening to music sometimes helped him feel better. The servants had heard about David and his beautiful songs. They sent a message to Jesse and asked him to send his youngest boy to play for the king.

Saul liked David the minute he saw him. He gave David the honor of carrying his sword and shield to all the battles. When Saul became sad, David would play music and sing to help him feel better. Soon Saul felt stronger, and he allowed David to return to his father. No one knew about the message God had given Samuel about David.

When Saul was king, Israel was always at war with the Philistine people who lived on the low land on the southwest border of his country. Three of David's older brothers were soldiers in Saul's army. One day Jesse sent David with food for his older sons. David was to find out how they were doing. David left his home in Bethlehem and found his brothers in their army camp near the Philistines' land. While he was talking with them, a giant came out of the Philistine camp and dared any Israelite to come forward and fight him. The giant's name was Goliath. He was nine feet tall and wore bronze armor from his head to his feet. He carried a spear twice as long and heavy as what any other man could lift. There was another big man who carried his shield and walked in front of Goliath.

Goliath came out every day and called out across the valley, "I am a Philistine, and you are servants of Saul. Choose one of your men to come and fight with me. If he can kill me, we will become your slaves. If I kill him, you will become our slaves. Come on! I dare you to send a man to fight with me!"

The giant had been coming to the valley and shouting these words at the Israelites for forty days, but no one had been brave enough to go down and fight him.

David looked around at his brothers and the other soldiers to see who would answer Goliath. None of

them ran forward to fight the giant. He could not believe it, so he asked, "Who is this man that dares the army of the Lord in such a proud way? Why doesn't someone just go out and kill him? Won't the man who does that get a great reward for stopping this Philistine from making fun of our army?"

The soldiers laughed at the little shepherd boy's brave talk. "Of course there's a reward for anyone who kills Goliath. King Saul has promised to make that hero and his family rich. He will get to marry

> *David told everyone, "If no one else will go, I will go out and fight this enemy of the Lord's people."*

the king's daughter." But the men didn't care what great things Saul offered. They weren't going to fight Goliath. They didn't think the person who went to fight would come back alive. That person would never get any of the rewards, because it looked as if no one was strong enough to beat the giant.

David's brothers told him to run along. They made fun of him. "Why did you leave your sheep and come down here to boast and watch the battle? Go back home and do your job instead of being lazy!"

But David didn't leave. He couldn't stand to hear the giant making fun of the Israelite army. He thought of a plan to stop Goliath. He told everyone, "If no one else will go, I will go out and fight this enemy of the Lord's people."

When they heard this, the soldiers brought David to the king. Saul looked at him and said, "You cannot fight this giant. You are still young and untrained. Goliath is a trained man of war."

David answered, "I am only a shepherd, but I have fought with lions and bears when they tried to steal my sheep. I am not afraid to fight with this Philistine. The Lord saved me from the lion's jaw and the bear's paw when I fought for my sheep. He will save me from this giant's sword when I fight for his people."

Saul agreed to let David fight Goliath. He gave David his own royal armor to wear. But Saul was almost a giant himself, and his armor was much too big for David. Saul's sword was too heavy for David, as well. The shepherd said, "I am not used to these kinds of weapons. Let me fight my own way."

So David left Saul's armor behind. He did not need it for the plan he had in mind. A quick eye, a clear head, a sure aim, and a bold heart were the weapons God had given him. David carried his shepherd's staff as if he were going to use it to fight the giant. But his secret weapon was really hidden in a bag under his coat. He had five smooth stones and a sling from which to shoot them. That was a weapon a shepherd knew how to use.

Goliath was angry when he saw who had come out to fight him. "What is this? You must think I'm a dog to send a boy with a stick to fight me! I'm going to tear him up and feed him to the birds like bread crumbs!"

Then he cursed David, using the names of the false gods of his people.

David answered, "You come against me with a sword and a spear, but I come to you in the name of the God of the whole earth, the Lord of the armies of Israel. Today God will give you to me. You and your army will be the crumbs the birds will eat. Then everyone will know there is a God in Israel. He doesn't need men's swords or spears to save us. The battle belongs to him."

Then David ran toward the giant as if he were going to fight him with his shepherd's staff. But when he came close enough, David took out his sling and hurled a stone at Goliath. David's aim was good, and his stone struck the Philistine right in the forehead.

The giant fell down to the ground like a tall tree. David ran up, grabbed Goliath's huge sword, and used it to cut off the giant's head.

The two armies just stood there for a moment, wondering what had caused the giant to fall so suddenly. Then the Philistines saw that their great war-

> *David answered, "You come against me with a sword and a spear, but I come to you in the name of the God of the whole earth, the Lord of the armies of Israel.*

rior was dead. They turned to run back to their homes, but the Israelites chased them and killed them by the thousands, all the way to the gates of their Philistine city.

David won a great battle that day, and everyone in the land knew he was the one who had saved his people from their enemies.

David Becomes King

2 SAMUEL 1–10

aul led Israel as king for forty years. At the beginning of his reign, his people were almost free from the Philistines, and it seemed as if King Saul were going to drive the enemy completely out of their land. But when Saul quit obeying the Lord and wouldn't listen to Samuel the prophet, the land fell back under the Philistines' power. David wanted to help Saul fight their enemy, but Saul became very jealous when the people sang songs about David's victories in battle. He liked it better when the people sang only about himself and his great battles. He even tried to keep David from seeing his son, Jonathan. David and Jonathan had become good friends. So when Saul drove David away, Saul lost a strong friend who could have helped him fight. In the end Saul and Jonathan died during a battle. The Philistines seemed to be taking over the land of Israel.

When David heard that King Saul and Jonathan were dead, he cried and felt very sad. He wrote a song that told what he felt in his heart about losing them.

The Song of the Bow

"In life Saul and Jonathan were loved and gracious.
In death they were not parted.
They were faster than eagles.
They were stronger than lions.

"Daughters of Israel, sob over Saul.
He dressed you in the finest clothes.
He decorated your clothes with ornaments of gold.

"Your mighty men have fallen in battle.
Jonathan lies dead on your hills.
My brother Jonathan, I'm filled with sadness
because of you.
You were very special to me....

"Israel's mighty men have fallen.
Their weapons of war are broken."

Even though Saul had treated David as an enemy, David wanted to be kind to Saul's grandchildren and family. He found out that Jonathan's son,

Mephibosheth, had been injured as a baby when a nurse had fallen down while she was carrying him. The boy had not been able to walk after the accident because his feet were hurt. His relatives had hidden Mephibosheth from David because in those days new kings often killed the families of the old kings so they wouldn't try to take back the throne. But David had a kind heart for Saul's family. He sent for Mephibosheth and invited him to live in the palace and eat at the royal table with David's own family. He made sure Mephibosheth was given all the lands that had belonged to Saul and Jonathan.

When David was thirty-seven years old, the elders of Israel made him their new king. He found the land in a helpless state because the Philistines and the Canaanites had taken over so much of their country. David fought them and took back the city of Jerusalem. Then he brought the ark of the covenant out of hiding and returned it to its rightful place on Mount Zion. The priests of the Lord kept it there in the tent of the tabernacle so the people could come and worship. Inside the tabernacle was the golden ark, and in the ark were the tablets of the Ten Commandments God had given Moses. The ark and all that was in it were blessed by God's Spirit.

David's home on Mount Zion was a beautiful palace. One day he had an idea. He asked a prophet named Nathan to tell him if God would be pleased by his plan. He said, "I live in a house of cedar wood, but the ark of God stands inside a tent made of cloth."

Nathan guessed that David wanted to build a beautiful cedar house for the ark of God. He thought it was a good idea, so he said, "Go do all that is in your heart. The Lord is with you."

But that night the Lord gave Nathan a message. He said, "Go tell my servant David, 'This is what the Lord says: "I have not dwelt in a house from the day I brought the Israelites up out of Egypt to this day. I have been moving from place to place with a tent as my dwelling. Did I ever say to any of their rulers, 'Why have you not built me a house of cedar?' I took you from the sheep pasture and made you a prince. I gave you great power. Now, because you have done my will, I will make you famous. When your days are over and you rest with your fathers, I will raise up your offspring to succeed you. Your son will sit on the throne after you, and he will build me a temple. I will give you and your children and your grand-children a throne and a kingdom that will last for-ever."'"

These promises of God came true. Solomon, one of David's sons, built a beautiful temple for the ark of God. And God gave David's family a kingdom that would last forever. Many years later Jesus Christ was born in Bethlehem, and he was one of David's grand-children. The kingdom of Jesus will last forever.

SOLOMON

The Wise King

1 KINGS 1:1–3:15

ing David put away a great treasure of gold, silver, brass, stone, cedar wood, and iron to be used in building a house for the Lord on Mount Moriah. This house for God would be called "the temple," and it was to be the most beautiful building in all the land. David wanted to build it while he was king of Israel, but God told him, "You have been a man of war and have fought many battles. A man of peace should build my house. When you die, your son Solomon will reign in peace and build my house."

So David stored up everything his son would need for the building. He told Solomon, "God has promised that there will be peace in the land while you are king. The Lord will be with you, and you will build a house where he can live among his people."

David commanded Solomon to ride out on the mule that no one but the king was allowed to ride. Solomon rode down to the valley of Gihon with the palace guards and nobles. This let all the people know that David had chosen Solomon to be the new king. A priest named Zadok poured holy oil on Solomon's head, and then the people called out, "God save King Solomon!" while priests blew trumpets. David said, "May the Lord make your name greater than my name has been! Blessed be the Lord, who has given me a son to sit this day on my throne!"

Soon afterward David sent for Solomon and gave his last words of advice to his son. David died in his own bed after reigning as king of Israel for forty years.

Solomon was just a young man when he became king. He worshiped and obeyed the Lord. One night God came to Solomon and spoke to him. "Ask me to give you anything you want, and I will give it to you."

Solomon said, "O Lord, you showed such kindness to my father, David. Now you have made me king in his place while I am only a child. I don't know how to rule so many people. I pray that you will give me wisdom and knowledge so I can judge the people well and rule them the right way."

The Lord was pleased with Solomon's choice. He said, "You have not asked for long life or great riches or victory over your enemies or great power. You have asked for wisdom and knowledge, so I grant you wisdom greater than that of any king who has come before you or who will come after you. Because you asked for this, I will give you not only wisdom but also honor and riches. If you obey my words, as your father obeyed, you will have long life and will rule for many years."

Then Solomon woke up and knew that he had been having a dream. But it was a dream that came true, for God gave him all that he had promised.

The Right Mother

1 KINGS 3:16–28

oon after the dream, Solomon showed the wisdom God had given him. Two women came to him with two little babies. One baby was dead, and the other was alive. Each woman claimed the living child as her own. One of the women said, "O my lord, this woman and I live in the same house. We both had babies. During the night this woman's son died because she rolled over on it and killed it. She put her dead child near me while I was asleep and took my living child. In the morning I saw that the baby beside me was not my child. But she says the dead child is mine and the living child is hers. Now, O king, command this woman to give me my own child."

Then the other woman said, "That is not true. The dead baby is hers, and the living one is mine. She is just trying to take my child from me."

The young king listened to both women argue. Then he told his guards, "Bring me a sword."

When they brought Solomon the sword, he held it up and said, "Take this sword and cut the living child in two pieces. Give half to each woman."

One of the women cried out, "O my lord, give her the living baby! Don't kill him."

The other woman said, "Neither I nor you shall have him. Cut him in two!"

Then Solomon said, "Give the child to the woman who didn't want us to kill it. She is the baby's true mother."

All the people of Israel were amazed at the wisdom of their young king. They agreed that God had given him a gift of understanding.

The House of God on Mount Moriah

1 KINGS 5:1–9:9

he great work of Solomon's reign was building a house for God on Mount Moriah. It became known as "Solomon's temple" or "the temple." The walls were made of stone and the roof of cedar. It covered the whole mountain peak of Mount Moriah. The cedar wood came from the forests on Mount Lebanon. Workman cut down trees and carried them to the city of Tyre on the seacoast. There they were made into rafts and floated in the Great Sea down to the town of Joppa. From the seaport of Joppa they were taken overland to Jerusalem. All this work was done by the men of Tyre at the command of their king, Hiram, who was a friend of Solomon, just as he had been a friend of King David.

All the stones for the building were hammered into shape and fitted together before they were brought to Mount Moriah. All the beams for the roof and the pillars of cedar were carved and made to fit each other before they were brought to the mountain. So as the great walls were built, there was no sound of a hammer or chisel in that special place.

Inside the temple there was a large altar made of rough, natural stones. No cut stones were allowed to be used to make the place where the priests offered animals as sacrifices for the sins of the people. In front of the altar was a big tank for water. It was so large, it was called a "sea." The tank was made of shining brass and stood on the backs of twelve oxen made of brass.

There was a long room called the Holy Place, which had a golden lamp. Behind a thick veil that hung down in the Holy Place was a smaller room called the Holy of Holies. The high priest was

allowed into that room only once a year. The ark of the covenant was kept in that room. The ark was a beautiful golden box with carved angels on top. The tablets with Moses' Ten Commandments were kept inside the box.

It took seven years for Solomon and his men to finish building the great temple. When it was finished, God came to the king in a dream and said, "I have heard the prayer you offered to me, and I have made this house holy. It shall be my house, and I will dwell there. If you do my will, as your father did, then your throne shall stand forever. But if you turn aside from following me, I will leave this house and turn aside from it. I will let the enemies of Israel come and destroy this house that was built for me."

The Golden Age

olomon's reign has been called "the Golden Age of Israel" because it was a time of peace and great riches. Kings and queens came from other lands to see all the beautiful things he had built there. Once the queen of Sheba traveled a thousand miles from the south to see Solomon's palace and hear his wise sayings. She asked him many hard questions, and God gave Solomon wise answers to tell her. After they talked, the queen said, "All that I have heard in my own land of your wisdom and your greatness was true. But I did not believe it until I came and saw your kingdom. Now I see that you are twice as wise and wealthy as in the stories I heard about you. Happy are those who are always with you to hear your wisdom! Blessed be the Lord your God, who has set you on the throne of Israel!"

Even though Solomon was very wise in the business of his country, he was foolish in some ways. Kings were allowed to have many wives in those days, and some of the wives Solomon chose were not Israelites. They came from countries like Egypt, where the people worshiped false gods. Some of these wives brought statues of their false gods, and Solomon allowed them to make places to worship these idols as they had in their own lands. The Lord was very angry with Solomon and told him, "Since you have done these evil things and have not kept your promise to serve only me, I will take the kingdom of Israel from your son and give it to one of your servants. But because your father, David, followed me, I will leave your son with one tribe of Israel to rule."

That was why Solomon's son Rehoboam ruled only the tribe of Judah, while Solomon's servant Jeroboam became king of ten tribes of Israel.

ELIJAH

A Jar of Flour and a Jug of Oil

1 KINGS 16:29–17:16

fter a time a man named Ahab became king of Israel. During his reign God told a prophet named Elijah to speak to the people for him. Although it was a great honor for Elijah to tell the people how to follow the Lord, it was not an easy job. Many of the kings who ruled after Solomon did not love and obey God the way King Solomon and King David had. These kings were more interested in becoming rich and powerful than in obeying God's laws. They often did not like the words God sent his prophets to speak to them. They became angry with the prophets. Of course, it was dangerous for anyone to have a king angry with him or her!

Elijah's troubles started with the very first message God sent him to give to King Ahab. God wanted

Ahab to change the way he was doing things. He was to obey God as King Solomon and King David had done. To prove that Elijah was a true prophet, the Lord had him go to Ahab and tell him, "As surely as the Lord God of Israel lives, no rain or dew will fall on the land until I call for it." After Elijah delivered his message, he turned and left the king as suddenly as he had come. He went out and hid in the wilderness, where Ahab could not find him.

It happened just as Elijah said it would. Rain did not fall on the land for many days, and no one could find Elijah. People began to run out of food. They could not grow more crops without rain. But God was taking care of Elijah in a special way all through the famine. God sent ravens to bring bread and meat to the prophet. In the wilderness there was a little brook where Elijah could drink water. As God held back the rain, the brook became smaller and smaller until it finally dried up. Then God told Elijah to go to a town called Zarephath and to ask a widow who lived there for help.

When Elijah saw the woman carrying some sticks for her fire, he said to her, "Would you bring me some water to drink and a little piece of bread to eat?"

But the woman was so poor that she told him, "As surely as the Lord your God lives, I don't even have a loaf of bread in my house to eat. All I have left is a handful of flour in a jar and a little olive oil in a jug. I am gathering these sticks to make a fire to bake it into one last meal for my little boy and myself. After we have eaten that, we will starve to death."

Then God told Elijah what he would do for the woman, and Elijah said, "Don't be afraid anymore. Go home and do as you planned. But before you bake your own bread, make a little loaf for me. God has told me, 'The jar of flour will not be used up and the jug of oil will not run dry until the day the Lord sends rain.'"

The woman believed Elijah's words. She made him the little loaf of bread, and then she mixed up some dough for herself and her son. When she was finished, she saw that the jar still had flour left and the jug still had oil in it. So Elijah and the woman and her son had enough food every day until God sent the rain again.

A Boy Gets Well

1 KINGS 17:17–24

One day the widow's son became very sick. He got worse and worse, and finally the little boy stopped breathing. His mother was very upset, and she asked Elijah to help. Elijah carried the little boy to the upper room where he was staying. Then he prayed to God, "O Lord my God, have you brought tragedy upon this widow I am staying with, by causing her son to die?" Then he stretched himself upon the boy three times and cried out to God, "O Lord my God, let this boy's life return to him!"

God heard and answered Elijah's prayer, and the widow's son began to breathe again. Elijah carried the boy to his mother and said, "Look, your son is alive!"

Then the woman said, "Now I know you are a man of God. The words you speak from God come true."

THE QUEEN OF SHEBA CAME
TO SEE KING SOLOMON

She traveled from her home because she heard of the
great wisdom and wealth God had given Solomon.

YOUNG JOASH BECAME KING OF JUDAH

He obeyed God. He collected money and
then he repaired the temple of the Lord.

God Sends Fire and Rain

he Lord God had stopped the rain for three years, and all the rivers stopped running. The ground was cracked and dry. No crops would grow, and there was hardly any food left for the people. All this time, the Lord had taken care of Elijah and the widow and her son by the miracle of the flour and oil that would not run out. Finally God told Elijah it was time to take another message to King Ahab and bring back the rain.

The king had a servant named Obadiah, a good man who worshiped God. Once Obadiah had saved all the prophets of God from the king and his evil queen, Jezebel, by hiding them in some caves. King Ahab sent Obadiah out to look for water in one part of his land while he searched for water in another part. While he was searching, Obadiah saw Elijah. The prophet told him to go tell King Ahab where he was. Obadiah was afraid that Elijah would hide again and the king would be angry. But Elijah promised to meet the king.

When King Ahab saw Elijah, he said, "So here you are, you troublemaker."

But Elijah answered, "I am not the one who has brought trouble on Israel. You and your family have turned away from God's laws and worshiped the false idols of Baal."

He told the king he would meet the false prophets at Mount Carmel and prove that their gods were not real, and he would show everyone that the God of Israel was the one true God.

So 450 false prophets who worshiped idols came to challenge Elijah, the only prophet of the true God of Israel. Two altars were set up, one to burn an offering to God and another to burn an offering to the false gods and idols of the 450 prophets. Everyone there agreed that the people of Israel would worship the god who proved he was real by sending fire to burn up the offering.

The 450 false prophets all prayed to their gods first. They shouted, danced, and prayed from morning until noon for their gods to send fire. But nothing happened.

Elijah laughed at their foolishness and said, "Call out louder! Maybe your gods are sitting and thinking. Maybe they have gone away on a trip! Or are they sleeping? Wake them up!"

But no matter what the false prophets did, nothing happened. So Elijah called everyone over to his altar. He took four barrels of water and poured them all over his altar. He filled them again and again and poured water over the whole offering until it was so wet that everyone thought it would be impossible for it to catch on fire. Then he prayed a simple prayer to

God. He didn't dance or shout. He just prayed, "O Lord, you are the God of Abraham, of Isaac, and of Israel. Show everyone this day that you are the true God and I am your servant. I pray that you would answer me so these people will know that you are the one and only God. Turn their hearts back to worship you again."

Then the fire of the Lord came down and burned up Elijah's offering. The fire was so strong that it burned up the water, the wood, and the whole altar. Even the stones were burned to dust. When the people saw this, they knew that Elijah worshiped the true God. They cried out, "The Lord is the one and only God!" They were angry with the 450 false prophets for tricking them with idols they had made. They grabbed the false prophets and put them to death.

Elijah told Ahab that God was going to send rain. So Ahab turned his chariot toward his city and began to drive it home. Elijah was so full of the power of God that he ran faster than Ahab's chariot to the city gate.

The Evil Queen

t last Elijah felt full of joy that the true God had won the challenge and the people had rejected the false gods at last. But trouble was waiting for him inside Ahab's city. When Queen Jezebel heard what Elijah had done, she was angry. She sent him a threatening message. "I promise to kill you tomorrow, just as you killed the prophets of Baal," she said.

Not one man in the kingdom dared help Elijah. He had to run away to save his life from the queen. He hid miles away from her in the desert. After walking all day, he sat down to rest under a juniper tree. Poor Elijah was tired and hungry and sad. He felt ashamed for running away from the queen. He thought the people he had rescued from the false prophets would go right back to worshiping idols without him to lead them. He cried out to God, "O Lord, I have lived long enough! Take away my life now because I am no better than my people."

He lay down to sleep under the tree. But the Lord cared for Elijah by sending an angel. The angel touched him and said, "Get up and eat."

When Elijah opened his eyes, he saw a campfire with a loaf of bread baking on it. There was a jar of water nearby. He ate and drank, and then he lay down to sleep again. Later the angel touched him once more and said, "Get up and eat. The journey is too long for you."

Elijah got up and ate again. Then he went on his way. The food the angel had made gave Elijah so much strength that he was able to walk for forty days through the desert without eating again. He came to Mount Horeb, the mountain where Moses had seen the burning bush and where he had received the Ten Commandments from God. Elijah found a cave in the side of the mountain and went inside to rest. In the cave he heard God's voice say to him, "What are you doing here, Elijah?"

Elijah answered, "O Lord God, the people have broken their promise to serve you. They have destroyed your altars and killed your prophets. Now I am the only one left, and they are trying to find me to kill me."

Then God told him, "Go out and stand on the mountain before the Lord."

Elijah stood on the mountain, and a great strong wind swept by. It tore the mountains apart and broke the rocks in pieces. But the Lord wasn't in the wind. Next an earthquake shook the mountains. But the Lord wasn't in the earthquake. A great fire passed by. But the Lord wasn't in the fire. After the fire passed, there was silence and stillness. Then Elijah heard a low, quiet voice, and he knew it was the voice of the Lord.

Elijah covered his face with his coat because he was afraid to look at God. The voice said, "What are you doing here, Elijah?"

And Elijah answered again, "O Lord God, the people have broken their promise to serve you. They have destroyed your altars and killed your prophets. Now I am the only one left, and they are trying to find me to kill me."

Then God told him, "Go back and anoint Hazael to be king of Syria and Jehu, the son of Nimshi, to be king of Israel. Anoint Elisha, the son of Shaphat, to take your place as my prophet. The swords of those two kings will kill all those who broke their promise to serve me. Elisha will kill any of them who escape. But you will find seven thousand men in Israel who have never bowed down on their knees to worship Baal. They have never kissed his statue with their lips."

It took the rest of Elijah's life to finish this work for God, but he was full of joy after he heard God's message. The Lord was sending him one thing he really needed: a friend to stand beside him so he wouldn't be alone. Elijah knew that his work had done some good when God told him there were seven thousand men who still served the Lord. And he knew Elisha would carry on God's work in Israel after he was gone.

The Little Boy Who Was Crowned King

2 CHRONICLES 21—24

hen Jehoram was king of Judah, he did many evil things. The prophet Elijah sent him a letter with a warning from God. He wrote: "The Lord God of David says 'You have led the people of Jerusalem and of Judah to worship idols instead of the Lord. You have killed your own brothers. Because of this the Lord will punish your family. He will send you a terrible disease no one can cure."

Elijah's words were true. Jehoram became sick and died from a disease no doctor could cure. The kingdoms around Judah attacked. They killed all of Jehoram's sons except for the youngest one, Ahaziah. But he did not sit on his father's throne for long, because an enemy killed him. Ahaziah's mother, Athaliah, heard that her son was dead. She fiercely killed all the princes she could find who belonged to the family of David. Then she took over Jehoram's throne herself. She was an evil queen. She taught the people to worship the idol Baal.

There was one prince of the house of David Queen Athaliah did not find. His name was Joash. His aunt hid him in the temple of the Lord for six years and kept him safe from the queen. His uncle, Jehoiada, was a priest of God. He taught Joash about the true God.

When Joash was seven years old, Jehoiada brought him out of his hiding place. He put a crown on his head in front of all the people and rulers in the temple. Everyone was tired of the cruel queen. They cheered for Joash: "Long live the king! Long live the king!" None of the queen's soldiers would arrest Joash. Instead they killed Queen Athaliah and obeyed

Joash as their king. All the people made a promise to serve the Lord, and they broke Queen Athaliah's idols and their altars into pieces. They worshiped the Lord in the temple. They were glad to have a king from David's family on the throne of Judah again.

King Joash wanted to make the temple beautiful once again. It had grown old, and the queen had broken many of its walls. She used its beautiful gold and silver on her idols' altars. Joash had a large box put by the door to the temple. Everyone who wanted to help fix up the temple put money into it. Soon the box was full. After they emptied it and put the money in a safe place, the people filled it up again. In the end, they had more money than they needed to pay for all the work that needed to be done. The king's uncle Jehoiada helped him make the temple look beautiful once again.

When Jehoiada grew old and died, the princes of Judah became King Joash's advisors. They loved to worship idols. They taught the king to do the same evil things they did. Their country became weak without God's protection. Soon the land of Judah was taken over by the Syrian kingdom from the north. Joash's life was soon over because his own servants killed him. They made his son Amaziah king instead.

Elijah Finds Elisha

1 KINGS 19:19–2 KINGS 2:12

ne day Elijah traveled to the place God sent him to meet a new friend. Elisha lived with his rich father on a large farm. Elijah found him plowing one of their fields with twelve strong oxen hitched to his plow.

Elijah walked right up to Elisha and tossed his rough leather cape around the younger man's shoulders. Then Elijah walked away. Elisha knew who Elijah was, and he knew what it meant for the prophet to give him his cape. It meant that Elijah had called Elisha to leave his beautiful home and become a prophet. Elisha believed in the true God of Israel, so he left his oxen standing right there in the field and ran after Elijah. Elisha was willing to live a dangerous life in the wilderness to serve the Lord. He didn't care if kings or queens tried to kill him. He just wanted to do God's work. After saying good-bye to his family, Elisha went with Elijah.

The two men worked together and did many great things for the Lord. They gave God's messages to King Ahab. Finally the king was sorry for the sins

he had done and asked God to forgive him. God said he would not bring disaster on the king himself but would bring it on his household when his son became king.

The two prophets knew that the Lord would come to take Elijah to heaven after his work for the Lord was finished. Elisha would go on living, and he would give God's messages to Israel in Elijah's place. One day the two men traveled to the Jordan River together. Elijah struck the water with his cape, and the waters parted. As they walked across on the dry path, he said to Elisha, "What would you like me to do for you before God takes me away?"

Elisha answered, "All I ask is for a double portion of your spirit to come upon me."

"You have asked a difficult thing," Elijah said. "Yet if you see me when I am taken from you, it will be yours. If you do not see me go, it will not come."

Suddenly a chariot of fire pulled by horses of fire came down between the two men. Elijah went up into heaven in a whirlwind on that fiery chariot. As Elisha watched him going up, he cried out, "O my father, the chariot of Israel and its horsemen!" And Elisha saw Elijah no more.

Elisha

God's Secret Army

2 Kings 2:13–6:23

hen Elijah was out of sight, Elisha saw the cape that had fallen from Elijah. He picked it up and then struck the water of the Jordan River with it. He said, "Where is the Lord God of Elijah?" When he did this, the water parted just as it had for Elijah. Elisha walked back across on a dry path.

Some men who believed in God watched him do this from the other side of the river. They told each other, "The spirit of Elijah now rests on Elisha." Some men known as the "sons of the prophets" came to meet Elisha and honored him as their leader that day.

Elisha did not live in the wilderness as Elijah had often done. Rather he went into the cities and told the people God's words. He did many miracles to show them that God was with them and that he was God's prophet. He made a city's bitter water become good. He healed a man with leprosy. And he brought a little boy back to life.

A man named Gehazi helped Elisha. He took care of him just as Elisha had cared for Elijah. One day

> *"Don't be afraid," Elisha answered.*
> *"There are more on our side*
> *than on theirs."*

Elisha and Gehazi found themselves surrounded by enemies. Soldiers sent by the king of Syria had surrounded the city where they were staying. They wanted to kill Elisha. They knew Elisha was helping the king of Israel by telling him all their plans for war. They couldn't keep their plans secret, because God kept telling Elisha what they were up to!

When Gehazi saw the soldiers, he was very afraid. He called Elisha and cried, "What will we do?"

"Don't be afraid," Elisha answered. "There are more on our side than on theirs."

Then he prayed that the Lord would open Gehazi's eyes so he could see God's secret army. The young man looked and could suddenly see something

ELIJAH HEALED THE WIDOW'S SON

Elijah carried the boy to his mother and said, "Look! Your son is alive!"
She thanked God for sending Elijah to help her boy.

ELIJAH WENT UP INTO HEAVEN
IN A WHIRLWIND

A chariot of fire pulled by horses of fire flew down
from heaven to Elijah—a man who walked with God.

other men could not see. The mountainside around the city was filled with horses and chariots of fire that God had sent to keep his prophet safe.

Elisha went out to the Syrian army and played a trick on them. He prayed that God would make the soldiers blind. Then he told them, "This is not the right city. Follow me, and I will show you the way." The soldiers could see only a mist around them, so they followed Elisha. He led them inside the city walls of Samaria, where the army of Israel could surround them. When God allowed the Syrian soldiers to see, they realized they had been captured. Elisha told the king of Israel not to kill these men but to send them back to their land with food and water. After that happened, the Syrian armies did not attack Israel again for a long time.

An Old Prophet and Young King Jehoash

hen Elisha was an old man, a good young king came to the throne in Israel. His name was Jehoash. Jehoash loved Elisha. He cried when he came to see him, because it seemed Elisha was about to die. King Jehoash said, "My father, my father, you more important to Israel than all our chariots and soldiers!"

Elisha's body was weak, but his soul was strong. He told the king to bring him a bow and arrows and open the eastern window that faced Syria. Then he placed his hands on the king's hands and helped him shoot an arrow out the window. As the arrow flew toward Syria, Elisha spoke his last prophecy: "This is the Lord's arrow of victory over Syria. You will strike the Syrians in Aphek and destroy them."

Soon after this Elisha died, and everyone remembered him as a man who had more of God's Spirit on his life than anyone during his time.

JONAH

The Big Fish

ne day God sent a message to a prophet named Jonah. He said, "Go to the great city of Nineveh. Preach to the people there because I see their sins."

But Jonah did not want to preach God's message to the people in Nineveh. They were enemies of Jonah's people, Israel. He decided it would serve them right to die in their sins and never turn to God and live. So Jonah tried to run away from God. He went to Joppa, a town on the shore of the Great Sea. There he found a ship sailing to Tarshish, and he paid to travel on the ship. Tarshish was about as far away from Nineveh as Jonah could get.

The Lord saw Jonah on that ship. God knew Jonah was running away. So he sent a big storm. The waves got so huge that it seemed the ship was going to be broken into pieces. The sailors were sure the ship was going to sink, and they were frightened. They threw things overboard to make the ship lighter. They prayed to their gods to save them. All this time Jonah was fast asleep in his room under the ship's deck. The captain came to him and cried, "How can you be sleeping while this storm is going on? Get up and pray to your god! Maybe he will take notice of us and we will not die."

But the storm kept getting worse and worse, and finally the sailors said, "Come, let us cast lots to find out who is responsible for our calamity."

So they cast lots, and the lot fell on Jonah. They all asked him, "What do you do? What is your country? Where do you come from? What have you done?"

Jonah told them the whole story. Then they asked him what they could do to stop the storm God had sent. Jonah said, "Pick me up and throw me into the sea, and it will become calm. I know it is all my fault that this great storm has come upon you."

The men didn't want to do something so dangerous to Jonah. They tried to save the ship by rowing it to land. Finally they prayed to the Lord, "O Lord, please do not let us die for taking this man's life. Do not hold us accountable for killing an innocent man, for you, O Lord, have done as you pleased."

So at last, because they could not save themselves, they threw Jonah into the sea. As soon as they did, the waves became still. When they saw this happen, the men all promised to serve the Lord themselves.

As soon as Jonah fell into the water, God commanded a big fish to swallow him alive. Jonah stayed inside the fish for three days and three nights. He finally called out to God to rescue him, and God heard his prayer coming from the fish's belly. He made the fish swim up to dry land and throw up Jonah on the beach.

God gave Jonah a second chance, and this time Jonah went to Nineveh as soon as he heard God tell him to go. The people of that city were sorry for their sins when they heard God's message from Jonah. God forgave them and didn't destroy their city. Jonah learned that men and women and little children are all precious in God's sight. The Lord sent Jonah to speak his word and save the people of Nineveh even though the people who lived there were not part of the tribes of the children of Israel.

ISAIAH

The Prophet Says, "Send Me!"

ISAIAH 6

I saiah was a young man to whom God sent a message. It was the year that Uzziah, the king of Judah, died. While Isaiah was worshiping in the temple, he saw a wonderful vision of the Lord sitting on a throne surrounded by angels. He also saw amazing creatures called "seraphim" that had six wings and flew through the air. They called out,

"Holy, holy, holy is the Lord of Hosts!
The whole earth is full of his glory!"

When the seraphim spoke, the walls and floor of the temple shook, and Isaiah saw smoke filling the temple. He was afraid and cried out, "Woe is me! I will be destroyed for seeing the Lord of Hosts, because I am a man who says sinful words. I live with people who speak sinful words."

But as soon as he said this, one of the seraphim flew to the altar and picked up a burning coal with a pair of tongs. He flew to Isaiah and touched the hot coal to his lips. Then he said, "This coal from God's altar has touched your lips. Now your sin is taken away, and you are clean."

Then Isaiah heard the Lord saying, "Who will I send to these people? Who will carry the words of the Lord to them?"

And Isaiah said, "Here I am. Send me!"

The Lord told him, "You will be my prophet and go to these people. I will give you my words. But they will not listen to your message or understand what you tell them. Your words will not do them any good. They will not hear with their ears or see with their eyes or understand with their hearts. They will not turn to me to be saved."

Then Isaiah asked, "How long must this be, O Lord?"

And the Lord told him that all the cities would be destroyed and the people carried away to another land before they would understand his message. In the end just a tenth of the people would come back to their land to rebuild the cities of Judah. Isaiah knew that he was being sent to give God's message even though it would seem as if no one were listening to his words.

Isaiah lived for many years and gave the people God's message. He spoke to four kings who did not always obey what God had sent Isaiah to tell them.

Good King Hezekiah

ne of Judah's best kings was Hezekiah. He listened to the words of Isaiah and obeyed the commands of God. He went through the temple and removed all the gold and silver idols that past kings had brought there. He had the priests give offerings only to the true God of Israel. The people worshiped the Lord and sang the psalms of David again. The people had not done this in years, because of the bad kings who worshiped false gods. Hezekiah had his servants go everywhere in the land of Judah and take down false idols and their places of worship. He told his people to turn back to the true God.

One day Hezekiah got a letter from the king of Assyria. It said that the Assyrian army was marching to his city to destroy it and take everyone prisoner. King Hezekiah took the letter to the house of the Lord and spread it out near the altar. He called on God to help him and save his people. Isaiah sent him this message: "God says, 'The king of Assyria will not come to your city. He will not even shoot one arrow against it. He will go back home by the same way he came. I will make him fall by the sword in his own land. I will defend this city and save it for my own sake and for my servant David.'"

Isaiah's words came true. The Assyrian army turned around because they heard that another army was coming out to fight them. Then many of the soldiers died of sickness as they marched back to Assyria. That king never tried to invade Judah again. He was killed by a sword in his own land, as Isaiah had said.

King Hezekiah became very sick, and his doctors could not help him with medicine. Isaiah came and told him, "God says, 'Get your house in order and be ready to die. You will not get well.'"

But Hezekiah prayed to the Lord that he might live. He said, "O Lord, I ask you to remember now how I have followed you in truth and with a perfect heart. I have done what is good in your sight. Let me live and not die, O Lord!"

The Lord heard King Hezekiah's prayer. As Isaiah was walking home, he turned around and went back to the king. He told Hezekiah that God had heard his prayer and seen his tears. He said the king would get well and live for fifteen more years.

Then Isaiah gave Hezekiah a sign that this would all happen as he had said. He asked the king, "Would you like to see the shadow on the stairs go forward ten steps or back ten steps?" If the shadow went back ten steps, it meant that time was going backward. Hezekiah thought it was normal for time to go forward, but only God could make it go backward. So he asked that the shadow go back ten steps, so he would know that Isaiah's words were from God.

Isaiah called on the Lord, and the shadow went back ten steps. Then Hezekiah praised God. He believed he would get well and live for fifteen more years. And that was what happened, just as Isaiah had told him.

EZEKIEL

What Ezekiel Saw in the Valley

fter the many warnings God gave his people about not worshiping idols, they at last were taken into captivity. The people of Judah were taken to Babylon. It was during this time that they first began to be called Jews, which means "people of Judah."

God was good to his people in the land of Babylon. He sent them prophets who showed them the way of the Lord. One of these prophets was Daniel, a young man who lived in the court of King Nebuchadnezzar. Another prophet was a priest named Ezekiel. He did not live in the king's court, but he lived right among the captive people.

God gave Ezekiel wonderful visions. Once he saw the throne of the Lord and the strange creatures with six wings that the prophet Isaiah had seen long before. He also heard the voice of the Lord telling him what was going to happen to the Jews in the years to come.

One time the Lord brought Ezekiel from his home and set him down in the middle of a great valley. It was full of bones. It looked as though a great battle had been fought and the bodies of those who had been killed had been left there. The bones were very dry.

Then the voice of the Lord said to Ezekiel, "Son of man, can these bones live?"

Ezekiel answered, "Lord and King, you are the only one who knows."

Then the Lord said to him, "Prophesy to these bones. Tell them, 'Dry bones, listen to the Lord's message. The Lord and King speaks to you. He says, "I will put breath in you. Then you will come to life again. I will attach tendons to you. I will put flesh on you. I will cover you with skin. So I will put breath in you. And you will come to life again. Then you will know that I am the Lord."'"

So Ezekiel did what the Lord told him to do, and as he was prophesying, he heard a noise. It was a rattling sound. The bones began to come together. One bone connected itself to another. He saw tendons and flesh appear on them. Skin covered them. But they did not breathe.

Then the Lord told Ezekiel to prophesy to the

bodies. "Tell the bones, now covered with tendons and flesh, 'The Lord and King says, "Breath, come from all four directions. Go into these dead bodies. Then they can live."'"

So Ezekiel did just as he was told, and that huge army came to life again. They stood up on their feet. The Lord then explained the vision to Ezekiel. He told him that the bones were like the people of Israel. They had dried up waiting for God to rescue them from their captivity. They had lost all hope.

The Lord told Ezekiel to prophesy to the people and tell them that God was going to give them his Spirit again and he would settle them once again in their own land.

That was very good news for the people to hear. Their hearts were lifted up with a new hope that they should see their own land again.

DANIEL

The King Has a Dream

ebuchadnezzar, the king of Babylon, took over the land of Judah with his great army. He took all the gold and silver from the temple. He also took to Babylon the princes and the best people from Judah as his prisoners. He ordered the men in charge of his palace to look over the prisoners and choose some young men who were stronger and smarter than all the others, to help him rule the land of Judah. He ordered that this group of young men live in his palace and be taught by the wisest men in his kingdom. He wanted them to grow up to be men who could help him lead the people.

There were four young men brought to the king's palace: Daniel, Shadrach, Meshach, and Abednego. For three years they studied all the wisdom of the country of Babylon. Then they were brought to work for the king.

Nebuchadnezzar found that the young men were wise and faithful in the work he gave them. Daniel was special to the king because God had given him the gift of understanding dreams and knowing what would happen in the future.

One morning the king had a dream that he couldn't remember. All he knew was that he woke up thinking he had dreamed something important. He called all his wise men and told them, "I have dreamed a wonderful dream. But I have forgotten what it was. Now tell me what my dream was and what it means. I am sure it has an important meaning."

The wise men told the king they could not tell him what he had dreamed. They said that only a god could do that. This made the king very angry because the wise men had said that their gods gave them the power to know all things. So he commanded them, "Tell me the dream and its meaning and I will give you a great reward. But if you can't tell it to me, I will know that you are liars. You will be put to death!"

Daniel and his three friends were part of the group of wise men. He asked, "Give me a little time.

GOD SAVED JONAH FROM A BIG FISH

Jonah tried to run from God. But God saw him and sent a
big storm. To stop the storm the sailors threw Jonah in the water.
A huge fish swallowed him. Then Jonah decided to obey God.
He prayed for God to help him. God heard him and made the
fish throw up Jonah on the land.

God Shut The Lions' Mouths

King Darius called, "Daniel, has your God been able to rescue
you from the lions? Out of the darkness Daniel answered,
"O king live forever! My God sent his angel and he shut the
mouths of the lions. They have not hurt me."
The king was happy.
He ordered his servants to let Daniel out of the pit.

I will pray to my God. I know that he will help me tell the king his dream and its meaning."

So Daniel was given some time to pray. That night the Lord told him the secret dream and its meaning. Daniel praised God for helping him. Then he told the king's guards not to kill all the wise men, because God had given him the dream. The guards took him to the king, and Daniel told him the dream God had shown him. He said, "The true God showed me your dream and the meaning of it. In your dream you saw a tall, beautiful statue. The head of it was made of gold, its chest and arms of silver, its waist and hips of brass, its legs of iron, and its feet

and toes of iron and clay mixed together. Next you saw a stone that rolled into the statue and broke it into pieces. The stone ground the statue into dust. Finally the stone became a mountain, and it filled the whole world."

Then Daniel told the king what this dream meant. He said, "This is the meaning of your dream, O king: God has shown you what will happen in the future. You are the statue's head of gold because your kingdom is great. The king who will come after you will have the kingdom that is like the statue's silver shoulders and arms. The next king will have a kingdom like the statue's waist and hips of brass. Then the last kingdom will be like the statue's iron legs. After that the Lord God will set up his kingdom. It will be like the great stone that knocked down all other kingdoms of men and filled the whole earth. God's kingdom will last forever."

When King Nebuchadnezzar heard Daniel's words, he was amazed. He made Daniel a ruler over part of his kingdom and gave him many presents. He also made Daniel's three friends rulers. After this Daniel lived in the palace near the king.

A Fiery Furnace

ing Nebuchadnezzar had a golden statue made. He set it up as an idol for all the people to worship. It was almost a hundred feet high and could be seen from far away. Then the king called everyone to come and dedicate the statue.

Daniel's three friends, Shadrach, Meshach, and Abednego, came when they heard about the king's command. For some reason Daniel was not there. He may have been busy with the work of the king in some other place.

At one moment during the dedication, musical instruments of all kinds were played. Trumpets were blown and drums were beaten. It was a signal for all the people to bow down and worship the big golden statue. But Shadrach, Meshach, and Abednego would not bow down. They worshiped only the one true God of Israel. They knew that statues were not real gods, and they refused to worship them. Some of the other rulers saw how the three young Hebrews did not worship the statue. They were happy to run and tell the king that the young men had disobeyed his order. They were jealous of all the good things the king had given Daniel and his friends. They knew that anyone who did not do what the king said would be thrown into a hot furnace full of fire.

Nebuchadnezzar was just as angry as the jealous rulers thought he would be. He ordered that Shadrach, Meshach, and Abednego be thrown into the fiery furnace. The three Hebrews were not afraid. They said, "The God we serve is able to save us from the fiery furnace. We know that he will save us. But even if it is God's will that we die, we will never worship the king's statue or any false god that you make."

The king became even more angry when he heard their answer. He told his servants to make the furnace ten times hotter than usual. He told the servants to tie up Shadrach, Meshach, and Abednego and throw them into the furnace. When they opened the door of the furnace to put the three men in, the flames were so hot that they burned up the servants.

King Nebuchadnezzar stood in front of the furnace and looked in through the open door. He could not believe what he saw. There were four men walking around inside. He saw Shadrach, Meshach, and

Abednego, and he saw another man walking around with them. He thought the other man looked like a god.

The king called to the three men, "Shadrach, Meshach, and Abednego, servants of the Most High God, come out of the fire. Come back to me."

They came out and stood before the king. Everyone could see they were alive and well. Not one hair on their heads had been burned. They didn't even smell like smoke after being in that huge fire!

The king told everyone, "Blessed is the God of these men! He sent an angel and saved their lives. I command that no one in my kingdoms shall say a word against their God. There is no other god who can save his people like this."

Daniel and the Lions

arius was king of Persia. When Daniel was a very old man, he was a powerful leader for King Darius and his people. King Darius thought Daniel was very wise, but the other rulers in the kingdom were jealous of Daniel. They tried to think of a way to get Daniel into trouble so they could be the king's favorite leaders instead of him. They knew that Daniel went to his room and prayed three times every day. He would open the window and look in the direction of his homeland and Jerusalem. Jerusalem had been torn down by war.

One day the jealous rulers went to the king and said, "We have all agreed to make a law that for thirty days no one can pray to any god or man except you, O king. If anyone does not obey this law, he shall be thrown into a den full of hungry lions."

The king was flattered by their plan because they made it sound as if they were giving their king a big compliment. He agreed that their idea should become a law of his land. He did not ask Daniel's advice. Later, when Daniel found out what had

happened, he still went to his room to pray. The jealous rulers watched him, and when they saw him praying, they went to the king to tell him that Daniel was breaking their new law.

The king was sorry he had made the law, because he liked Daniel. But he said, "The law has been made, and it must be obeyed." Sadly he commanded that Daniel be thrown into the den of lions. The king told Daniel hopefully, "May your God, whom you serve continually, rescue you."

Then the king's servants took Daniel to the lions' pit and threw him in. They rolled a stone over the top, and the king sealed the den with his own seal. No one would be able to take the stone away and rescue Daniel—no one except God.

That night the king was so sad that he couldn't eat, sleep, or even sit and listen to music, as he usually did. Early the next morning he got up and went to the lions' den. He broke the seal and took the stone away himself. He called out, "Daniel, servant of the living God, has your God been able to rescue you from the lions?"

Out of the darkness came Daniel's voice. "O king, live forever! My God sent his angel, and he shut the mouths of the lions. They have not hurt me, because the Lord saw that I had done nothing wrong."

The king was happy. He ordered his servants to let Daniel out of the pit. Then ordered them to throw the jealous rulers into the pit instead. As soon as they did this, the hungry lions' mouths were opened, and they killed the jealous rulers.

King Darius wrote to the people in all his lands, telling them that everyone everywhere should worship the God of Daniel. He said, "Daniel's God is the living God—the only one who can save."

ESTHER

A Brave and Beautiful Queen

After King Darius died, his son Ahasuerus took his place on the throne of Persia. The new king was not as wise as his father had been. He had a quick temper and did many foolish things.

One night the king held a dinner in the garden of his great palace. He invited all the nobles and officials in his kingdom, along with the kings and princes from other lands nearby. At the same time, his wife, Queen Vashti, held another dinner party for all the women. Everyone ate as much as they wanted and got as much as they wanted to drink. King Ahasuerus was in a happy mood, and he showed the men his palace and his treasures. Then he wanted them to see his beautiful queen. He sent his servants to tell

Queen Vashti that the king commanded her to come to his garden.

But the queen told his men that she would not come. The king was very angry and embarrassed that his queen would not obey the command he had given in front of his friends and nobles. He asked his wise men what he should do about the problem. One of them said, "The queen has done wrong to you and to all the nobles. She has even done wrong to all the people in your kingdom. When the other women hear how she refused to come, they will not do as their husbands ask them, either. You should command that Vashti not be queen any longer. Since she would not come to see you when you asked her to, she should not ever be allowed to see you again. You should choose another woman to take her place."

All the wise men and nobles agreed with this advice. The king commanded that Vashti not be queen any longer. He sent messengers to tell everyone that he was going to choose a new queen. Every part of the kingdom was searched to find and send to the palace of King Ahasuerus the most beautiful young women in the land. He would choose his new queen from among these beautiful women.

The king's chief servant, Hagai, took care of all the young women who came to the palace. He gave them everything they needed to look their best as they stayed at the palace and waited to see which of them the king would choose. A young Jewish woman named Esther was chosen from among all the girls in her part of the land to go to the palace. Her name means "star," and she was as beautiful as a star in the night sky. The moment the king saw Esther, he fell in love with her. He gave her the royal crown of Persia and commanded that she be made his new queen.

Esther's parents had died when she was a child, so her older cousin Mordecai had raised her as if she were his own child. He told her not tell anyone at the

palace that she was Jewish, because the Jewish people had powerful enemies there. Esther obeyed her cousin, so no one knew that a Jewish girl had been made queen.

Queen Esther was given fine clothes, royal servants, and beautiful rooms in the palace. Whenever the king wanted to see her, he sent a message to her, and Esther put on her most beautiful clothes and came to see him. No one was ever allowed to see the king of Persia without being invited by the king. Anyone who came to see him without an invitation would be killed unless the king held out his golden scepter.

Mordecai missed Esther very much, so each day he sat outside the palace gate, hoping to hear from her. He was not allowed to come in and see the new queen, but Esther had her servants take him messages. One day Mordecai heard two men whispering together. He heard them making plans to kill the king. He told Queen Esther's servants to tell her about it. When she told the king, he sent his guards to arrest those men, so he was saved from their plan to kill him. The man who wrote all the news of the kingdom in the king's book wrote the story of how Mordecai the Jew saved the king's life.

One day when Mordecai was sitting outside the palace gate, Haman, a powerful man who came to the palace to serve the king, saw him. Everyone in the palace showed great respect to Haman because he was a friend of the king. Whenever he went by, they all bowed down as if they were worshiping him. But Mordecai worshiped only the one true God of Israel, and he would not bow down to any man. Haman noticed this. He became angry with Mordecai. He went to the king and asked that Mordecai and all the Jewish people in the land be put to death. Haman offered to pay money to the king's treasury to have this awful thing done.

King Ahasuerus lived in his palace and never went out among his people. He didn't know anything about the Jews. He believed what Haman told him. Haman said that the Jews were a dangerous problem in his land. The king took the royal ring from his own hand and gave it to Haman. That meant Haman could do anything he wanted with Mordecai's people. And he wanted to kill them all. He and the king still did not know that the beautiful Queen Esther was a Jew.

Mordecai heard that Haman had given orders to have all the Jews in Persia killed on a certain day. He prayed and cried out to God loudly in front of the palace. Queen Esther heard him and sent her servant, Hatach, to find out what was wrong. Mordecai told him about the trouble. He sent a message with Hatach to Queen Esther: she must go to the king and beg for help for her people. But Esther explained that it could mean death to go to the king if he had not called her. She was afraid that if she came to the

"Don't think you are safe in the king's palace. If you don't save your people, God will save them in some other way. But you and our family will be destroyed. It may be that the whole reason God has brought you to the palace is for such a time as this. You can be the one to save your people."

king's court without being invited, Ahasuerus would be angry and not hold out his golden scepter to her.

Mordecai sent back a message to Esther that said, "Don't think you are safe in the king's palace. If you don't save your people, God will save them in some other way. But you and our family will be destroyed. It may be that the whole reason God has brought you to the palace is for such a time as this. You can be the one to save your people."

When Esther heard his answer, she agreed to go to the king if Mordecai and all the Jews would pray for her for three days without eating any food. She bravely told her cousin that she was ready to die to save all her people.

So Mordecai and his people prayed and fasted for three days. Then Esther put on her royal robes and dressed as a queen. She went to the throne room of King Ahasuerus. As soon as the king saw her standing before him in all her beauty, his heart was touched with love for her. He held out the golden scepter, and Esther came over and touched the top of it. She was safe. The king said, "What do you wish, Queen Esther? I will give you anything, even up to half my kingdom!"

But Esther did not ask just then for what she wanted. She wisely said, "If it pleases the king, I have come to ask that the king and Haman come to a dinner I have made ready for them today."

The king sent for Haman to dine with them. As they sat at the table with the queen, the king repeated his offer. "What do wish, Queen Esther? I will give you anything, even up to half my kingdom!"

And Esther invited the men to another dinner! She said, "My wish is that the king and Haman come to dinner with me again tomorrow."

QUEEN ESTHER CAME TO SEE THE KING

The king was glad she had come to his throne room.
He held out his scepter to welcome her.

GOD SHOWED EZEKIEL A STRANGE VISION

Ezekiel commanded a valley of bones to stand up.
They stood up and became an army for the Lord.

Haman walked out of the palace happy about being so honored by the queen. But he saw Mordecai sitting near the gate, and he became angry. He commanded that a gallows be made so when he came to dinner, he could ask the king to hang Mordecai.

That night the king could not sleep. He called for his servants and asked that one of them read aloud his book of news from the kingdom. A servant read him the story that told how Mordecai had discovered the plan to kill him and told Queen Esther. Ahasuerus realized that this man had saved his life, and he asked, "What reward was given to Mordecai for saving my life from these men?"

"O king," his servants answered, "nothing has been done for Mordecai."

Then the king asked, "Is any of my princes standing outside in the court?"

Haman was outside at that moment. He had just finished having the gallows built and was waiting to ask that Mordecai be hanged on it. The king sent for him to come in and said, "What should I do for the man I wish to honor in a special way?"

Haman thought to himself, *I must be the man the king wants to honor.* So he answered, "Let that man be dressed in the king's clothes and let him sit on the

king's throne. Have him ride around the city's main
street while one of the nobles calls out, 'This is the
man the king delights to honor!'"

Then the king commanded Haman, "Hurry and
do all the things you have just said to Mordecai the
Jew, who is sitting near my gate. See that you give
him everything you suggested."

Haman was stunned. He did not dare disobey the
king's command. Haman dressed Mordecai in the
king's robes, then ran through the streets in front of
him, calling, "This is the man the king delights to
honor!"

Later Haman sat down to the queen's dinner with
a sad heart. Of course, he had never been able to tell
the king about wanting to hang Mordecai on the
gallows.

The king could tell that his queen still had something she wanted to ask him, so he said again, "What
do wish, Queen Esther? I will give you anything,
even up to half my kingdom!"

This time Esther knew she must ask for the thing
she really wanted. She replied, "If I have found favor
in your sight, O king, and if it please you, spare my
life and the lives of my people. We have been sold to
be destroyed. If we had only been sold as slaves, I

would have been silent. But we are to be killed just to please our enemy."

Then the king cried out, "Who is the man, and where is he that has dared to do this thing!"

Queen Esther told him, "Our enemy is this wicked Haman!"

When the king heard this, he was so angry that he got up and walked out into the garden. When came back, he saw that Haman had fallen onto the couch where Esther was. He was begging for his life. One of the officers told the king about the gallows Haman had built to hang Mordecai. The king said, "Hang Haman on the gallows he had made for Mordecai."

That day the king gave Haman's house to Mordecai and made him a prince over all the other leaders. Then he gave Mordecai his royal ring.

When the day came for the Jews in Persia to be killed, most of the people who had wanted to kill them didn't dare do it. They knew that all of Mordecai's people were under the protection of the king. Anyone who did try to carry out Haman's plan was destroyed. From then on, all Jews everywhere celebrate that day as a time to remember how God protected them. They call it the feast of Purim, and they tell the story of beautiful and brave Queen Esther.

NEW TESTAMENT

THE BIRTH OF JESUS

God Sends an Angel

t the time when the stories of the New Testament began, a wicked king named Herod ruled the land of Israel. He was the first of several kings who were all named Herod. But these kings were not the highest rulers in the land. All of them reported to the emperor of Rome. Years before this time, the Romans had marched in with armies and taken over the Jewish kingdom and many other nearby lands. At the time Jesus was born, the Roman emperor's name was Augustus Caesar.

One day God sent an angel named Gabriel to the Jewish city of Nazareth. Gabriel came to a young girl named Mary and said, "Greetings, you who are highly favored! The Lord is with you."

Of course, this surprised Mary. So the angel said, "Do not be afraid, Mary. God is very pleased with

you. You will give birth to a son. You must name him
Jesus, because he will save his people from their sins.
He will be great and will be called the Son of the
Most High God. The Lord will make him a king like
his father David of long ago. He will rule forever
over his people."

Mary could not understand how all this would
happen. She was engaged to Joseph but not yet married. Then the angel said, "The power of the Most

High God will cover you and cause this to happen. So the holy one who is born will be called the Son of God."

Then the angel told Mary that her cousin Elizabeth, who was very old, would have a child soon through the power of the Lord. Mary knew that only God's power could help someone as old as Elizabeth have a baby. So when the angel said this, she said, "I serve the Lord. May it happen to me just as you said it would."

Mary Visits Elizabeth

Soon after the angel left, Mary went to visit her cousin Elizabeth. She could see that the angel's message was true. Elizabeth was pregnant. When Elizabeth heard Mary's voice, the baby inside her seemed to jump for joy. Then the Holy Spirit filled Elizabeth and gave her these words to say to Mary: "God has blessed you more than other women! And blessed is the child you will have! You have believed that what the Lord has said to you will be done!"

Then the Holy Spirit filled Mary, and she sang a song of praise:

> *"My soul gives glory to the Lord.*
> *My spirit delights in God my Savior.*
> *He has taken note of me*
> *even though I am not important.*
> *From now on all people will call me blessed.*
> *The Mighty One has done great things for me.*
> *His name is holy."*

Mary stayed with Elizabeth for nearly three months. Then she went home to Nazareth.

The Manger in Bethlehem

MATTHEW 1:18–25; LUKE 2:1–7

ary was engaged to marry Joseph, a carpenter from Nazareth. One night Joseph had a dream. In his dream an angel told him something important. The angel said, "Joseph, don't be afraid to take Mary home as your wife. The baby inside her is from the Holy Spirit. She is going to have a son. You must give him the name Jesus, because he will save his people from their sins."

Then Joseph knew that the angel meant that Jesus would be the King of Israel. All his life Joseph had heard the words of the prophets of the Old Testament. The prophets had told the people of Israel that a special baby would be born. The baby would be God's chosen King to save his people.

So Joseph and Mary were married in Nazareth. Soon afterward the emperor Augustus Caesar commanded all the people to go to the city from which their families had come. There they would be counted. Joseph's and Mary's families were from Bethlehem, the city of King David. The two of them traveled about eighty miles to Bethlehem from

Nazareth. They went down the mountains and followed the Jordan River almost to its end and then went back up again through the mountains to Jerusalem. It was almost time for Mary's baby to be born.

When they got to Bethlehem, all the inns were full of people. The only place they could find to

spend the night was a stable. It was in the stable that their little baby was born. Mary wrapped him in soft cloths. For his bed, she laid him in a large box called a "manger," where the oxen and donkeys were fed.

The Angel Tells the Shepherds

That same night some shepherds were tending their sheep in a field near Bethlehem. Suddenly a bright light shone down from heaven, and they saw a shining angel standing before them. They were scared, but the angel said, "Do not be afraid! I bring you good news of great joy! It is for all the people. Today in the town of David a Savior has been born to you. He is Christ the Lord. You will know him by this sign: you will find a baby wrapped in soft cloths lying in a manger."

Suddenly the sky above them was full of angels. They were praising God and singing,

> *"Glory to God in the highest,*
> *and on earth peace to men on whom*
> *his favor rests."*

While they looked and listened in wonder, the angels went out of sight as suddenly as they had come. The shepherds said to each other, "Let's go to Bethlehem. Let's see this thing that God has told us about."

The shepherds ran to Bethlehem as quickly as they could. There they found the new baby in a manger, just as the angel had said. They told Mary and Joseph about the angels and how they had heard about their baby boy. After the shepherds left the stable, they told everyone they saw about what God had done. All who heard their story were amazed at what the shepherds said. Mary said nothing. She kept all these things like a secret treasure in her heart, and she thought about them over and over.

The Star and the Wise Men

Matthew 2:1–12

After Jesus was born, his family stayed in Bethlehem for a while. After a few days the family moved from the stable to a room in a house. One day another group of visitors, from a land far away, came to see Jesus. They had received a special message from God.

These visitors lived in a country far east of Bethlehem. They were very wise men who studied the stars. One night they had seen a strange new star shining in the sky. They had learned that the coming of this star meant that a king would soon be born in the land of Judea near Bethlehem. They felt as if God had given them a secret message telling them to travel far from their homes to see this newborn king.

They rode a long, long way on camels and horses. As soon as they got to Judea, the part of the country where Bethlehem was, they asked everyone they met, "Where is the child who has been born to be king of the Jews? When we were in the east, we saw his star, and now we have come to worship him." But no one had ever seen or heard of this king!

Someone sent news to King Herod about the coming of these wise men. Now, old Herod was an evil man. When he heard about someone who had been born to be a king, he was afraid that his throne would be taken away from him. If that happened, he would no longer be king. Herod made up his mind to kill this new king before the baby could grow up. He sent for the priests and the scribes. Scribes were the men who studied and taught the writings of the Old Testament. He asked them where Christ was going to be born.

"He is to be born in Bethlehem of Judea. This is what the prophet has written."

Then Herod met secretly with the wise men. He asked them exactly when the star had appeared. Then he told them to go to Bethlehem. He said, "Search carefully for the child. When you find him, come back and tell me. Then I can come and worship him, too."

The wise men went on their way toward Bethlehem. Suddenly they saw the star again, shining on the road before them. They followed it until the star came to a stop over the very house where the child lived. They came into the house. There they saw Jesus with Mary, his mother. They knew at once that this was the King. They fell to their knees and worshiped Jesus as the Lord. Then they gave him royal gifts of gold and expensive perfumes called "frankincense" and "myrrh."

That night God sent a dream to the wise men, telling them not to go back to Herod. They were told they must go home by a different way so Herod could not find them. They obeyed the Lord and went to their own country without passing through the city where Herod lived.

An Angel Tells Joseph to Flee

MATTHEW 2:13–23

oon after the wise men went home, the Lord sent another dream to Joseph. In the dream an angel told Joseph, "Get up! Take the child and his mother and escape to Egypt. Stay there until I tell you to come back. Herod is going to search for the child. He wants to kill him."

Joseph got up in the middle of the night. He left with his wife and baby for Egypt. They stayed there

until Herod died. Then God sent an angel to tell Joseph he could return home to Nazareth.

Nazareth was ruled by one of Herod's sons, King Herod Antipas. He was not a good man, either, but he was not as cruel as his father had been. So Joseph the carpenter and Mary his wife lived in Nazareth with their little boy, Jesus. They lived there many years and had other sons and daughters, who grew up with Jesus.

JESUS IN NAZARETH

Growing Up in Nazareth

LUKE 2:40–52; MATTHEW 18:1–6;
MARK 9:33–37

esus came to live in the town of Nazareth with his family when he was a small child. He lived there until he was about thirty years old. The Bible tells very little about his boyhood. It says that Joseph was a carpenter and that he taught Jesus to work with wood. In those days almost all boys grew up and worked in their fathers' trade. Most houses had only one room and often had dirt floors. There was no glass in the windows or pictures on the walls. Many homes did not even have tables, chairs, or beds. People sat and slept on the floor or sometimes on pillows or rugs. Since Joseph was a carpenter, he may have made furniture for his family, but we can only guess.

Jesus probably learned to read at the village school. This was usually held in the building the people used for worship. It was called a "synagogue." Lessons were taught from rolls of special paper that had many words from the Old Testament written on them. Jesus and the other students never had a Bible of their own. Joseph and other men of the village took their sons to worship at the synagogue twice each week. They sat on the floor on pillows or mats. The priests and scribes read the Old Testament and explained what the reading meant. Jewish boys learned almost the whole Old Testament by heart. The women of the village, like Mary and her daughters, listened to the teaching while sitting behind a screen so they could not be seen.

Every spring Jews from all parts of the country went to the great city of Jerusalem to worship during the feast called "Passover." When he was twelve, Jesus went with his family to the Passover Feast. There he saw the holy city of Jerusalem and the temple of the Lord on Mount Moriah. For the first time he walked through the courts of the temple and saw its altar. He saw the priests in their white robes and the Levites blowing silver trumpets.

Jesus was only a boy, but he felt how special this place was. He knew he was the Son of God, and he knew this house belonged to his heavenly Father. His heart was filled with the beauty of worship in the temple. He loved hearing everyone talking about God. He loved the words of the teachers. His thoughts were filled with the things of God.

Somehow, when it was time for his family to go home to Nazareth, Jesus was left behind. At first no one noticed he was missing. There were so many people traveling together in one big group. Everyone thought he must be there somewhere. But night came, and the boy could not be found.

His mother, Mary, was very afraid for her son. She and Joseph left their group and hurried back to Jerusalem to look for him. They checked with their friends and family who lived in the city, but no one had

seen him. They were sad as they looked for their boy. On the third day they went back to the temple. Then all at once they found him! Jesus was sitting with a group of teachers of the Jewish law. He had been listening to their words and asking them questions. Everyone there was surprised to hear the wisdom of this young boy as he talked about the Word of God.

Mary spoke to him a little sharply. She felt that her son had not been thoughtful of his duty to his parents. She said, "Child, why have you treated us this way? Don't you know we have been searching everywhere for you with troubled hearts?"

"Why did you search for me?" asked Jesus. "Didn't you know I would be in my Father's house?"

They did not understand his words at the time. But Mary thought often about them later. She knew her son was no ordinary child. His words had a deep meaning. Though Jesus was wise beyond his years, he obeyed Joseph and his mother in all things. He went back with them to Nazareth and lived a very simple life in their country home.

As he grew to be a man, Jesus grew in knowledge and in wisdom. He grew in love and the favor of God and all the people who knew him. There was something about him that drew all hearts, both young and old, to him.

Jesus remembered what it was like to be a child and to grow up in a family. He always seemed to have a special place in his heart for children. He often told his disciples that they should trust God the way children trust their parents. One day the disciples were arguing about who was the greatest and best follower of God. Jesus told them, "If anyone wishes to be first, he should put himself last. He should try to serve everyone else instead of himself."

Then he took a little child in his arms and held him up for everyone to see. He said, "Unless you change your ways and become like little children in spirit, you won't enter the kingdom of heaven. The one who is gentle and humble like this little child is the greatest in heaven. Whoever welcomes a little child like this because of me, welcomes me. Don't reject one of these little ones. Be careful because their angels are always standing before my Father in heaven. The Son came to save that which was lost. It is not the Father's will that even one of these little ones should be lost."

JOHN THE BAPTIST

The Voice in the Wilderness

LUKE 1:5–17; MATTHEW 3; MARK 1:1–11

hen Elizabeth and Zacharias had a baby boy, an angel told Zacharias to name him John. The angel said, "He shall bring joy and gladness to many. He shall be great in the sight of the Lord. He must never taste wine or strong drink as long as he lives. He shall be filled with God's Holy Spirit. He shall lead many people of Israel to the Lord. He shall go before the Lord in the power of Elijah the prophet. He shall turn the hearts of the fathers to the children. And he shall cause those who are disobeying the Lord to do his will."

John was six months older than Mary's son Jesus. The two boys had never met, because they lived about eighty miles apart. When Jesus was about thirty years old, news spread all over the land that a real prophet had come. This prophet was John, the son of Elizabeth and Zacharias. He listened to God's voice and then told the people what God had said.

It had been more than four hundred years since God had sent a prophet to his people. Those who heard John said they could tell that God was giving him words to speak to them. From all parts of the land people came to the wilderness beside the river

Jordan to listen. He spoke about the Messiah who was coming soon to save his people.

John looked very different from other men. He wore clothes made of rough cloth that had been woven from camels' hair. He had a thick leather belt. Even the food he ate was different: locusts and honey from wild trees. He lived in wild lands where he could be alone with God. His message was different from what the people usually heard at the synagogue. John said, "Stop sinning and do good. The kingdom of heaven is near, and the King is coming soon."

The people came to hear his words, and they asked him what they should do. He said, "Whoever has two coats should give one away to someone who has none. Anyone who has more food than he needs should give some to those who are hungry. Do not cheat people or rob them. Do not harm anyone or lie about them."

John Baptizes Jesus

LUKE 3:1–22

hen the people who heard John's words wanted to serve God, John baptized them in the Jordan River. It was a sign that their sins were washed away. Because he baptized people, he was called John the Baptist.

Some people thought John might be the Messiah who would save the people. But when John heard their talk, he said, "I baptize you with water. But someone is coming who is greater than I. He will baptize you with the Holy Spirit and with fire. He is so high above me that I am not worthy to stoop down and untie the strings of his shoes."

Nearly all the people in the land came to listen to John and to be baptized by him. Among the last who came was Jesus, the young carpenter from Nazareth. When John saw Jesus, God told him that this was the one who would save the people. He said to Jesus, "I need to be baptized by you! Why are you coming to me?"

Jesus answered him, "Let it be so for now. It is right for us to do this. It is part of God's plan."

Then John baptized Jesus as he had baptized all the others. When Jesus came up out of the water, John saw the heavens open and the Holy Spirit coming down upon Jesus like a dove. John heard a voice from heaven say, "This is my Son, whom I love; with him I am well pleased."

Then John told everyone that Jesus was the Son of God—the one God had promised to send to save the people.

Jesus Is Tempted

MATTHEW 4:1–11; MARK 1:12–13;
LUKE 4:1–13; JOHN 1:29–51

oon after Jesus was baptized, the Spirit of God led him into the desert to be tempted by the devil for forty days. During that time Jesus ate nothing. He did not even want any food. But at the end of the forty days, he was very faint and hungry.

At that moment the devil came to Jesus and put a thought in his mind. It was this: "If you are the Son of God, tell this stone to become bread."

Jesus knew he could do this, but he also knew the power that had been given to him was not for himself, but to help others. So he said to the devil, "It is written, 'Man doesn't live only on bread.'"

Then the devil led Jesus up to a high place and showed him all the kingdoms of the world. He said to Jesus, "I will give you all their authority and glory. It has been given to me, and I can give it to anyone I want to. So if you worship me, it will all be yours."

Jesus was not going to listen to that temptation. He said, "It is written, 'Worship the Lord your God. He is the only one you should serve.'"

The devil was not through yet. He took Jesus to the highest point of the temple and said to him, "If you are the Son of God, throw yourself down from here. It is written,

"'The Lord will command his angels
    to take care of you.
They will lift you up in their hands.
Then you won't trip over a stone.'"

Jesus knew that this would not be right because it would not be done to please God. So he told the devil: "Scripture says, 'Do not put the Lord your God to the test.'"

When the devil found that Jesus would not listen to him, he left him alone. Then the angels came to Jesus in the desert and took care of him.

Jesus Was Born in Bethlehem

All the inns were full of people, so Mary and Joseph stayed
in a stable. When their baby boy, Jesus, was born, Mary wrapped
him in soft cloths and laid him in a manger for a bed.

JESUS TOLD HIS FRIENDS WHERE TO FISH

Simon Peter obeyed Jesus, and his net was filled with fish.
Then Jesus told them, "Follow me and I will make you fishers of men.

Jesus Calls His Disciples

Fishers of Men

MATTHEW 4:18–22;
MARK 1:16–20; LUKE 5:1–11

esus was walking by the Sea of Galilee when he saw some men fishing. He called to them and told them they could become fishers of men. They were Andrew, Peter, James, and John. Some other men, Philip and Nathanael, also became disciples.

One morning Jesus went by the place where the fishermen disciples were washing their nets to get ready to go fishing. Jesus stepped into the boat that belonged to Andrew's brother Simon Peter. He asked Peter and Andrew to push it out from the shore a little so he could talk to the people without being crowded too closely. They did as he asked, and from the fishing boat Jesus taught the people who sat on the beach.

After he finished teaching, he said to Simon Peter, "Go out into the deep water and let down your nets."

"Teacher," said Simon, "we have fished all night and caught nothing. But if you say so, I will let down the net again."

When Peter obeyed Jesus, his net caught so many fish that the men could not pull it up! They made signs to the two brothers, James and John, to bring their boat over to help them. They poured the fish from the nets into the two boats. There were so many fish that the boats almost sank!

When Simon Peter saw this, he was amazed at the power of God. He fell down at the feet of Jesus and said, "O Lord, I am full of sin. I am not worthy of all this. Please leave me, O Lord."

But Jesus said to them, "Don't be afraid. Follow me, and I will make you fishers of men!"

A Man in a Tree

esus was teaching and healing people. A large crowd of people had gathered around him. A very short man named Zacchaeus wanted very much to see Jesus, but he couldn't see over the people in front of him. Then he had an idea. He ran ahead of the crowd and climbed a sycamore tree beside the road. He waited there for Jesus and the others to pass by.

When Jesus got to the tree, he stopped walking. He looked up. Then he called out, "Zacchaeus, hurry and come down. Today I must visit your house!"

Zacchaeus was so glad! He came down at once and took Jesus to his house for a meal. Some people were angry that Jesus had decided to go to Zacchaeus's house, because he was a tax collector. Sometimes Zacchaeus had charged people too much money and kept it for himself. They thought of him as a thief. But Jesus changed Zacchaeus's heart so he suddenly wanted to help others. He told Jesus, "Lord, I am going to give half of my money to the poor. If I have wrongly taken anything from any man, I will give him back four times as much as I took."

Jesus said, "Today salvation has come to this family. This man is also a son of our ancestor Abraham. I have come to seek out and to save those who are lost."

The Tax Collectors

ne day Jesus was going out of Capernaum to the seaside. A large crowd of people followed him. He passed a tax collector who was seated at his table and taking money from those who came to pay their taxes. This man's name was Matthew. Jesus could look into people's hearts, and he saw that Matthew was a person who could help him as one of his disciples. So he looked at Matthew and said, "Follow me!"

At once Matthew got up from his table and left everything behind to go with Jesus. All the people were amazed that Jesus would ask a tax collector to join his group. Everyone hated tax collectors because they often took too much money from people and kept it for themselves. But Jesus knew that Matthew would do work that would bless the world forever. It was Matthew who later wrote the gospel of Matthew that we now have in our Bibles.

That day Matthew had a great feast for Jesus at his house. He invited many tax collectors and other kinds of people that the rulers of the Jews hated. Those rulers asked his disciples, "Why does your teacher sit at a table and eat with tax collectors and sinners?"

Jesus heard them and said, "Healthy people do not need a doctor to cure them. It is the sick who need help. I want to show mercy to these people, because they know that they are sinners and need to be saved. I didn't come to call those who are good; I came to call those who are sinners."

The Twelve Disciples

MARK 3:13–19; LUKE 6:12–16

ne evening Jesus went to a mountain near the town of Capernaum. He walked to the top of the mountain, where he could be alone. There he stayed all night, praying to God. In the morning he chose twelve men from among all his followers to walk very closely with him and learn how to teach others. They became known as "the Twelve," or "the disciples." After Jesus went to heaven, these men were called "the apostles" because that means "those who were sent out." Jesus sent them out to tell his good news to the world.

The names of the twelve men were Simon Peter and his brother Andrew; James and John, the two sons of Zebedee; Philip of Bethsaida; Nathanael, who was also known as Bartholomew; Thomas, who was also called Didymus; Matthew the tax collector; James the son of Alphaeus, who was also called James the Less; Thaddeus, who was also called Judas; another man named Simon, who was called the Canaanite, or Simon the Zealot; and Judas Iscariot.

These men watched and remembered the stories of Jesus' life on earth and his teachings. They taught them to others so we could have them in our Bible today.

Jesus' disciples were

Simon Peter

Andrew

James

John

Philip of Bethsaida

Nathanael

Thomas

Matthew

James the Less

Thaddeus

Simon the Canaanite

Judas Iscariot

Jesus Heals

A Leper

MATTHEW 8:2–4;
MARK 1:40–45; LUKE 5:12–16

esus traveled through all the towns in Galilee. His disciples always traveled with him. He taught the people, and he healed all kinds of sicknesses. Great crowds followed him everywhere. People came to hear his wonderful words and to see his wonderful works.

One day a man with a disease called leprosy came to Jesus for help. In those days there was no medicine to cure leprosy, so those who had it became very sick. They had sores all over their bodies, and after a while they usually died.

Well, this poor leper fell down before Jesus and cried out, "O Lord, if you are willing, I know that you can make me well!"

Jesus was so sorry for the poor man. He reached out his hand and touched him. In a moment he was

330

cured. Jesus said to him, "Don't tell anyone." But the leper did not obey the command. He couldn't keep quiet about his joy. He told everybody what a great prophet and healer Jesus was.

The Man Let Down Through the Roof

Matthew 9:2–8;
Mark 2:1–12; Luke 5:17–26

hen Jesus came to a town called Capernaum, there was a great crowd of people waiting to hear him. Many sick people hoped he would heal them. They filled the house, the yard, and the streets all around the place where he was staying. Suddenly part of the roof over Jesus' head was taken away. Everyone looked up and saw that four men were letting a man down from above.

This man was paralyzed. He couldn't walk or even stand up. His friends had tried to carry him to Jesus but couldn't get through the large crowd. Then they had an idea. They lifted him to the top of the house and opened the roof! They really believed that Jesus could cure their friend.

Jesus said to the sick man, "Son, your sins are forgiven!"

Jesus' enemies didn't like what he said. They thought he was wrong to say he could forgive sins.

Jesus knew what they were thinking, and he said, "Is it easier to say to this man, 'Your sins are forgiven'? Or to say, 'Get up, take your mat, and walk'? I want you to know that the Son of Man has authority on earth to forgive sins." Then Jesus spoke to the sick man and said, "Get up, take your mat, and walk!"

At once new life and power came into the sick man. He stood up, rolled up the mat he used for a bed, and carried it out through the crowd. He went back to his own house, strong and well and praising God as he walked.

The Crippled Man by the Pool

hile Jesus was in Jerusalem, he came to a pool called Bethesda. Beside this pool were five arches or porches. There were a great many sick people lying there waiting. They believed that when the water in the pool bubbled up, an angel was stirring the pool. It was said that the first person to get into the pool after it bubbled would be healed.

One of the sick people lying there near the pool was a man whose legs had been crippled for many years. Jesus looked at him and said, "Do you want to get well?"

The man did not know who Jesus was. He answered, "Sir, I have no one to help me into the pool when the angel stirs up the water. I try to get in, but someone else always goes down ahead of me."

Then Jesus said to him, "Get up! Pick up your mat and walk!"

The man had never heard anyone say words like this before. As Jesus spoke, he felt power shoot

through his legs. Suddenly he stood up! Then he picked up the mat he had been lying on, rolled it up, and walked toward his home.

This healing happened on the Sabbath, the day the Jews went to their synagogues to worship. They had laws that said no one could work on that day. The people did not even make their beds on the Sabbath! So when the religious leaders saw the man carrying his mat home, some of them stopped him and told him he was breaking the law. He replied, "The one who made me well said to me, 'Pick up your mat and walk.'"

The people were angry and tried to find out who had done this. But Jesus had already disappeared into

> *"The one who made me well said to me, 'Pick up your mat and walk.'"*

the crowd. The man who was healed didn't even know Jesus' name. He saw Jesus later in the temple, and he spoke with him. Jesus told the man, "See, you are well again. Stop sinning, or something worse may happen to you."

The Widow's Son

LUKE 7:11–17

ne day Jesus and his disciples and many other people came to a city called Nain. Just as they came near the city gate, they saw a group carrying out the body of a dead man to be buried. He was a young man and the only son his mother had. She was a widow. All the people felt very sad for her because her husband died first and now her only son was dead. When Jesus saw the mother crying, he felt sorry for her, too. He said, "Don't cry."

He came near and touched the frame of the bed on which the young man's body was lying. The people carrying it stopped. Then Jesus said, "Young man, I say to you, get up!"

The young man sat up and began to talk! Jesus gave him back to his mother. The people were filled with wonder. They praised God and said, "God has come to his people! He has given us a great prophet!"

The news that Jesus had raised a dead man was told everywhere in the land.

The Little Girl Who Was Raised to Life and the Woman Who Touched Jesus' Robe

MATTHEW 9:18–26;
MARK 5:21–43; LUKE 8:40–56

hen Jesus and his disciples came across the Sea of Galilee to Capernaum, they saw a crowd of people waiting for them to land their boat. One man came forward from the crowd and fell at Jesus' feet. His name was Jairus, and he was one of the leaders of the synagogue. He cried out, "O Master, please come to my house at once! My little daughter is dying. But I know if you come and touch her, she will live."

Jesus and the disciples went with Jairus. All the people followed him. One woman in the crowd was very sick. She had spent all her money going to doctors, but no one could make her well. This woman had heard of Jesus and came to see if he could help. She could not get a chance to talk to him with all the people crowded around. She thought, *If I can just touch his robe, I know that I will be healed.* So as Jesus passed by, she reached out her hand and touched the hem of his robe. At that very instant she felt completely well! But suddenly Jesus asked, "Who touched me?"

Peter said to him, "Teacher, there is a crowd pushing all around you. How can you wonder that someone touched you?"

But Jesus said, "Someone has touched me. I felt power go out from me."

He looked around to see who it was. Then the woman came forward. She was afraid and shaking because she thought she might have done something wrong. She fell down before Jesus and told him what she had thought and done. But Jesus wasn't angry. He said, "Daughter, be comforted. Your faith has made you well. Rise up and go in peace." From that hour on, the woman was free from her illness.

All this time Jairus, the father of the dying girl, stood beside Jesus. He was very worried that his little daughter would die before they came to his house. Then someone ran up and said, "It is too late. Your daughter is dead. Don't bother the teacher anymore."

But Jesus said to Jairus, "Do not be afraid. Only believe, and she will be healed."

Soon they came to Jairus's house. They could hear

people crying loudly. Jesus said to them, "Why do you make such a noise? The little girl is not dead. She is only sleeping."

Jesus would not allow any of the crowd of people to go into the room where the dead child was. He took three of his disciples—Peter, James, and John— and the father and mother of the child. He closed the

door to keep the rest of the people out. He went to the bed where the body of the child was lying. He took her hand and said, "Little girl, rise up!"

Suddenly the life of the little girl came back! She opened her eyes and sat up. Jesus told them to give her something to eat. Then he said, "Do not tell anyone how the girl was brought back to life."

Lazarus

wo sisters, Martha and Mary, and their brother, Lazarus, were friends of Jesus and his disciples. They lived in the town of Bethany. Word came to Jesus that Lazarus was very sick. But Jesus did not hurry to their village. He stayed where he was for two more days before he told his disciples they would go. He said, "Our friend Lazarus has fallen asleep. I'm going there to wake him."

The disciples thought that if Lazarus had fallen asleep, it meant that he might be feeling better. But Jesus told them he knew Lazarus was dead. He said, "I am glad that I was not there to cure him of his sickness. Now you will see something that will help you believe. Let us go to him."

When they came to Bethany, they learned that Lazarus had been in the burial tomb for four days. As soon as Martha saw Jesus, she said to him very sadly, "Lord, if you had been here, my brother would not have died. Even now I know that God will give you whatever you ask."

Jesus replied, "Your brother shall rise again."

Martha said, "I know the dead will be raised at the end of the world."

But Jesus told her, "I am the resurrection and the life. Anyone who believes in me will live, even if he dies. Those who live and believe in me will never die. Do you believe this?"

She answered, "Yes, Lord! I believe that you are the Christ, the Son of God who came into this world."

Then Martha went home and said quietly to her sister, "The teacher is here. He is asking for you!"

At once Mary got up to go to Jesus. Her friends thought that she was going to her brother's tomb to cry, so they followed her. Jesus was still on the road to their house when Mary met him. She fell down at his feet and said, "Lord, if you had been here, my brother would not have died!"

When Jesus saw Mary weeping and her friends weeping with her, he was touched. His spirit was very sad. When he went with them to see the tomb, Jesus wept. They all said, "Look how much he loved Lazarus!"

And some asked, "If this man could heal people, why didn't he keep his friend from dying?"

Jesus stood before the cave and said, "Take away the stone!"

They did as Jesus commanded. Then he looked up to heaven and said, "Father, I thank you for hearing me. I know that you always hear me. I say this so the people standing here will believe that you sent me."

Then he called, "Lazarus, come out!"

And Lazarus, who had been dead for four days, came out of the tomb. It must not have been easy for him to walk, because he was wrapped around and around with long strips of cloth. Another cloth was covering his face.

Jesus told them, "Take off the clothes he was buried in and let him go."

When they saw the wonderful power of Jesus, many people believed he was the Christ. But others went away and told the rulers what Jesus had done. They called a meeting of the great council of the Jews. They said, "What shall we do? This man is doing many wonders. If we let him alone, everyone will believe in him. They will try to make him king. Then the Romans will destroy us and all our people."

But the high priest, Caiaphas, said, "It is better that this one man should die than that our whole nation should be destroyed. Let's put him to death."

The other rulers agreed. From that day on, they made plans to kill Jesus.

Stories Jesus Told

Jesus and the Children

MATTHEW 18:1–9; 19:13–15;
MARK 9:33–37; 10:13–16

ne day Jesus came into the house where he was staying, and he said to his disciples, "What was it that you were talking about among your-selves while we were coming here?"

They looked at one another and said nothing, for on the way they had been arguing about which one of them should have the highest place of honor in the Lord's kingdom. Then Jesus said to them, "If anyone among you wishes to be first, let him be willing to be the last of all."

Then Jesus took a little child in his arms and held him up before all his disciples. He said to them, "You need to change and become like little children. If you don't, you will never enter the kingdom of heaven. Anyone who becomes as free of pride as this child is the most important in the kingdom of heaven. Anyone who welcomes a little child like this in my name welcomes me. But what if someone leads one of these little ones who believe in me to sin? If he does, it would be better for him to have a large millstone hung around his neck and be drowned at the bottom of the sea."

Another time, mothers brought their children to Jesus so that he might place his hands on them. But before the mothers could get close to Jesus, the disciples told them to stop.

Jesus saw what was going on, and he was angry with the disciples. He said, "Don't keep them away. The kingdom of heaven belongs to people like them." Jesus placed his hands on the children and blessed them.

The Parable of the Sower

Matthew 13:1–23;
Mark 4:1–20; Luke 8:1–15

 esus traveled through Galilee, teaching people and healing those who were sick. One day he went to a place by the Sea of Galilee where the beach rose up gently from the water. He sat in Simon Peter's boat and spoke to a great crowd of people who stood on the beach.

He taught them by telling parables—stories that show the truths of the gospel. Everybody liked to hear stories, and the stories would often cause people to think. Then they could learn about the truth of God's love. The first of these stories Jesus told was the parable of the sower.

"Listen to me," Jesus said, looking out at the big crowd. "A farmer went out to sow his seeds. And as he scattered the seeds, some of them fell on the path and the birds ate it. Some fell where the soil was hard and rocky. These seeds grew up quickly, but when the sun became hot, they dried up and died. They had no roots. Other seeds fell among briers and thorns, where there was not enough room for them to grow. The thorns choked out the young plants. But there were some seeds that fell on good ground. These seeds put down deep roots and grew tall. The tall plants grew fruit with seeds in them. Then the farmer gathered up thirty, sixty, or even a hundred times as many seeds as he started with. Whoever is listening with his ears open will hear my story."

Jesus' disciples were listening while he told the parable, but they didn't understand why he told a story about a farmer and seeds. When they were alone with him, they asked, "Why do you speak to the people in parables? What does this story about the man and his seeds mean?"

Jesus said to them, "You have been given under-standing about the secrets of the kingdom of heaven. But others don't understand. They are like the

people Isaiah the prophet told about: They have eyes, but they do not see. They have ears, but they do not hear. They do not wish to understand with the heart and turn to the Lord and have their sins forgiven.

"But your eyes are blessed because they do see. And your ears are blessed, for they really do hear what God wants to say. Now listen again, and I will tell you the meaning of the parable of the sower.

"The farmer is the one who speaks the word of God. The seeds are the word which he speaks. The hard path upon which the seeds fell are those who hear, but the Evil One comes and snatches away the truth. The rocky ground on which the seeds fell are those who hear the word with joy but grow no roots. When trouble comes, they quickly give up following God. Others who hear are like the ground where the seed couldn't grow because of the thorns. The worries of life and the desire for riches and enjoyment crowd out the gospel from growing in their hearts. But the good ground where the seeds grow tall are like those who hear the word of God and understand it. They hold on to it, and a crop of good fruit grows in their lives."

JESUS LOVES LITTLE CHILDREN

He told his disciples to let the children come to him. He told them
God wants his people to have hearts like little children.

A Boy Gave Jesus His Lunch to Share

Jesus blessed the boy's lunch and then divided it.
Soon there was enough to feed five thousand people.
It was a miracle!

The Mustard Seed and the Yeast

MATTHEW 13:31–35; MARK 4:30–32

 esus also told the crowd the parable of the mustard seed. He said, "The kingdom of heaven is like a grain of mustard seed that a farmer took and planted in his field. This is the smallest of all seeds, but it grows up to be almost as big as a tree. Birds even land upon its branches."

Another story he told was the parable of the yeast. Jesus said, "The kingdom of heaven is like yeast, or leaven, that a woman mixed with dough when she was making bread. It is worked all through the dough, and it grows. It changes flat, heavy dough into good, light bread."

The Treasure, the Pearl, and the Net

hen they were alone, Jesus gave his disciples three more parables to think about. He said, "The kingdom of heaven is like a treasure which a man found hidden in a field. He was glad when he saw it, but he hid it again. Then he went home, sold all he had, and used the money to buy that field with a treasure in it.

"The kingdom of heaven is also like a businessman who was looking for the best pearls to buy. When he found the expensive pearl he really wanted, he bought it—even though he had to sell everything he owned to get enough money.

"The kingdom of heaven is like a net that was cast into the sea and took in all kinds of fish. When it was full, the fishermen dragged it to the shore. Then they sat down and picked out the good fish. They put them away in baskets for safekeeping and threw away the bad fish that were not good for eating. That's how it will be at the end of the world. The angels will separate the bad people from the good."

The Weeds and the Wheat

MATTHEW 13:24–30, 36–43

esus told the crowd of people another parable about seeds: the parable of the weeds.

"The kingdom of God is like a farmer who has an enemy," Jesus said. "The farmer planted good seeds in his field, but while people were asleep, that enemy came and threw weed seeds among the good seeds. When the shoots of grain began to have heads of wheat, then the weeds came up with them. The farmer's servants asked, 'Sir, didn't you sow good seeds in your field? How did the weeds get in there?'

"The farmer answered them, 'An enemy has done this.'

"'Shall we go and pick out the weeds from among the wheat?' the servants asked.

"'No,' answered the farmer. 'If you pull up the weeds, you may also root up the wheat with them. Let both grow together until the harvest. At that time I will tell the reapers to take out the weeds first and tie them in bundles to be burned. Then they will gather the wheat and bring it into my barn.'"

Jesus did not tell the people what the story meant. When he and the disciples were alone, they asked him, "Tell us the meaning of the parable of the weeds."

So Jesus said, "The one who sows the good seeds is the Son of Man. The field is the world. The good seeds are those who belong to God's kingdom, but the weed seeds are the children of the Evil One. The enemy who planted them is the Devil. The servants who harvest the plants are God's angels.

"One day the end of the world will be like the day when the farmer harvested his crop. Like the weeds the farmer separated from the good plants and burned in the fire, people who do evil will be separated from the people of God and thrown into a furnace of fire. But the people of God will be like the good plants that shine like the sun in their Father's kingdom. Everyone who has ears to hear—listen!"

The Good Shepherd and the Good Samaritan

JOHN 10:1–18; LUKE 10:25–37

ne day Jesus told the people in Jerusalem two stories called parables. He had been talking about how to be a good follower of God. Jesus often told stories to teach people truth about God.

First he gave them the story of the good shepherd. He said, "Here is the truth. Anyone who does not go into the sheep pen by the gate but climbs in another way is a robber. The one who comes in through the door is their shepherd. The gatekeeper opens the gate for him. The sheep know him and listen for his voice. He calls them by name. He goes in front of them in case there is danger. He leads them out to fields of good grass to eat. They follow their shepherd because they know his voice. They won't follow a stranger with a voice they don't know."

The people did not understand what the story meant. So Jesus explained it to them. He said, "I am the gate that leads to the sheep pen. If anyone comes to the sheep through any other way than through me, he is a robber. Those who are really my sheep will not listen to him. The thief comes to the pen to rob the sheep and kill them. But I come to give them life. I give them all the good things they need. I am the good shepherd. The good shepherd will give up his life to save his sheep. I will give up my life so my sheep will live.

"I am the good shepherd. Just as a real shepherd knows all the sheep in his flock, so I know my own sheep. And my sheep know me, just as I know the Father and he knows me. I lay down my life for the sheep."

Some of the Jewish leaders were angry because they heard Jesus call God his father. But others

wanted him to tell them more about how to follow God. Jesus told them they should obey the Old Testament commandment that says, "You shall love the Lord your God with all your heart and all your mind and all your strength. And you shall love your neighbor as yourself."

Then a man asked, "Who is my neighbor?" Some people thought caring for a neighbor meant to care for their relatives or close friends. But Jesus told them the parable of the good Samaritan so they would understand that they should care about everyone.

He said, "One day a man was traveling the lonely road from Jerusalem to Jericho. Suddenly some robbers attacked him. They took everything he had. Then they beat him up so badly, they thought he was dead. A priest soon came down the same road. When he saw the man lying there, he crossed to the other side and walked by. Later a Levite also came down road. He passed by on the other side of the road, the same way the priest did.

"Then a man from Samaria came down the road. He stopped as soon as he saw the hurt man. He felt sorry for him. He helped the man by putting ointment and bandages on his wounds. Then he lifted the man and put him on his own donkey. He took the man to an inn. There he took care of him all night. The next morning he took out money and gave it to the innkeeper. He said, 'Take care of him. If you need to spend more than this, do so. I will pay you back when I come again.'"

Then Jesus asked, "Which of these men do you think was a neighbor to the man who was robbed?"

The man answered, "The one who showed kindness."

Jesus said, "Go and do the same."

Jesus taught that our neighbor is the one who needs the help that we can give, whoever it may be.

Miracles of Jesus

Calming the Sea

MATTHEW 8:18–27;
MARK 4:35–41; LUKE 8:22–25

fter teaching all day by the Sea of Galilee, Jesus saw that the crowds were still coming and there was no time to rest. He said to his disciples, "Let's go over to the other side of the lake. There we can be alone."

So the disciples took Jesus into the boat and began to row across the water. Other little boats were with them, for many people wished to go with Jesus. While they were rowing, Jesus fell asleep on a pillow in the back of the boat. Suddenly a storm came up and drove great waves of water into their boat.

Soon the boat was in danger of sinking. But Jesus was still asleep. The disciples were very frightened because of the storm. They woke Jesus, saying, "Master, Master, we are lost! Help us or we will die!"

Jesus woke, got up, and looked out at the sea. Then he spoke to the waves. "Peace, be still!"

The wind stopped! The waves became quiet and calm! Then Jesus said to his disciples, "Why were you afraid? Where is your faith?"

They all were amazed at Jesus' power. They said to each other, "Who is this man? Even the wind and the sea obey him!"

A Wonderful Picnic

MATTHEW 14:13–21; MARK 6:30–44;
LUKE 9:10–17; JOHN 6:1–15

ne day Jesus taught a huge crowd of people in an open place near the town of Bethsaida. As it began to get late in the day, the disciples said to him, "This is a lonely place. There is nothing here for such a crowd of people to eat. Send them away before it is too late to get some food in the town."

But Jesus replied, "They don't need to go away. You can give them food to eat."

The disciples were surprised at that. They asked, "Shall we go into town and buy bread? We could not buy enough for each person here to have one bite!"

Jesus looked at one of the disciples. "Philip," he asked, "where can we find enough bread so all these people may eat?"

Philip looked at the crowd. There were about five thousand men and a lot of women and children who had also come. He said, "Eight months' pay would not buy enough bread so all these people could have a little piece."

"How many loaves do you have?" Jesus asked them.

Andrew, another disciple, found a young boy and brought him to Jesus. He said, "Here is a boy who has five loaves of barley bread and two dried fish. But how far can that little lunch go to feed such a large crowd?"

Jesus said to all the disciples, "Go out among the people. Divide them into groups." So the disciples had the people sit down on the green grass in groups of fifty or a hundred.

The people in their colorful robes looked like beds of flowers arranged in rows and squares. Jesus

took the boy's five loves and the two little fish in his hands. He looked up to heaven and gave thanks for the food. Then he broke the loaves and the fish and gave pieces to each of the twelve disciples. The disciples went among the groups of people and gave the bread and fish to the people. They found they had enough food for everyone. They just kept breaking off pieces and breaking off pieces until everyone had eaten enough. Then Jesus said, "Gather up the extra food so none of it is wasted."

The disciples carried their baskets around and asked people to put in any leftover food. When they came back to Jesus, all twelve of their baskets were filled with bread and fish!

Walking on Water

MATTHEW 14:22–33;
MARK 6:45–51; JOHN 6:16–69

hen the people saw that Jesus could give them food to eat, they all wanted to make him an earthly king. But Jesus knew that the kind of king the people wanted was the kind the Romans had. He also knew that he was God's chosen King. The people wanted a king who would take over the world by power, but Jesus had been sent to take over the world by love. His kingdom would be in the hearts of people who loved him, not on a golden throne in a palace on earth.

He commanded his disciples to get into their boat and row across the lake, away from the excited crowd. He stayed behind to send the crowd away. Then he went up into the mountain to pray. While he was praying in the night, a great storm arose on the lake. From the mountain Jesus could see his disciples working hard to row against the waves. After midnight the storm was the strongest. Jesus went to his disciples by walking on the water. He walked right on top of the waves as if they were dry land!

The men in the boat saw a person coming toward them on the sea. They cried out in fear because they thought it must be a ghost. But Jesus called to them, "Don't be afraid! It is I." Then they saw that it was their teacher!

Peter called to Jesus, "Lord, if it is really you, let me come to you on the water."

Jesus answered, "Come."

Simon Peter leaped overboard, and he too walked on the water—until he noticed how big the waves

> *When he began to be afraid, he began to sink! He cried out, "Lord, save me!" Jesus reached out his hand and caught hold of Peter. He lifted Peter and helped him back onto the boat.*

had become. When he began to be afraid, he began to sink! He cried out, "Lord, save me!"

Jesus reached out his hand and caught hold of Peter. He lifted Peter and helped him back onto the boat. Jesus said, "O man of little faith, why did you doubt my word?"

When they landed on the shore, many people

came to see Jesus because of the miracle of the bread and fish. They wanted Jesus to feed them too. But he told them, "Look for food that will cause you to live forever, not for food that doesn't last. I am the bread of life."

But the people wanted to see a miracle, so they wouldn't listen to Jesus teach. They decided to go away. Jesus asked his disciples, "Now do you want to go away and leave me, too?"

Then Simon Peter answered for all the disciples, "Lord, who else could we follow? Only you have the words of eternal life."

Palm Sunday

The Precious Perfume

MATTHEW 26:6–16; MARK 14:1–11;
LUKE 22:1–6; JOHN 12:1–11

esus and his disciples left the city of Jericho and went up the mountain to Bethany. That was the home of his friends Martha, Mary, and Lazarus. While everyone ate dinner together, Mary came into the room carrying a sealed jar of very precious perfumed oil. She opened it and poured some on Jesus' head and some on his feet. Then she bent down and used her own long hair to wipe up the oil and clean the dust of the road from Jesus' feet.

Some of Jesus' friends were surprised and didn't know what to think about this. Only kings got to wear such expensive oil or use it to wash their feet. Ordinary people got to use perfumed oil only when they were about to get married or when they had died. Their families poured it on their bodies before the funeral.

Judas spoke up and said, "Why did she waste the perfume? It could have been sold for a lot of money to help the poor."

Later the disciples found out that Judas had been stealing money for himself, when he said he was giving it to the poor. Jesus already seemed to know that when he looked at Judas. He said, "Let her alone. She has done a good thing for me. There will always be people among you who need money. Mary did what she could with this perfume. Its purpose was to prepare my body to be buried. All over the world, everywhere the good news will be told, the thing that this woman has done today will be told. She will be

remembered for it." Mary seemed to believe what the others did not. Jesus was going to die soon. She showed her love for him by giving such a rich gift. She showed how much she would miss him by the way she gave it.

This was the day Judas went to see the rulers of the Jews. The rulers were afraid of the things Jesus

> *"All over the world, everywhere the good news will be told, the thing that this woman has done today will be told. She will be remembered for it."*

said and did. Because of their fear, they wanted to kill Jesus. They even wanted to kill Lazarus, because of the miracle that raised him from the dead. They worried because all the people were so excited about what happened to him. His story made the people decide to follow Jesus. Judas was very angry with Jesus, so he plotted with the rulers. They offered Judas thirty pieces of silver to help them arrest Jesus.

The Borrowed Colt

MATTHEW 21:1–11; MARK 11:1–11;
LUKE 19:28–40; JOHN 12:12–16

ne morning soon after the supper at Bethany, Jesus called two of his disciples and told them, "Go into the next village. At a place where two roads cross, you will find a donkey tied next to a colt. Untie the colt and bring him to me. If anyone asks why you are doing this, say, 'The Lord needs him,' and they will let you take him."

The disciples went to the place and found the donkey and her colt. While they were untying him, the owner came out and said, "What are you doing?"

The disciples said just what Jesus had told them to say: "The Lord needs him."

Then the owner gave it to them. They brought the colt to Jesus. Although it had never been ridden, the colt was quiet when the disciples put their own robes across its back as a cushion. It obeyed when they helped Jesus get on to ride.

Jerusalem was just two miles from Bethany. That was the town where Lazarus lived. Many people came to see Jesus. They were also curious to see

Lazarus, because they heard about how Jesus raised him from the dead. As Jesus rode over the mountain

> *They waved palm tree branches like green flags and shouted together, "Blessed be the Son of David! Blessed is the King who comes in the name of the Lord! May there be peace and glory in the highest heaven!"*

toward Jerusalem, the huge crowd of people who had come to see Jesus threw their clothes on the road in front of him, so it looked like a giant, colorful carpet leading into the city. They were so happy to see him that they welcomed him the way they would a king or a great hero. They waved palm tree branches like green flags and shouted together, "Blessed be the Son of David! Blessed is the King who comes in the name of the Lord! May there be peace and glory in the highest heaven!"

They said these things because they really believed that Jesus was the Messiah, the King sent from God. They hoped that he would come into the city and set up a golden throne right then.

Some of the teachers and rulers who did not believe said to Jesus, "Master, stop your disciples."

But Jesus said, "I tell you, if they keep quiet, the stones will cry out instead."

When he came into Jerusalem surrounded by the crowd, everyone was amazed. They asked, "Who is this?"

The crowd answered, "This is Jesus, the prophet of Nazareth in Galilee!"

Today we remember that Sunday. We call it Palm Sunday because of the palm branches the people waved for Jesus.

THE LAST SUPPER

The Disciples Find an Upper Room

MATTHEW 26:17–19;
MARK 14:12–16; LUKE 22:7–13

t was almost time for the special feast of the Passover, and the disciples asked Jesus what they should do to celebrate together. Jesus told them, "Go into the city, and a man carrying a pitcher of water will meet you. Follow him. Go into the house where he goes and say to the owner, 'The Master says, "Where is my guest room, where I can eat the Passover meal with my disciples?"' Then he will show you a large room upstairs with furniture set up. That is where you can prepare for us to eat."

So Peter and John went into Jerusalem, and just as Jesus said, they saw a man walking toward them, carrying a pitcher of water. They followed him into the house and spoke to the man who owned it, saying,

"The Master says, 'Where is my guest room, where I can eat the Passover meal with my disciples?'"

Then the man led them upstairs and showed them a large room, with the table and couches around it—all ready for guests and dinner, just as Jesus had said! The disciples went out and brought back all the food that was used for the feast of Passover: a roasted lamb, vegetables, and a special thin bread made without any yeast.

Breaking Bread

MATTHEW 26:26–29;
MARK 14:22–25; LUKE 22:14–20

n Thursday afternoon Jesus and his disciples walked to the house and went upstairs to the large room where the Passover meal was ready. When they were all at the table, Jesus told them, "I have really looked forward to eating this Passover meal with you. I wanted to do this before I suffer. I tell you, I will not eat the Passover meal again until we eat it together in God's kingdom."

While they were eating, Jesus took bread and gave thanks. Then he broke it and passed a piece to each of the Twelve, saying, "Take and eat; this is my body which is broken for you. Do this and remember me."

Then he took the cup of wine and passed it to each one, saying, "This cup is my blood, shed for you and for many, that your sins may be taken away. Whenever you drink this, remember me."

Jesus Washes the Disciples' Feet

JOHN 13:1–17

hile they were still at the table, Jesus stood up and took off his outer robe. He tied a long towel around his waist, as a servant would. He poured water into a bowl and carried it to the feet of one of the disciples while they all wondered what he would do next. When he began to wash the first disciple's feet, they were surprised. He went around to each of them and washed their feet, as a house servant would do for his master's guests.

Simon Peter tried to stop Jesus when he came to him. "Lord, are you really going to wash my feet?"

Jesus answered him, "You don't understand what I am doing now, but you will later."

Peter argued, "No, Lord, don't wash my feet."

"If I don't wash you," said Jesus, "then you don't really belong to me."

Then Peter said, "Oh, Lord, not just my feet! Wash my hands and my head, too."

Jesus smiled at his friend. "A person who has taken a bath needs only to wash his feet. The rest of

his body is clean. And you are clean. Except for one of you."

Jesus knew what was in Judas's heart. He knew that one of those disciples whose feet he was washing would turn him over to his enemies.

"Do you know what I have done for you? You call me 'Master' and 'Lord.' You are right. That is what I am. Now I, your Lord and Master, have washed your feet. I have given you an example to follow. You should do as I have done and wash one another's feet."

Jesus wanted all who follow him to help and serve each other. He wanted them to think of others instead of seeking great things for themselves.

Judas Betrays Jesus

MATTHEW 26:20–25; MARK 14:17–21;
LUKE 22:21–23; JOHN 13:18–30

hile Jesus was talking, he became very sad. Suddenly he said, "The truth is, one of you is going to hand me over to my enemies."

The disciples were looking at one another and wondering whom Jesus was talking about. One after another they asked, "Am I the one, Lord?"

Jesus didn't tell them who it was. He just said, "It's one of you twelve who are dipping your hands into the same dish and eating with me."

When he passed a piece of bread to Judas, Jesus said to him, "Do quickly what you are going to do."

No one realized what this meant then. They thought Jesus was sending Judas on an errand, because he was in charge of the money. He often went out to buy things they needed or give money to the poor. But once Judas went out, he knew that he had to carry out his plan now or never. Jesus seemed to know all about it. Judas went to the rulers and told them he would lead them to Jesus.

Praying in the Garden

MATTHEW 26:36–46;
MARK 14:32–42; LUKE 22:39–46

t the foot of the Mount of Olives there was an orchard of olive trees called the Garden of Gethsemane. The word *Gethsemane* means "oil press." Jesus often went to this place with his disciples because of its quiet shade. Jesus now took his disciples there. He asked eight of the disciples to wait outside the orchard, saying, "Sit here while I go inside and pray."

He took the other three disciples, Peter, James, and John, into the orchard. Jesus knew that in a little while Judas would be there with a band of men. He knew they would arrest him. He also knew he would be beaten and led out to die. The thought of what he was about to suffer came to him and filled his soul with sadness.

He said to Peter, James, and John, "My soul is filled with sorrow, a sorrow that almost kills me. Stay here and watch while I am praying."

Then he went a little farther into the olive trees. Jesus fell to his knees on the ground. He cried out,

"O my Father, if it's possible, take this cup away from me. But I want to do your will, not my own."

As Jesus prayed, his feeling was so strong that great drops of sweat poured from his face. They looked like drops of blood falling there on the ground. After he had prayed for some time, he went back to his disciples. He found them all asleep. He woke them and said to Peter, "What is this? Couldn't you watch with me even for one hour? Watch and pray. It will keep you from falling into sin when you are tempted. Your spirit is willing, but your flesh is weak."

Jesus left them. He went back into the woods and fell on his knees and prayed again. "O my Father, if this cup cannot be taken away and I must drink it, then your will be done."

He went back to the three disciples. They were asleep again! This time he didn't wake them. He

The word Gethsemane means "oil press." Jesus often went to this place with his disciples because of its quiet shade.

turned around and went back to where he had been praying in the woods. He prayed the same words as before, but this time an angel came down from heaven to give him strength.

Jesus Is Arrested

Judas Brings Soldiers

MATTHEW 26:47–56; MARK 14:43–52;
LUKE 22:47–53; JOHN 18:1–11

ow Jesus was ready for the work he had come to do. His heart was strong. He went back to the three disciples again and said, "Are you still sleeping and resting? Enough! The hour has come. Look! The Son of Man is about to be handed over to sinners. Get up! Let us go. Here comes the one who is handing me over to them."

The disciples woke to the noise of a crowd. They saw the flashing torches and the gleaming swords and spears. In the middle of the crowd they saw Judas. They remembered what Jesus had told them the night before at the Passover meal. He had said that one of the disciples would turn him over to his enemies. Now they knew that Judas was the one who had done it.

Jesus Came to the Disciples' Boat by Walking on Top of the Water

Peter tried to walk out on the water like Jesus, but he began to sink.
Jesus held Peter by the hand and saved him from sinking.

MANY PEOPLE CAME TO SEE
JESUS RIDE INTO JERUSALEM

A huge crowd threw their clothes on the road. They were so happy
to see him that they waved palm tree branches like green flags.
They shouted, "Blessed is the king who comes in the name of the Lord!"

Suddenly Judas came rushing forward and kissed Jesus as if he were glad to see him. This was a secret signal Judas had given the soldiers so they would know which man to arrest. Jesus looked into Judas's eyes and said, "Judas, do you betray the Son of Man with a kiss?"

Then Jesus turned and asked the crowd and the soldiers, "Who is it that you want?"

The crowd replied, "Jesus of Nazareth."

Jesus said, "I am he."

When Jesus said this, a sudden fear came on his enemies. They drew back and fell to the ground.

After a moment Jesus said again, "Who is it that you want?"

They answered again, "Jesus of Nazareth."

Jesus said, "I told you, I am he." Then he pointed to his disciples and said, "If you are seeking me, let these men go their own way."

The crowd came forward to take Jesus. But Peter drew his sword and struck at one of the men and cut off his right ear. The man's name was Malchus, and he was the high priest's servant.

Jesus stopped Peter by saying, "Put your sword away! Shouldn't I drink the cup my Father has given me? Don't you know I could call to the Father and he would send armies of angels to defend me?"

Jesus touched the man's ear and healed it. Then he said to the armed men, "Do you come with swords and clubs to arrest me as you would a robber? I was with you every day in the temple courtyard. You didn't lay a hand on me. But now is your hour. This is when darkness rules."

When the disciples saw that Jesus would not let them fight for him, they did not know what to do. They were afraid and ran away. They left their teacher alone with his enemies.

Jesus Is Taken Prisoner

MATTHEW 26:69–75; MARK 14:66–72;
LUKE 22:54–62; JOHN 18:12–27

he crowd of men arrested Jesus and bound him. They led him away to the high priest's house.

Simon Peter and John followed after the crowd to the high priest's house. John knew Annas, the high priest, so John went into the courtyard where they were questioning Jesus. Peter stayed outside until John came to bring him in. Inside he waited with others who were keeping warm by a charcoal fire.

In the courtyard, Annas asked Jesus about his disciples and teaching. Jesus answered him, "I have taught openly in the temple. Why do you ask me? Ask those who heard me. They know what I said."

Then one of the officers struck Jesus on the mouth. He said, "Is that the way you answer the high priest?"

Jesus answered the officer calmly and quietly. "If I said anything evil, tell what the evil is. But if I told the truth, why did you strike me?"

Annas and his men kept doing things to show that they hated Jesus. He stood bound and alone among his enemies. Peter stayed with the group around the fire in the courtyard. He was worried about his friend and teacher but dared not go inside. A serving woman from the high priest's house looked at Peter sharply. Finally she said, "You were one of those with this Jesus of Nazareth!"

Peter was afraid to tell the truth. He answered, "Woman, I don't know the man. I don't know what you are talking about."

He went out to the porch of the house to get away from her. But another woman saw him there and said, "This man was one of those with Jesus!"

Peter again said that he did not know Jesus at all. Soon a man came by who was a relative of Malchus, the man whose ear Peter had cut off. He looked at Peter and listened to him talk. He said, "You are certainly one of this man's disciples. I can tell by your accent. You are from Galilee."

Then Peter began to curse and to swear. He declared that he did not know the man they were talking about.

Just at that moment the loud, shrill crowing of a rooster startled Peter. Then he saw Jesus. The soldiers were dragging him through the hall to the council room of Caiaphas, the other high priest. Jesus turned and looked at Peter as he was passing by. Jesus' words from the evening before flashed into Peter's mind: "Before the rooster crows tomorrow morning, you will say three times that you don't know me at all."

Peter went out into the street and cried bitterly.

Peter and the Rooster

Matthew 26:31–35; Mark 14:27–31;
Luke 22:31–34; John 13:31–14:4

s soon as Judas was gone, Jesus said to the eleven disciples, "My little children, I shall be with you only a short time. I am going away to a place where you cannot come now. But when I have gone, remember this new commandment I am giving you: Love one another as I have loved you."

Simon Peter said, "Lord, where are you going?"

Jesus answered, "Where I'm going, you cannot follow now. But you will follow me there one day."

Peter argued, "Lord, why can't I follow you now? I am ready to lay down my life for you!"

Jesus replied, "Will you really lay down your life for me? The truth is, Peter, before the rooster crows tomorrow morning, you will say three times that you don't know me at all."

But Peter couldn't believe that! "Even if they try to kill me," he promised, "I will never deny you, Lord."

All the disciples were upset by what Jesus had told Peter, so Jesus said, "Don't let your hearts be troubled. Believe in God. Believe also in me. There are many rooms in my Father's house. And that is where I am going. I will make a place ready for you. When it is ready, I will come back for you. I will take you with me so you will also be where I am."

Jesus talked with the disciples for a long time and prayed for them. About midnight they all left together and went to the Mount of Olives.

Pilate Meets Jesus

Matthew 27:11–30; Mark 15:1–19;
Luke 23:1–25; John 18:28–19:16

t was early morning when the Jewish leaders brought Jesus to Pilate at the Fortress of Antonio. Pilate came out to them and asked, "What charge do you bring against this man?"

They answered, "If he were not an evil-doer, we would not have brought him to you."

Pilate did not wish to be bothered, and he said, "Take him away and judge him yourselves by your own law."

The leaders said to Pilate, "We are not allowed to put any man to death unless we bring him to you. We have found this man teaching evil and telling men not to pay taxes to Emperor Caesar. He said he is the Christ, a king."

Then Pilate went into his courtroom and sent for Jesus. He looked at Jesus and asked, "Are you the king of the Jews? Your own people have brought you to me. What have you done?"

Jesus replied, "My kingdom is not of this world. If it were, then those who serve me would fight to save me from my enemies."

Pilate asked, "Are you a king, then?"

Jesus answered him, "You have said it. I am a king. For this I was born. For this I came into the world, that I might speak the truth of God to men."

"Truth," said Pilate. "What is truth?"

He didn't wait for Jesus to answer. Pilate went out to the crowd and said, "I find no evil in this man."

Pilate thought that Jesus was a harmless man. He could see no reason why the rulers and the people should be so bitter against him. But they cried out all the more, saying, "He stirs up the people everywhere, from Galilee even to this place."

When Pilate heard the word *Galilee*, he asked if Jesus had come from that land. They told him yes. So Pilate said, "Galilee and its people are under the rule of Herod. He has come up to Jerusalem. I will send this man to him."

So they took Jesus to Herod's palace. Now, Herod was very glad to see Jesus, for he had heard many things about him. He hoped to see Jesus do a miracle. But Jesus would not work wonders as a show for anyone. When Herod asked him many questions, Jesus didn't answer one word. Herod would not give a judgment about Jesus. He knew Jesus had not done anything wrong. To please the angry crowd, Herod and his soldiers dressed Jesus in a royal robe and made fun of him. Then they sent him back to Pilate.

So even though he didn't want to, Pilate was forced to judge Jesus' case. As Jesus stood in front of Pilate with his hands bound, a message came to Pilate from his wife. She wrote, "Do nothing against that good man. I suffered many things in a dream about him last night."

Pilate said to the Jews, "You have brought this man as one who is leading the people to evil. I have seen that there is no evil in him. Herod agreed. It is the custom to set a prisoner free at the Feast. Now I will order that he be beaten and then set free."

But the Jewish leaders and the crowd called out to set free a murderer and robber named Barabbas instead of Jesus.

Pilate said, "What shall I do with Jesus?"

And they all cried out, "Crucify him! Let him die on the cross!"

Pilate wished to spare Jesus' life. To show how he felt, he sent for water. He washed his hands before all the people. He said, "My hands are clean from the blood of this good man!"

Then the angry crowd cried out, "Let his blood be on us and on our children after us! Crucify him! Send him to the cross!"

To please the people, Pilate gave them what they asked. He set Barabbas free even though he was a robber and a murderer. He tried one more time to save Jesus' life. He had Jesus beaten until he was bleeding. He hoped the crowd would be satisfied with that. One of the soldiers put a crown made of thorns on Jesus' head to mock him about being called a king. They put a purple robe on him and pretended to bow before him. They called out, "Hail, king of the Jews!"

Pilate brought Jesus out to the crowd this way, hoping they would feel some pity for him. Pilate said, "Look at this man!"

But the crowd cried out again, "Crucify him! Send him to the cross!"

At last Pilate gave in to the people. He sat down on the judgment seat. He knew Jesus was a good man and had done nothing evil. But he commanded that Jesus be put to death.

The Jewish Rulers Question Jesus

Matthew 26:57–68;
Mark 14:53–65; Luke 22:63–71

esus' enemies led him away from Annas's house. They took him to Caiaphas, the man the Romans considered to be the high priest. There all the rulers of the Jews tried to find someone who had heard Jesus say something they could use against him. They wanted to find a reason to put Jesus to death. But they could find nothing. Some men said one thing. Some men said another thing. But their words did not agree. Finally the high priest stood and said to Jesus, "Do you have nothing to say? What about the things these men are saying against you?"

Jesus stood there silent.

The high priest spoke again. "Are you the Christ, the Son of God?"

Jesus said, "I am. And the time shall come when you will see the Son of Man sitting on the throne of power and coming in the clouds of heaven."

These words made the high priest very angry. He said to the rulers, "Do you hear these evil words?

He says he is the Son of God. What do you think of words like these?"

They all answered together, "He deserves to die!"

Then the high priest's servants and the soldiers who held Jesus mocked him. They spit at him. They blindfolded him and hit him with their fists. They said, "If you are such a great prophet, tell us who hit you!"

The Jewish rulers and priests decided that Jesus should be put to death. But the Romans ruled their land. No man could be put to death unless the Roman governor, Pontius Pilate, commanded it. So the crowd took Jesus to Pilate at the fortress.

Judas Dies

Matthew 27:1–10

 udas Iscariot saw how Jesus did nothing to protect himself from the angry crowd. He saw that Jesus did not save himself or do any miracles. Judas watched as Jesus allowed the people to tie him up and beat him. It looked as if they were going to put him to death after all. Judas brought back the thirty pieces of silver that the Jewish leaders had given him to help them arrest Jesus. He said, "I have sinned. I betrayed someone who has done nothing wrong."

But they answered, "What does that matter to us?"

Judas saw that they wouldn't take back the money and let Jesus go free. He threw the thirty pieces of silver on the floor of the temple. Then he went away and hanged himself. That was how the man who once had been a friend of Jesus died.

The leaders didn't know what to do with the money Judas had thrown away. They said, "We can't put it in our temple treasury. It is the price paid for a man's blood."

They decided to use it to buy a piece of ground called the potter's field. They set the land apart as a place for burying strangers who died in the city. But everyone in Jerusalem called the place the Field of Blood.

THE DARKEST DAY
OF ALL THE WORLD

The Road to Calvary

MATTHEW 27:31–33; MARK 15:20–22;
LUKE 23:26–32; JOHN 19:16–17

ontius Pilate, the Roman governor, gave the order that Jesus must die on the cross. The Roman soldiers took Jesus and beat him again very cruelly. Then they led him out of the city to the place where criminals were killed. This place was called Golgotha in the Hebrew language and Calvary in the Roman language. Both words mean "the place of the skull."

A great crowd of people followed the soldiers. Some of them were Jesus' enemies, and they were glad to see him suffer. Others were Jesus' friends. The women were crying as they saw him wounded from his beatings and going to die.

The soldiers forced Jesus to carry the heavy cross, but soon he could not carry it. He was too weak from all the injuries they had given him. They forced a man named Simon, who had come into town from the country, to carry Jesus' cross to its place at Calvary. It was a sad, sad day.

At the Cross

MATTHEW 27:34–44; MARK 15:23–32;
LUKE 23:33–43; JOHN 19:18–27

hen the procession arrived at Calvary, the soldiers laid the cross down and stretched Jesus upon it. They drove nails through his hands and feet to fasten him to the cross. Then they stood the cross up. Jesus prayed for the soldiers who put him on the cross. He prayed, "Father, forgive them. They do not know what they are doing."

The Romans had a custom of giving men about to die on the cross some medicine to numb the pain of that awful death. They offered some to Jesus, but he knew what it was when he tasted it and wouldn't take any. He wanted to be able to think clearly, even if it meant he would suffer more.

The soldiers took Jesus' clothes and divided them among themselves. They gambled for his robe, which was woven in one long piece. They didn't want to cut it up to share it.

Two robbers who had been sentenced to die were led out and hung on crosses on each side of Jesus.

Over Jesus' head the soldiers put up a sign, as Pilate had ordered. It read, "This is Jesus of Nazareth, the King of the Jews." It was written in three languages: in Hebrew, which was the language of the Jews; in Latin, the language of the Romans; and in Greek, a language read by many other people of that area.

The chief priests of the Jews were unhappy with the sign. They asked Pilate to have its writing changed from "the King of the Jews" to "He said, 'I am King of the Jews.'" But Pilate would not change it. He said, "What I have written, I have written."

People who passed by on the road mocked Jesus. Some called out to him, "You said you would destroy the temple and build it again in three days! Save yourself! If you are the Son of God, come down from the cross!"

The priests and scribes said, "He saved others, but he cannot save himself. Come down from the cross, and we will believe in you!"

Then one of the robbers who was on a cross beside Jesus joined in. He said, "If you are the Christ, save yourself and save us!"

But the other robber scolded him. "Don't you have any fear of God? You are under the same sentence as this man. We deserve to die, but this man has done nothing wrong."

Then he said to Jesus, "Lord, remember me when you come into your kingdom."

And Jesus answered him, "Today you will be with me in paradise."

Mary, Jesus' mother, stood near the cross. She was filled with sorrow. John, the disciple Jesus loved best, stood next to her. Jesus said to Mary, "Dear woman, here is your son." Then he said to John, "Son, here is your mother." From that day on, John took the mother of Jesus home to his own house and cared for her as his own mother.

Jesus Dies

MATTHEW 27:45–56; MARK 15:33–41;
LUKE 23:44–49; JOHN 19:28–37

t about noon a sudden darkness came over the land. It lasted for three hours. In the middle of the afternoon, after Jesus had endured six hours of terrible pain on the cross, he cried out, "My Lord, my God, why have you forsaken me?" Those words are at the beginning of Psalm 22. Though this psalm was written long before Jesus' death, it told about the suffering of the Messiah, the Son of God, who would come.

After this Jesus said, "I am thirsty."

Someone dipped a sponge in a cup of wine vinegar and put it on a long stick, then lifted it to Jesus' lips for him to drink.

Jesus spoke his last words on the cross: "It is finished! Father, into your hands I give my spirit!"

Then Jesus died. At the same moment, the heavy curtain of the temple that hid the Holy of Holies was torn in two from top to bottom. The earth shook. Rocks split open.

When the Roman officer in charge of the soldiers saw what was happening, he said, "Surely this was the Son of God!"

To be sure Jesus was dead, one of the soldiers stuck a spear into his body. Everyone saw that blood and water came pouring out. They all could see that Jesus had really died.

Jesus Is Buried

Matthew 27:57–66; Mark 15:42–47;
Luke 23:50–56; John 19:38–42

esus had friends and followers who were rulers of the Jews. They did not dare follow him openly, but they secretly believed he was the Christ. One of these was Nicodemus, who had once come to see Jesus at night. Another was a rich man named Joseph from the town of Arimathaea. Joseph went boldly to Pilate and asked that the body of Jesus be given to him. Pilate wondered how it happened that Jesus died so soon. Often men lived on the cross for two or three days before they died. He checked and made sure that Jesus really had died. Then he allowed Joseph to take the body away.

Joseph and his friends took Jesus' body down from the cross. They wrapped it in fine cloth. Nicodemus brought expensive spices, myrrh, and aloes to wrap up with it. Then they placed the body in Joseph's own new tomb. It was a cave dug out of the rock in a garden near the place of the cross. They rolled a large stone in front of the cave's opening to cover it like a door.

Some of the rulers of the Jews went to Pilate and said, "Sir, we remember that Jesus told the people, 'After three days I will rise again.' Give orders that the tomb shall be watched for three days, or else his disciples may steal his body and tell everyone that he is raised from the dead. If that happens, he may do more harm than he did while he was alive."

So Pilate told them, "Set a watch, and make it as secure as you can."

Then they placed a wax seal on the stone in front of the opening of the cave. That way if anyone tried to open it, the Romans could see that the seal had been broken. They commanded a group of soldiers to guard the door to the tomb at all times.

Jesus' body lay in the tomb from the Friday evening that he died until the dawn of Sunday, the first day of the week.

THE BRIGHTEST DAY
OF ALL THE WORLD

At the Tomb

MATTHEW 28:1–8; MARK 16:1–8;
LUKE 24:1–12; JOHN 20:1–9

he events that happened on the first Easter Sunday are a little bit confusing. While all of the following events did happen, in some cases we are not sure what happened first, then next, and so forth. Even though we may not know what happened first, second, third, we are sure they did happen, and they happened so that God could show his love to us.

Two days after the death and burial of Jesus, some women walked to the tomb. It was very early that Sunday morning. Mary Magdalene, Salome, and another woman named Mary came to the garden as soon as it was light. They brought sweet-smelling spices to put in Jesus' grave. As they walked, the women asked each other, "Who will roll away for us the great stone that covers the door of the tomb?" They didn't know what they would do.

But when they came to the cave where Jesus was buried, they were surprised. Someone had already rolled the huge stone away. The soldiers who had been guarding the tomb were gone. The tomb of Jesus stood open!

The women did not know about the amazing thing that had happened before they got there. A great earthquake had shaken the ground and rocks. An angel had come down from heaven and rolled the stone away. When the soldiers saw the angel sitting on the stone with his bright face and shining robe, they fell to the ground as if they were dead! When

they could get up, the men ran away in terror. That was why no guards were in sight when the women got there.

Without stopping to look inside, Mary Magdalene ran back to tell the disciples about the open tomb. The other two women looked into the tomb. They saw that Jesus' body was gone. Then they saw two young men wearing long white robes sitting at each end of the tomb. Their faces shone like angels. When the women saw them, they were filled with fear. One of the angels said, "Do not be afraid. You are looking for Jesus of Nazareth, who was crucified. He is not here. He has risen from the dead, as he said he would do. Come see the place where the Lord lay. Go and tell his disciples and tell Peter, too. Jesus will go before you to Galilee. You will see him there."

The women left that place full of both joy and fear. They ran to bring this news from the angel to the disciples.

While the two women had been looking into the tomb, Mary Magdalene had been looking for the disciples. She did not know that Jesus had risen from the dead. She knew only that the tomb was open and his body was missing. She found Peter and John and cried, "They have taken away the Lord out of the tomb. We do not know where they have laid him!"

Peter and John ran at once to the garden. John outran Peter. He looked at the tomb first and saw the broken seal and the stone rolled to one side. He stood still. Then he stooped and looked into the cave. He could see lying there the linen cloths that had been wrapped around the body. When Peter arrived, he did not wait. He passed John and went into the tomb. Then John followed him. They could see that the strips of linen cloth had been rolled up and the cloth that had covered Jesus' face had been neatly folded.

Suddenly a thought flashed through John's mind: *Jesus has risen from the dead!* He had not seen the angel or heard his words. But from that moment, John believed Jesus was alive again. The men walked away thinking about the strange things they had just seen.

Jesus Is Alive

John 20:10–18; Mark 16:9–11;
Matthew 28:8–10

oon Mary Magdalene came back to the tomb. No one was there, because the other two women and the disciples had left. Mary still didn't know about the angel's message. She didn't know that Jesus had risen from the dead.

She wept as she thought of her Lord. Wicked men had killed him and not even allowed his body to rest in peace in his grave. As she wept, Mary stooped and looked into the cave. Then she saw the two young men in long white robes sitting where Jesus had lain. One of them said to her, "Woman, why do you weep?"

She answered, "Because they have taken away my Lord, and I do not know where they have laid him."

Then she turned around and saw a man standing beside her. It was Jesus, but Mary did not know it was him. He said to her, "Woman, why do you weep?"

She supposed that he was the gardener and said, "Sir, if you have carried him out of this tomb, tell me where you have laid him. I will go and get him."

Then the stranger spoke her name. "Mary!"

That was when she knew he was Jesus. She turned to him and fell down before him. She knew he was no longer dead but risen and living. She cried, "My teacher!"

Jesus said, "Do not hold on to me. I have not yet returned to the Father. But go to those who believe in me. Tell them I am going to my Father and to your Father, to my God and to your God."

Mary Magdalene went and told the disciples how she had seen the Lord. She told them what he had

> *Jesus said, "Go to those who believe in me. Tell them I am going to my Father and to your Father, to my God and to your God."*

said to her. It was the first time anyone had seen Jesus after he rose from the dead. Mary was the first believer to speak with Jesus after he had risen.

The other two women, Salome and another woman named Mary, were the second believers to see Jesus. After they saw the angel who told them Jesus was alive, they went into the city. The angel had said Jesus would meet his disciples in Galilee. They wanted to tell their friends the good news. As they were looking for them, Jesus himself suddenly stood before them. When he greeted them, the women fell down before him and worshiped him. Jesus told them, "Do not be afraid. Find those who believe in me, and tell them to go into Galilee and they shall see me there."

Jesus Died on the Cross

Jesus' last words on the cross were: "It is finished! Father, into
your hands I give my spirit!" When Jesus died, the heavy curtain
of the temple was torn in two from the top to the bottom.
The earth shook. Rocks split open. A Roman officer said,
"Surely this was the Son of God!"

JESUS CAME BACK TO LIFE

Jesus came to visit his friends. He said, "May peace be with you!"
They were surprised and afraid. They didn't know he would
come back to life after dying on the cross. He showed them the places
where the nails had made holes in his hands. They could hardly believe
it and were filled with joy to see him again.

On the Road to Emmaus

MARK 16:12–13; LUKE 24:13–35

hat same day Jesus appeared for a third time. Two of his followers were walking out of Jerusalem to a village called Emmaus. While they were talking over the strange happenings of the day, they saw a stranger walking beside them. It was really Jesus, but they didn't know it was him at first. The stranger asked them, "What are you talking about? Why are you so sad?"

Cleopas, one of the men, answered, "You must be a visitor to Jerusalem. If you lived there, you would know the things that have happened."

"What things?" Jesus asked.

"About Jesus of Nazareth," they told him. "He was a mighty prophet. He did and said powerful things in front of all the people. The chief priests and our rulers caused him to be put to death on a cross. But we had hoped that he would be the one to set Israel free. Now it is the third day since all this happened.

"Today some of our women surprised us with news that his body was not in his tomb early this morning. They had seen a vision of angels who said Jesus was alive. Some of our companions went to the tomb and found it just as the women had said. But they did not see Jesus."

The stranger said, "O foolish men, how slow of heart you are to believe the things the prophets said! Didn't the Christ have to suffer these things and then receive his glory?"

Then he told them the meaning of what was written ahead of time about Christ. He started in the books of Moses and went through the books of the prophets. As they walked, they came to the village. He seemed about to say good-bye and walk farther. The two men did not want him to leave them. "Stay with us. It is now almost evening. The day is at end," they said.

So Jesus went inside with them and sat down to eat supper. As they were about to eat, he took the loaf of bread and blessed it. He broke it and gave it to them. Then their eyes were opened, and they knew he was the Lord. At that moment Jesus disappeared!

They said to each other, "Didn't our hearts burn inside us while he talked on the road and opened the Scriptures to us?"

They ran to Jerusalem that night to tell the others what they had seen. When they found them gathered together, they were all saying, "The Lord has risen indeed! He has appeared to Simon Peter." We don't know what Jesus said to Peter then, but it was the fourth time Jesus showed himself to his friends that day.

A Surprise Appearance

MARK 16:14; LUKE 24:36–49;
JOHN 20:19–23

s the disciples talked together in a room, Jesus himself suddenly stood among them. He said, "May peace be with you!"

They were surprised and afraid. Some thought he might be a ghost. But he said to them, "Why are you frightened? Why do you doubt? Look at the wounds in my hands and my feet. Touch me and see. A spirit does not have skin and bones as I do."

He showed them his hands and his side where the spear had pierced him. They could hardly believe it and were filled with joy to see him again. He asked, "Do you have anything to eat here?"

They gave him a piece of broiled fish and some honey. He ate it right there. Then he said, "This is what I told you while I was with you. Everything written about me in the Law of Moses and in the Prophets and the Psalms must happen." Then he helped them understand the Scriptures. He told them, "This is what is written: The Christ will suffer.

He will rise from the dead on the third day. His followers will tell others to turn away from their sins and be forgiven. People from every nation will hear the good news, beginning in Jerusalem. You have seen these things with your own eyes.

"I am going to send you the promise of my Father. But for now stay in Jerusalem. Stay there until the power comes to you from heaven."

When the disciples saw that it was really the Lord and he was alive, they were glad. Jesus said to them, "Peace be to you. As my Father has sent me, so I send you. May the Spirit of God come upon you."

Doubting Thomas

John 20:24–31

he disciple Thomas was not with the other disciples when Jesus appeared to them. So the others told Thomas, "We have seen the Lord!"

Thomas said, "I cannot believe that he is alive. I must see the nail marks in his hands with my own eyes. I must touch him with my own hands."

A week passed. On the next Sunday evening the disciples got together again. This time Thomas was with them. The doors were shut. But suddenly Jesus stood in the middle of the room. He said, "Peace be with you."

Then he turned to Thomas. "Thomas, come here. Touch my hands with your finger. Put your hand into my side. Stop doubting and believe."

Thomas answered, "My Lord and my God!"

Jesus told him, "Because you see me, you believe. Blessed are the people that have not seen me but still have believed."

Gone Fishing

eter and the other disciples went to Galilee. The angels at the tomb had told the women that Jesus would come and meet them there. The disciples waited a few days but did not see Jesus. Finally Peter said, "I'm going fishing."

"We will go with you," said the others. Peter, the two brothers James and John, Thomas, Nathanael, and two other disciples all got into a fishing boat. They sailed out onto the lake. All night they threw out their fishing nets, but they did not catch one fish. When the sun started to come up, they saw someone standing on the beach. They did not know it was Jesus.

He called out to them, "Friends, have you caught anything?"

They answered, "No."

He told them, "Cast the net on the right side of the ship, and you will find some fish."

They did what the stranger told them. Suddenly they could not pull the net into the boat, because it was so full of fish. John's quick eyes saw who the stranger really was. He told Peter, "It is the Lord!"

The minute Peter heard this, he leaped into the water and swam to the shore. The other disciples stayed in the boat and rowed it to shore, dragging the heavy net full of fish. When they came to land, they found a fire of charcoal burning. Jesus was broiling a fish with a loaf of bread beside it. He said, "Bring some of the fish you have just caught."

Simon Peter waded out to the net full of fish. He pulled it to shore. Later they counted the fish in the net. There were 153 large fish. The disciples were surprised that their old net had not broken with such a huge catch.

Jesus called them, saying, "Come now and have breakfast."

He gave them bread to go with their fish. They ate breakfast on the beach with Jesus. Their teacher and friend was alive again. This was the third time Jesus came to a large group of his disciples after rising from the dead. It was the seventh time he was seen after he had risen.

Jesus' Lambs and Sheep

fter breakfast Jesus turned to Simon Peter, the disciple who three times had said that he didn't know Jesus. Jesus asked, "Simon, son of John, do you love me?"

Peter answered, "Yes, Lord, you know that I love you."

Jesus said, "Feed my lambs."

After a time Jesus asked him again, "Simon, son of John, do you love me?"

Peter answered him as before, "Yes, Lord, you know that I love you."

This time Jesus said, "Take care of my sheep."

The third time Jesus said, "Simon, son of John, do you love me?"

Peter was troubled that Jesus had asked the question again. He answered, "Lord, you know everything. You know that I love you."

Jesus said, "Feed my sheep." And he added, "Follow me."

Peter had once denied three times that he knew Jesus. Now he had declared his love to Jesus three times. Jesus had called Peter back to his place and work as one of the disciples.

Jesus on the Mountain

Matthew 28:16–20; Mark 16:15–20;
Luke 24:50–53; Acts 1:1–11

he disciples met on a mountain in Galilee. Many people came to see Jesus. He showed himself to them all. He told them, "All power is given to me in heaven and in earth. Go out and tell everyone in all nations about the good news of the Son of God. Baptize them in the name of the Father, Son, and Holy Spirit. Teach them to live by my commandments, as I have taught you. Know that I am with you always, even to the end of the world." This was the eighth time Jesus was seen after he rose from the dead.

The ninth time he was seen, Jesus came to a man named James. This wasn't the same James who was listed as one of Jesus' twelve disciples. He may actually have been a son of Joseph, the carpenter of Nazareth, and his wife, Mary—a half brother to Jesus. People think this because he was known as "James, the Lord's brother." We don't know what Jesus said at that meeting, but James became a strong believer from that time on.

The tenth time Jesus came to his disciples may have been in the city of Jerusalem. He told his followers to wait there until God sent down the gift of the Holy Spirit. He said, "When the Holy Spirit comes to you, you will have a new power. You will speak in my name in Jerusalem, in Judea, in Samaria, and in the farthest parts of the earth."

Jesus led his disciples out of the city. They walked over the Mount of Olives to near the village of Bethany. He lifted up his hands to bless them. While he was blessing them, he began to rise in the air. He rose higher and higher until a cloud covered him. The disciples could no longer see him.

They stood there looking up toward heaven. Suddenly two men who looked like angels in shining robes stood there beside them. They said, "Men of Galilee, why do you stand here looking at the sky? Jesus has been taken away into heaven. But he will come back in the same way you saw him go."

Then the disciples were happy. They worshiped Jesus there. They walked together back to Jerusalem. They kept going to the temple to praise and give thanks to God.

Stories of the First Christians

The Mighty, Rushing Wind

Acts 1:12–2:47

fter the Lord Jesus went up to heaven, the eleven disciples and others who followed Jesus met together. They were not sad that he had gone. They were very happy because Jesus had left them a promise. He said he would send them power from God. Every day they met together and praised God. They prayed in the large upstairs room in Jerusalem where Jesus had eaten his last supper with the disciples.

The eleven disciples chose a twelfth man to take the place of Judas Iscariot. His name was Matthias. Mary, Jesus' mother, and his brothers and the women who had been at the cross were there with a number of others who believed in Jesus.

Ten days after Jesus went to heaven, there came the Jewish feast day called Pentecost. On that day the believers in Christ were together in the upstairs room. Suddenly they heard a sound from heaven that was like the rushing of a mighty wind. They saw something that looked like tongues of fire. A flame seemed to be over the head of each of them. Then the Spirit of God came on all the believers gathered there. They began to speak in languages they had not known before.

People all over town came to see what was happening. When they did, they heard these Jewish people speaking all the different languages that people in the city knew. The followers of Jesus were praising God and telling the good news about his

Son in the languages of Jews from all over the world. Everyone heard the message in his own language.

Then Peter got up and explained that God had given Jesus' followers a gift. The ancient prophet Joel had told about this gift in the holy writings of the Jewish people. God had said through his prophet Joel, "In the last days I will pour out my Holy Spirit on all people." Peter told the crowd the good news that Jesus had come to forgive their sins.

Many Jews believed and were baptized and became followers of Jesus. About three thousand people joined the faith that day. They all met together and loved each other. They shared everything they had and were filled with joy. They told everyone they could the good news about Jesus.

THE MAN AT THE BEAUTIFUL GATE WAS HEALED

Peter told the man: "I don't have silver or gold, but I'll give you
what I do have. In the name of Jesus Christ of Nazareth,
get up and walk." Peter helped him up. The man stood on his feet,
and then he began to walk! He had never walked before.

HOW THE IRON GATE OPENED

King Herod kept Peter in prison. All the Christians prayed to God
to help Peter. Suddenly a bright angel from the Lord stood by Peter.
Peter followed the angel right out through the great iron gate of the prison.
It opened for them as if unseen hands were pushing it.

The Man at the Beautiful Gate

Acts 3:1–4:31

ne afternoon the apostles Peter and John were going to the temple for the hour of prayer. They walked across the court of the Gentiles. It was a large, open square paved with marble. The eastern side had a row of pillars with a roof that was named Solomon's Porch. The main entrance to the temple was at the front of the porch, and it was called the Beautiful Gate.

Some people were carrying to the gate a sick man who could not walk. He had been born unable to walk, and every day some friends would bring him to the gate. Then he would sit there and hope that people who were going into the temple to pray would notice him. He hoped they would give him money to help him live, since he could not work.

Peter and John did notice him. Peter said, "Look at us." The man looked at them and hoped they were going to give him something. Peter said, "I don't have silver or gold, but I'll give you what I do have. In the name of Jesus Christ of Nazareth, get up and walk."

Peter took hold of the man's right hand and helped him up. At once the lame man felt a new power entering his feet and anklebones. He jumped up and stood on his feet! Then he began to walk! He had never done this before in his life. He was so happy that he went into the temple court with Peter and John. He was not just walking. He was jumping up and down and praising God. The people there recognized him as the man who sat at the Beautiful Gate every day. They knew that he had never been able to walk before. Everyone was filled with wonder at what had happened to him.

After prayer and worship time Peter and John went out to the porch again. The man who had been healed stayed with them. A great crowd had gathered to see what had happened to him. They wanted to see the two men who had healed him.

Peter spoke to them. "Men of Israel," he said, "why does this surprise you? Why are you staring at us? We haven't made this man walk by our own power or goodness. The God of Abraham, Isaac, and Jacob has done this. He wants you to see the power and glory of his Son Jesus."

He told the people about how Jesus died for them. He explained how Jesus wanted to forgive their sins.

He told them how God had sent Jesus to be the Messiah that their holy writings and prophets had said would come. Many people believed them, but some of the rulers of the temple were angry. They did not believe that Jesus was God's Son. They arrested Peter and John. They locked them up in a guardroom so they would stop telling the good news.

But it didn't stop them. This gave Peter and John a chance to tell the story of Jesus to a group of rulers who came to judge their case. Even those high priests who had sentenced Jesus to death had to admit that God had given these men power. The man they had healed was standing right there beside them! But the rulers didn't want the apostles to keep healing people and telling the good news. They told them to stop or they would be punished.

Peter and John answered, "Which is right? Should we obey you or obey God? You decide. As for us, we cannot be silent. We must tell the truth we have seen and heard."

The rulers weren't happy with their answer. But they had to let them go, because they were afraid of the people, who all praised God for the good work Peter and John had done. When the two men went back to the other believers, everyone there rejoiced. They praised and thanked God for helping them speak his word without fear.

Philip and the Magician

ACTS 8:4–24

 ew groups of believers in Christ began to form all over the land. People from the first church in Jerusalem scattered all over, telling everyone the good news about Jesus. Some people believed when they heard it. Others were angry. A young man named Saul was very angry with the Christians. He went around trying to make trouble for them. He had some arrested. He even helped put some believers to death. But these problems made the followers of Jesus move from one town to another to hide from Saul and people like him. Then whenever they went to a new town, they would tell the good news to more people who hadn't yet heard about Jesus. So the number of believers kept growing.

One of the Christians on the run from Saul was a believer named Philip. He went to the city of Samaria and told people about Christ. The Lord gave Philip power to speak his word to people, to heal them, and to drive away evil spirits that were bothering them. The Samaritans were not Jews, but many of them believed Philip's words. He baptized many people, and the whole city was full of joy.

There was in that city a magician named Simon. He made people believe he had power to do miracles. When Philip came, everyone said that the Christian power was greater than the magician's. So Simon pretended to listen to Philip and to believe in Jesus. He even asked to be baptized. But his heart hadn't really changed. He just wanted to find out how Philip got the power to do miracles. He thought it was some sort of trick he could learn.

When Peter and John heard about Philip's work in Samaria, they came to help him. They were glad when they saw how people who weren't Jews could become believers. The same power of the Holy Spirit that came to the disciples in Jerusalem came to the Samaritan believers. It happened when Peter and John prayed for the people by laying their hands on them.

Simon the magician saw this happen. He still thought it was some sort of trick. He asked Peter and John to sell him some power for money. He wanted to be able to do the same things they did. But Peter answered him, "May your silver be destroyed with you! Do you think you can buy God's gift with money? You do not really belong to Christ. Your heart is not right with God. Turn from this sin and pray to God for forgiveness. It is a chain of evil around your heart."

Simon didn't really understand what being a believer was about. He asked the apostles to pray for him.

The Man in the Chariot

eter and John finished working with Philip. They went on to more villages and told the good news about Jesus as they went back to Jerusalem. After they left, an angel of God visited Philip. He told him, "Get up and leave this city. Go south to the desert road toward Gaza."

This road went through a place without villages or people. But Philip obeyed the angel. While he was walking, he saw coming toward him a chariot pulled by horses. There was an African man from Ethiopia sitting in it reading a scroll of paper. He had an important job. He controlled all the riches of Candace, queen of Ethiopia. He had come a thousand miles to worship in the temple at Jerusalem. He believed in the Lord God of Israel even though he wasn't Jewish. Now he was going back to his own land. The scroll he was reading had the writing of the words of the prophet Isaiah. He read them aloud as he traveled.

As the chariot came into sight, God's Holy Spirit said to Philip, "Go near and stand close to the chariot."

Philip obeyed and ran toward it. Then he said to the man, "Do you understand what you are reading?"

The Ethiopian nobleman answered, "How can I understand it unless someone tells me what it means? Can you show me? If you can, come up into the chariot and sit with me."

So Philip did. The Ethiopian was reading the fifty-third chapter of Isaiah. It says,

> *"He was led like a sheep to be killed.*
>> *Just as lambs are silent while their wool*
>>> *is being cut off,*
>> *he did not open his mouth.*
> *When he was treated badly, he was refused a fair*
>> *trial.*
> *Who can say anything about his children?*
>> *His life was cut off from the earth."*

The man asked Philip, "Tell me, please. Who is the prophet talking about? Himself or someone else?"

Then Philip told the Ethiopian all about Christ. The man believed and opened his heart to the good news of Jesus Christ. As they traveled the road, they came to a place where there was water. "See, here is water!" the nobleman said. "Why shouldn't I be baptized?"

Then the he gave the order for the chariot to stop. Philip went down into the water with him and baptized the Ethiopian as a follower of Christ. When they came up out of the water, the Spirit of the Lord took Philip away. The man didn't see him anymore! He went on his way home full of the joy of the Lord.

Philip was next seen at Azotus. From there he traveled northward through the towns by the Great Sea and preached about Jesus in them all.

Surprises at the Gate

ACTS 12:1–19

ing Herod wanted to please the Jews in Jerusalem. So he arrested James, one of the apostles who had been close to Jesus. He ordered his guards to kill James with their swords. When he saw how much this pleased the Jewish priests and rulers, he had Simon Peter put in prison also. Herod planned to put him to death in front of the crowds at the next great feast, the Passover.

Peter was kept in prison with sixteen soldiers around it to guard him. Four soldiers watched him all the time. All the Christians prayed to God to help Peter. The night before Peter was to be brought to trial, he was sleeping in the prison. He was bound with two chains, and the four guards stood watching before his door. Suddenly a bright light shone in Peter's cell, and an angel from the Lord stood by him. The angel struck him on the side to wake him, then said, "Rise quickly!"

As soon as Peter stood, the chains fell from his hands. The angel said, "Wrap your coat around you and follow me." Peter followed the angel, but he thought that he was dreaming! They passed the first guard of soldiers and the second also. Not one of the soldiers tried to stop them. When Peter and the angel came to the great iron gate outside the prison, it opened for them as if unseen hands were pushing it. They walked out of the prison into the city. Then the angel left Peter as suddenly as he had come. By this time Peter was fully awake. He said, "Now I am sure that the Lord has sent his angel and has set me free from the power of King Herod."

Peter thought about what he should do and where he should go. He turned toward the house of a woman named Mary. That was where many of the

Christians were praying for him. When he came to the house, he knocked on the outside door and called to those inside. A young woman named Rhoda came to the door. She listened and at once knew the voice of Peter. She was so excited that she didn't open the door. She just turned and ran back inside the house, where the group was praying. She told them that Peter was standing at the door.

The Christians in the house said to her, "You are crazy!"

She said that she was sure that Peter was there, for she knew his voice.

Then they said, "It must be an angel who has taken Peter's form."

All the while Peter kept on knocking! At last they opened the door and saw that it was really he. They were filled with wonder. Peter told them all how the Lord had sent an angel and brought him out of the prison.

PAUL'S STORIES

Paul on the Road to Damascus

ACTS 9:1–22

ew believers in Christ from the first church in Jerusalem traveled to other towns to tell everyone about the good news of Jesus Christ. Many people believed that Jesus was the Messiah. But others were angry and did not believe. A young man named Saul thought the Christians were telling lies. He wanted to stop them. He had them put in jail. He even had some believers killed. But it didn't stop the Christians from being joyful and wanting to tell everyone how Jesus had changed their lives.

Saul heard that some believers were teaching about Christ in a city called Damascus. He wanted to stop them, so he went to the Jewish high priest. He asked the priest for a letter to give him power to arrest all the believers he could find in that city. The priest gave him the letter, and Saul started on his journey.

As he was going down the road, Saul thought about these strange people who angered him. No matter how badly they were treated, the Christians seemed to have joy and peace in their hearts. No matter how mean people were to them, the Christians forgave and loved their enemies. Deep in Saul's heart he had a strange feeling. He wondered if he should keep trying to stop people who had so much love for others. He tried to forget about the feeling and kept going toward the town.

Suddenly a bright light flashed from heaven. It was brighter than the sun. It blinded Saul's eyes and knocked him to the ground. Then he heard a voice call his name. It said, "Saul, Saul, why are you fighting against me?"

Saul asked, "Who are you, Lord?"

Then the answer came: "I am Jesus. I'm the one you are trying to stop. Get up and go into the city. You will be told what to do."

Saul's friends had seen a light, but they didn't hear the voice Saul heard. When Saul opened his eyes, he couldn't see. He was blind. They led him by the hand to the house of a man named Judas. Saul stayed there for three days. He didn't eat or drink anything. He sat in the darkness praying to God and Christ with all his heart.

A believer named Ananias lived in Damascus. He was praying, too. The Lord spoke to him and said, "Ananias."

Ananias answered, "Here I am, O Lord."

"Get up and go to the street called Straight and find the house of Judas. Ask the people there for a man named Saul from Tarsus. This man Saul is praying. He has seen a vision of a man named Ananias. In the vision Ananias lays hands on Saul and gives him back his sight."

This command from the Lord surprised Ananias. He answered, "Lord, I have heard from many people about this man Saul. He has done evil things to all your people in Jerusalem. He has an order from the high priest to arrest anyone here who follows you.

Paul Told the Sailors, "Don't be afraid."

An angel told Paul that no one would drown in the storm.
Paul told the sailors to eat some bread: "You will need it
to keep your lives safe. You will all be saved."
He took some bread and gave thanks to God in front of them all.
Later, they all made it safely to shore.

PAUL WAS A PRISONER FOR A LONG TIME

Even though Paul was a prisoner he told a scribe what to write down
in letters to his friends who were praying for him. The letters Paul
and the scribe wrote are now part of our Bible.

Should I go and visit such a man?"

But the Lord said, "Go to this man. I have chosen him to take my name to people of all nations. He will speak to kings and to the children of Israel. I will show him how many things he must suffer for my sake."

Ananias obeyed the Lord. He found the house and Saul, just as the Lord had said. He laid his hands on Saul's head and said, "Brother Saul, the Lord Jesus met you on the road as you were coming. He has sent me that you may have your sight and be filled with the Holy Spirit. Wait no more. Get up and be baptized and call on the name of Jesus. He will wash away your sins."

Then something like scales fell off Saul's eyes. At once he could see. They baptized Saul as a believer. He ate and became strong in body and in soul. He had come to do harm to the Christians, and now he was one of them. He went to the synagogues where the Jews in Damascus worshiped. He preached about Jesus there. He told the Jews how Jesus was their Messiah. Everyone who heard him was amazed. They said, "Isn't this the same man who did everything he could to stop Jesus' followers in Jerusalem? Didn't he come here with orders to arrest them?"

Paul Escapes in a Basket

ACTS 9:23–31; GALATIANS 1:11–24

aul's faith and words were so strong that none of the Jews could argue with him. Soon he went to the desert of Arabia. While he was there, he thought about the good news, and God taught him. Afterward, when he came back to Damascus, he preached to both Jews and Gentiles and people from other nations. Some Jews were angry about this and planned to kill him. They watched for him to try leaving by the city gate. But his friends, who were believers, saved Saul. They secretly let him down over the city wall in a basket. His enemies didn't know where he had gone. Saul escaped from Damascus.

He traveled back to Jerusalem. When he had left three years before, he was an enemy of Christ. Now he came back as a follower. The Christians in Jerusalem didn't know that Saul had changed. They were afraid of him and hid from him. Finally a man named Barnabas heard Saul's story and believed him. He brought Saul to the apostle Peter. When Peter heard how Saul had become a believer, he accepted Paul as a disciple of Christ.

Saul stayed for a few weeks and preached about Jesus. Some of the Jews were angry because Paul said Jesus had come to save the Gentiles as well as the Jewish people. Saul knew why they felt that way. He had been angry about the same thing before he met Jesus on the road to Damascus. He had helped kill Christians who taught such things. Now these same angry people wanted to kill him. One day while Saul was praying in the temple, God warned him about his enemies. The Lord said, "Go from this place. I want to send you far away to preach to the Gentiles."

The disciples in Jerusalem helped him get away from his enemies, on a ship that was going to the city of Tarsus. That was the city where Saul had been born. There he made tents for a living and preached the gospel of Christ. Saul the enemy had become Saul the friend of the gospel and of all the churches in the land.

New Names

hen Saul was helping the Jewish leaders arrest and kill believers in Jerusalem, many believers fled from the city. Everywhere they went, they told the good news about Jesus. At first they only told the Jews that Jesus had come to save them. But soon many Gentiles, or people who were not Jewish, heard about the gospel. They wanted to hear more. So believers began to tell them about Jesus and how to be saved from sin.

The Lord helped their work, and in a short time a great number of people, both Jews and Gentiles, believed in Jesus. People from every nation worshiped together at the city of Antioch in the country of Syria. All the believers in the church at Jerusalem had been Jewish, and they heard about the Syrian Gentiles coming to Christ. They weren't sure if the Gentile believers should be allowed to worship beside the Jewish believers. In the Jewish temples the Gentiles who believed in the one true God had to worship in a room outside the place where the Jews worshiped. The believers in the church at Jerusalem decided to choose one wise man to send to Antioch to see this new church of Jews and Gentiles.

They chose Barnabas, a good man who had given land to help the poor. He was the one who had brought Saul to the church when the disciples were still afraid of him. Barnabas traveled to Antioch and saw many new disciples who were very strong in their love for Christ. They were united in spirit and serious about the gospel. He was glad and spoke to them all. He told them to stand firmly in the Lord. He was full of faith and the Holy Spirit.

Barnabas knew that the growing church at Antioch needed leaders and teachers. He went to Tarsus and found Saul. He brought Saul to Antioch and stayed with him there for a year. They preached and taught at the church. Antioch was the place where the disciples were first called by the name Christians. The name means "those who are like Christ." The disciples liked their new name because they were always trying to follow Christ's way of living. They wanted to say the things Jesus would say about everything. They even wanted the thoughts in their hearts to be the kinds of thoughts he would have.

God blessed them and helped them be strong followers filled with his Holy Spirit. He sometimes told people what would happen in the future, to help the church be ready. The people he told were called prophets because they spoke aloud for God. One of them was a man named Agabus. He said God's Holy Spirit had shown him that a great famine, or need for food, would soon come to all the lands. His words were true. Food became difficult to find, and many people were hungry.

Christians in Antioch heard that believers in Jerusalem and Judea needed food. They gave as much money as they could to Saul and Barnabas to take to the people there so they could buy food. The men took the gifts to Jerusalem and stayed there for a while. When they returned to Antioch, they brought a young believer named John Mark with them.

Once when the church members in Antioch were praying, God's Spirit told them to send Saul and Barnabas to do a special work. The leaders laid their hands on the heads of Saul and Barnabas and sent them traveling. They took John Mark with them and sailed to the island of Cyprus. There they preached about Christ in all the synagogues.

At a place called Paphos they met the Roman ruler named Sergius Paulus. He sent for them because he wanted to learn about Christ. But a Jewish man named Elymas was there with the ruler. He claimed to be a prophet. But he said things against the disciples and didn't want the ruler to hear the gospel.

Saul was full of the Holy Spirit. He looked at Elymas, the false prophet, and said, "You are a man filled with evil, a child of the Devil. You are an enemy of what is right. Why won't you stop doing things against the word of the Lord? Now God's hand is on you. You will be blind for a time and not see the sun."

At once a mist and darkness fell on Elymas. He reached around with his hands, looking for someone to lead him. When the ruler saw what had happened, he was amazed and believed in the gospel of Christ.

From this time on, Saul was called Paul. He was Paul the apostle. He had all the power that belonged to Peter and John and the other apostles of Jesus. He traveled to many other cities and preached the gospel.

In a city called Lystra Paul met a disabled man who had never walked in his life. He looked at the man and said loudly, "Stand on your feet!" At those words the man jumped up and walked. The people who lived there were so amazed, they thought Paul and Barnabas must be Roman gods who had come down from heaven. They thought Barnabas was Jupiter and Paul was Mercury. They even wanted to worship them and give them the kinds of gifts they offered to their statues of gods. Paul stopped them. He told the people that they were just men and that their power came from the one true God. He explained the gospel to them.

Some Jews from another town came and told the people lies about Paul. By the time the liars had finished, the people of Lystra had changed their minds about Paul. Instead of worshiping Paul, they decided to kill him. They threw stones at him and hit him until it looked as if he were dead. Believers came there after the angry crowd was gone. They gathered around Paul's body. They prayed and cried about what had happened to their friend. Suddenly Paul got up! He was alive. He stayed with his friends in Lystra for another day. Then he traveled with Barnabas and preached in more cities. They taught and helped believers everywhere they went.

The Song in the Prison

aul wrote letters to all the churches he visited as he traveled. Sometimes he wrote them from prison. He was arrested more than once because he wasn't afraid to tell about Jesus even if people got angry about his words. Paul believed that everything that happened to him would work out so more people would hear about Jesus.

Once when he and his friend Silas were beaten and put in jail, they sang songs to God all night. They just knew God would do something good because of their arrest. The other prisoners listened to them. At midnight there was a great earthquake. It shook every door in the prison open. All the chains on the prisoners fell off. When the jailer in charge of the prison saw the doors open, he pulled out his sword. He was going to kill himself because he thought all the prisoners had escaped. By Roman law, a guard who didn't stop his prisoners from escaping would be put in prison in their place. But Paul called out, "Don't hurt yourself! We are all still here."

The jailer called for lights. He saw Paul and Silas and the other prisoners still sitting there. He fell down at their feet and cried out, "Sirs, what must I do to be saved?"

They told him, "Believe in the Lord Jesus Christ. You and those in your family will be saved."

The jailer brought Paul and Silas to his house and washed their wounds. He and his family accepted Christ as their Savior and were baptized as believers right then. Afterward he kept Paul and Silas at his home instead of in the prison.

The Storm and the Snake

ne time Paul spent two years in prison for preaching the gospel. The guards in charge of him finally had to take Paul to Caesar to be judged. Paul had rights as a Roman citizen. He had asked to have his case heard by Caesar. So he and his guards had to travel a long way to Rome. Paul knew he would get to talk about Jesus to many Romans and Jews and others if he did this.

While he was sailing on a large ship, a great storm blew up. It drove the ship out into the open sea. The sailors thought they were going to die, but Paul told them, "Don't be afraid. This night an angel of the Lord I serve stood by me. He said, 'Don't be afraid, Paul. You are going to stand before Caesar. God has given you the lives of all those who are sailing with you.' So be brave and happy. Things will happen just as he told me."

The ship and all its passengers were lost at sea for fourteen days. Then Paul told them to eat some bread. He said, "You will need your strength to keep your lives safe. Don't be afraid. You will all be saved.

Not a hair on your heads will be lost." He took some bread and gave thanks to God in front of them all. There were 276 people on board. As soon as day dawned, they could see land. They rowed toward it, but rocks and waves broke up the ship. All the people swam or floated on pieces of wood from the ship and made it safely to the shore. Not one life was lost.

They had landed on the island called Malta. The people there were very kind to these strangers whom the sea had thrown upon their shore. They made a fire to warm the visitors. Paul gathered a bundle of sticks to burn. As he put them into the hot fire, a poisonous snake popped out of the pile and bit Paul's hand. The snake hung there for a few seconds until Paul shook it off. The people watched him. Usually

anyone bitten by that kind of snake would swell up and drop dead. But nothing happened to Paul. They thought he must be a god, because the snake's poison had not killed him.

Paul preached the gospel on that island. He prayed for sick people, and they were healed. After a while Paul and the others were able to leave the island, and he continued on to Rome.

Paul spoke God's word to many leaders of the Gentiles and Jews. Usually this was because he was on trial for being a Christian. In every place he was in prison or arrested, he was able to tell someone new about Jesus. He was full of joy even though he was sometimes sick from being in prison. He was an innocent man and had been put in jail as if he had done something wrong. At the end of many years an evil Roman emperor named Nero finally decided to put Paul to death. Some of Paul's last words show that he was still full of joy about serving Christ. He wrote, "I have fought a good fight; I have run my race. I have kept the faith. Now there is a crown that the Lord himself will give me. It is waiting for me in heaven."

GOD'S KINGDOM

Heaven—The City of God

REVELATION 7:9–17; 21; 22:1–17

he apostle John had a vision about heaven. He saw the throne of God and all the people wearing white robes gathered in front of it. These people were waving palm branches were calling out, "Salvation belongs to our God, who sits on the throne. Salvation also belongs to the Lamb."

All the angels were standing around God's throne, and there were some others there called elders. There were twenty-four of them. Then the angels fell down on their faces and began worshiping God. They said, "Amen, May praise and glory and wisdom be given to our God for ever and ever. Give him thanks and honor and power and strength. Amen!"

Then one of the elders asked John, "Who are these people dressed in white robes? Where did they come from?"

Then John said, "Sir, you know."

And the elder said, "They are the ones who have come out of the time of terrible suffering. They have washed their robes and made them white. So they are before the throne of God to serve him day and night in his temple. They will never be hungry or thirsty again. The sun will not beat on them and the heat of the desert will not harm them. The Lamb, who is at the center of the area around the throne, will be their shepherd forever. He will lead them to drink at springs of living water."

And then the elder gave the best part, "And God will wipe away every tear from their eyes." In heaven there will be no more crying. There will be no more

death. There will be no more pain. God is going to make everything brand new in heaven.

Then John saw a new Jerusalem coming down from heaven. It was a beautiful city, and it shone with the glory of God. It gleamed like a valuable jewel. It was as clear as crystal.

The city had a huge, high wall with twelve gates made of pearl, and there was an angel at every gate. On the gates were written the names of the twelve tribes of Israel. The wall also had twelve foundations made of precious stone. On them were written the names of the twelve apostles of the Lord. The city resting on this foundation was made of gold so pure it looked like glass.

John said that he didn't see a temple or a church in the city because it didn't need one. You see, God, who rules over all, is its temple. The city didn't even need the sun or moon to shine on it because God's glory provides the light.

The gates of the city will never be shut. And all the nations of men will walk in the light of the city. But only those whose names are written in the Lamb's Book of Life will enter the city.

The angel said to John, "You can trust these words. They are true."